Peanuts and Cracker

Peanuts and Crackerjacks

A *Baseball* Novel

M. Z. RIBALOW

McFarland & Company, Inc., Publishers
Jefferson, North Carolina, and London

LIBRARY OF CONGRESS CATALOGUING-IN-PUBLICATION DATA

Ribalow, M.Z. (Meir Z.)
    Peanuts and crackerjacks : a baseball novel / by M.Z. Ribalow.
      p.   cm.

    ISBN 978-0-7864-6598-9
    softcover : 50# alkaline paper ♾

    1. Baseball stories.   I. Title.
    PS3568.I16P43   2012
    813'.54—dc23   2011040304

BRITISH LIBRARY CATALOGUING DATA ARE AVAILABLE

Cover design by Mark Durr.

Manufactured in the United States of America

*McFarland & Company, Inc., Publishers
  Box 611, Jefferson, North Carolina 28640
   www.mcfarlandpub.com*

For HUR and Donna, who left the game too soon;

AND

for SSR, Rhona, Glen and LSC, who kept the rally going

Acknowledgments

THE AUTHOR WOULD LIKE to express his profound gratitude to all the wonderful friends who were so supportive of this novel. In addition to those to whom it is dedicated, that would include Tom and Emily Hyde, who were enormously helpful with insights into Buffalo; Chris Modrzynski, another invaluable source of Buffalonian lore; Ellen Barber, who was endlessly encouraging; Dasha Shenkman, who always is; N. Scott Momaday, as much a fan of the game as I am of him; Stephen Collins, an inspiration even when he's unaware he is; Shaiel Ben-Ephraim, a perfect companion in any ballpark; Peter Brown, a brother in every way but blood; Greg Diskant, a terrific teammate; Patricia Randell, a true ace; Sharon Pomerantz, an all-star friend; Annie Shaw who is in a league of her own; "The Great" Ann Vellis, whose nickname says it all; Mark Woods, who laughed; Sam McGregor, the best there is; Spencer Humphrey, a first-ballot Hall of Famer; Jim McLure, my favorite bench coach; and Laura, Jenna, Nellie, Kati and Hilary, who make each at-bat worthwhile.

Warming Up

I REGARDED THE BASEBALL I held in my hand and heard my dead father's voice echoing in my head, as I did most every day. Today, his ghost was repeating—in a low, encouraging tone—one of his favorite mantras.

"It's a simple game. You throw the ball, you hit the ball, you catch the ball. It isn't easy. But it *is* simple."

I turned the handle and entered the Manager's office. Pepper sat there in the dark communing with the invisible phantoms of players past. I closed the office door, which made it almost impossible to see anything. But I knew my way around the room, so I rambled over to the old leather easy chair and relaxed into it. I liked that chair. It was pretty beat-up, but I felt comfortable reclining in it. I closed my eyes. Wasn't much point in keeping them open; you couldn't see a damn thing anyway.

Pepper's voice floated at me in the disembodied dark. You could tell he was in a philosophical mood because the usual aggressive edge in his rasp of a voice was as far below the surface as you were ever likely to hear it. Of course, you could tell he was in that kind of mood just by seeing him sitting there in the dark, too.

"Mike," he said to me, "you and me know each other a long time."

Well, there was no arguing with that, so I didn't say anything. I was going to miss that chair when he took it away with him. Of course, if Pepper did get fired, I'd probably be out of a job anyway, and why I was sitting there in the dark with my eyes closed thinking about a chair at all was something of a mystery to me.

"Mike," Pepper asked me, "Do you remember Bob 'Death to Flying Things' Ferguson?"

"Sure," I said. Actually, Ferguson was way before our times: an infielder from baseball's earliest years, before my grandfather was even born, probably. "Death to Flying Things" earned his nickname because he had a legendary ability to catch line drives barehanded, in the days before they developed fielders' gloves. But even though I never saw him, or know anyone who ever did, I did *remember* him in the same way that Pepper did. He was part of our heritage, Pepper's and mine. I knew that if Pepper was thinking about baseball's original days, he was really brooding about something. Of course, I had figured that out already from his sitting in the dark.

"He can catch that ball," said Pepper.

"Yeah," I said, just to say something.

He was quiet for a minute, then he said as if discovering the fact, "Y'know, my name's not really Pepper."

"I know that, Pepper."

"No, I mean my *nickname's* not really Pepper. I mean it is now, but it isn't a real nickname, I just made it up myself. Back when I am a kid when I always think a real ballplayer—you know, the kind every kid really wants to be—has a great nickname. Like Lefty, or Dutch, or The Georgia Peach, something like that. You know."

"Sure. Like Still Bill Hill."

"Yeah. Or Candy LaChance."

"Or Bunny Brief."

"Or Bow Wow Arft."

"Thumper DeMerit."

"Chicken Wolf."

"Suitcase Simpson."

"Creepy Crespi."

"Peek-A-Boo Veach."

"Phenomenal Smith."

"Mysterious Walker."

"Schoolboy Rowe."

"Preacher Roe."

"Cuddles Marshall."

"Duster Mails."

"The Wild Hoss of the Osage."

"The Wild Elk of the Wasatch."

"Yeah, all those boys. So when I start out on my first semi-pro team and the manager asks me what my name is, I tell him—real cocky, you know—'they call me Pepper.' Well, hell, at the time nobody ever calls me

Pepper. I just always wish they do. So I tell him that's what they call me, and they don't know any better, so they refer to me by this moniker. And they continue to do so ever since."

"Well, hell, Pepper, if they've been calling you that for—what is it, forty years?"

"Forty-four. I am only seventeen then."

"Well, then, wouldn't you say that by now, that *is* your name?"

"Well, sure it is. But not my real name. I mean, no one ever gives it to me. I make it up myself."

"That still counts."

"No, it doesn't."

"It does to me."

His voice continued to float through the blackness like a satellite through space.

"Thumper DeMerit. Jesus. Remember Thumper DeMerit?"

"I'm the one who mentioned him."

"Yeah. Jeez. Five years in the bigs with all of three home runs, and they call him Thumper." His sigh filled the room and made me feel unaccountably elegiac, but I wasn't sure about what exactly.

"Ah, Mike ... baseball's a helluva game, isn't it?"

"The best there ever was."

"The best there ever will be."

"Yup."

"When it's played the way it oughta be."

Now we both knew what was bothering him. Well, that was okay. We had both been aware of it anyway. He sighed again and flicked on his desk lamp.

I opened my eyes. Pepper was a little guy, five-seven though he always claimed to be five-nine, which he never was, a skinny big-jawed ugly mug whose face looked like a map crowded with details that were easier to read than understand. He was a good man, though. He had no tact at all, but he was honest, which isn't as common as it might sound. He was as tough as a fast-food steak, but he was loyal, too; he would give you what-for if you didn't do your job, but he would never fault you if you always gave it your best shot. He was an opinionated big-mouthed troublemaking redneck hard-ass peckerwood, but he was okay with me. And he knew his baseball; no one could say otherwise.

"Guess we better go out there and do our jobs, huh?" He rose to his feet, stretched his short arms, yawned and started to put on his fierce game face. Pepper did this before every game. He always wanted the boys to see him ready for bear, whether it was our bear or the other team's. Before he opened the door, though, he stopped and faced me. He looked a little bit nervous.

"Say, Mike. About what I say about being called Pepper. You're not gonna say anything about that, are you? To anyone at all, I mean."

"Hell no, Pepper."

"I mean, it's no one's fucking business, right?"

"Right."

"So just forget I ever say it, okay?"

"Ever say what?"

He gave me a mean little grin and opened the door, ready now to go out and face whatever awaited him. As I watched the world-weariness invade his baseball-lifer spirit, I suddenly recalled the time my father, toward the end of his career, was told by a reporter that my dad no longer appeared to be throwing his fastball as hard as had previously been his custom. My dad had given him a twisted smile and said,

"I'm throwing as hard as I ever did. The ball's just taking longer to get there."

The Golden Egg

PEPPER WAS THE MANAGER of the Buffalo Bears, and I was his new pitching coach as well as his temporary bench coach ever since Mojo Mendoza had left to manage the Denver Desperadoes in the other league. The Bears were an expansion team, and since this was only our fourth year in the majors, we had been pretty bad so far: stocked mostly with kids who weren't ready yet, over-the-hill guys who weren't ready any more, and run-of-the-mill players who never would be. That's the way it usually is with expansion clubs. It takes time. This is a game of time; that's part of the beauty of it. It's not a game with a clock, like football or basketball or hockey or soccer or all those others. In baseball, if you keep getting hits and don't make outs, you can bat forever. It's the only game I know in which you can theoretically defeat time. I mean, you can't really, but you could if you were able to, if you see what I mean. Baseball demands patience, but it demands more than that: it requires an appreciation of the nature of time.

But we had hopes for this season. For one thing, we had a couple of promising young pitchers. Also, a couple of our regulars showed some signs of being able to hit more than their weight. And mostly, we had hopes this year because it was spring, and every ballclub that's ever been has glowing hopes every spring. In baseball, as in other walks of life, contemplating one's fondest hopes is what spring is about.

Now, there are a lot of Buffalo jokes out there, and the players had heard most of them already; but the Nickel City is underrated. She has hidden treasures. The Thursday in the (Lafayette) Square concerts were a civic treat, though Donna had to review them for me after she went; as they were summer events, the Bears were usually playing those nights. Martin's Fantasy Island was an endearingly second-rate amusement park with only about ten rides, but Jenna always wanted to go there because they held Wild West Shootouts every couple of hours; and Laura loved Loganberry Juice, a local drink made from, she had informed me, a nonexistent fruit ("but who cares, so long as it tastes good"). And how can't you appreciate a town whose residents call it "the city of no illusions?"

Still, even at its best Buffalo was not an obvious choice for an expansion team. The only reason the city had a major league baseball team—the only reason anyone associated with the Bears lived in Buffalo and spent their waking and working hours in the Lumpe Dome—was because of the obsession and bankbook (both of the same oversized proportions) of Simon Lumpe, majority owner of the Buffalo Bears Baseball Club, Inc.

Simon's name wasn't originally Lumpe. He had changed it many years ago from Lumpenkopf, but he didn't like to be reminded of that; and most people were not anxious to remind him of whatever he didn't wish to be reminded of. That was because Simon had enough money to buy and sell everyone in Buffalo. Twice. He had inherited most of it from his father Herman (who had not changed *his* name). Herman had arrived in America a penniless Austrian refugee, but he had parlayed a shrewd knowledge of pharmaceutical medicines and a ruthless business acumen into a considerable fortune. What he'd done, in its simplest terms, was steal patents. He'd recognize the real value of some poor inventor's medicine for headaches or upset stomachs or whatever; and while the big companies were dismissing the novel idea, whatever it was, as useless, Herman would buy the rights to it for a song. If he could put his own name on it first without paying for it at all, that was of course preferable; but if he absolutely had to, he would pay the poor sucker whose idea it actually was, something—as little as possible—and then take it over from there.

Herman had died a detested but extremely rich man, and Simon was doing his best to live up to both aspects of that image. True, he had changed the name of Lumpenkopf Enterprises to Lumpe and Lumpe (the second Lumpe being his only son and heir, twenty-year-old Jefferson Washington Lincoln Lumpe, generally known as Junior). But to give Simon his due, his talent for administering a corporation matched Herman's for building one; and his gift for smelling a profit was fully the equal of his old man's.

Simon had his obsessions, though. One of them was baseball, a game he didn't understand at all, mostly because he confused it with football. He had been the manager of his high school football team (apparently he had had a nice sideline selling the team's towels and replacing them with cheaper ones) and he had somehow developed the notion that baseball, with its elaborate historical fabric and pastoral pace, was similar to football, with its hyped-up motivational frenzy and its lack of any sense of history. Football is a game that exists entirely in the moment; it makes no difference who did what how long ago. Whereas in baseball every ball you hit and every pitch you throw conjures echoes and images of past legions of fabled predecessors doing the same things in their days. There's a big difference. How big a difference became vividly clear by the way Simon ran the club.

But before we get into all that, you need to know about Simon and Buffalo. Lumpe and Lumpe had its headquarters right there where Herman had founded the place. It was the city where Simon had been born and raised, until he'd been sent to prep school at St. Paul's (he couldn't get into Exeter) and to college at Ithaca (he couldn't get into Princeton; he was even on Ithaca's waiting list until Herman gave the place a sensational contribution for their fundraising campaign). I knew all this because I'd looked it up. History interests me, and I enjoy research; and while knowledge isn't always power, it can be sometimes. Also, I like to know who I'm working for. The more you know about where someone's coming from, the better idea you have where he (and therefore you) may be going. Besides, I was desperate for a job that would let me coach anywhere at all, especially in Buffalo—I had managed to get a job coaching and teaching history at Emily Andrews High—because Donna's law practice was there, so that was home for us and our two daughters.

Simon had an obsession about Buffalo. He had heard most of the jokes, and he didn't think they were funny. He took them, as he took most things, personally. If you laughed at Buffalo, you were laughing at him; and Simon was not a man who liked being laughed at. "He always likes a good joke," Pepper once said to me, "as long as it's about other people." So he decided to do Buffalo so proud that no one, not even the despised citizens of that famous metropolis in the southern part of the state, could laugh at her any more. Buffalo already had a pro football franchise, and of course a hockey team, but the latter was more for the Norks (a Canadian might also be called a Gordy by residents of The Buff); but baseball was, after all, the national game. The all–American pastime. So Simon bid for a major league expansion club.

As I already mentioned, Buffalo was hardly the most obvious city to which the league might award a new franchise. But as it happened, the Commissioner of Baseball, Clyde Wallingford, had political ambitions. Everyone knew that, because every so often, he would make sure the papers printed a denial that he was running for Governor. Then again, maybe the private huddle between Wallingford and Simon before Simon's formal meeting with the other owners had nothing to do with Buffalo being awarded a franchise, or with how much the Lumpe Corporation might contribute to a Wallingford campaign. Might be it was all coincidence. As we say when we're nine runs down, anything is possible in this game.

Since Simon was richer than many of the other owners, they were glad to let him into their exclusive club. The only substantive objection raised to a baseball team in Buffalo was the weather—and Simon was ready for that one. He unveiled his plans for the Lumpe Dome, which he built right on schedule. He had the dome painted gold so that it shone in the sun like a great golden egg. The players on the team called it The Egg, in fact. Most of them thought it looked pretty silly, and almost all of them hated the artificial turf. But they loved those large, regular paychecks; and they knew they were, after all, playing baseball in the bigs. Some of us will put up with a lot to do that. Put up with almost anything. It just seemed that sometimes Simon was out to prove the truth of that proposition.

Brown Rice

THE LOCKER ROOM WAS pretty much emptied out as Pepper and I walked through it. Most all the Bears were out on the field stretching, warming up, tossing a ball, and in general letting their muscles know they were about to be called on for some more substantial activity. The only ones we saw in the locker room were Charlie Luposo and Tad Strain. Charlie, a grizzled, small man in his sixties who was the team's equipment manager, was collecting used towels. Tad, a twenty-four-year-old reserve outfielder who had fair power but who was overweight and couldn't handle hard inside stuff, sprawled in his uniform across a chair, reading a paperback mystery novel. Pepper looked at him.

"Why aren't you on the field warming up?"

Tad barely glanced up from the book. It seemed to be holding his interest pretty well, so I checked out the title. *Blondes Will Be Blondes*, by a writer I'd read a couple of times.

"I don't want to overdo the warm-ups," he explained. "It could be bad for me. Wouldn't want to get hurt just practicing."

"*What?*" You could hear the mounting rage approaching quickly on the highway of incomprehension in Pepper's voice.

"Well, Skip, you did tell me I should take care of myself."

"I tell you you should get in shape! Sitting around on your ass is not getting in shape!"

"My agent told me too much exercise could cause me serious damage."

"You're a professional ballplayer!" Now he *was* screaming.

"My agent says—"

"Fuck your agent!" The veins on Pepper's neck were competing to see which one would first burst through the reddened skin.

Tad looked hurt and mad at the same time. "You shouldn't talk like that about my agent."

15

Pepper's mouth opened twice, but nothing came out. He stomped away and stood quivering on the other side of the room, trying to regain control of himself. I leaned over to Tad and tried to sound as friendly as possible.

"Tad, I *know* your agent. The most exercise he's ever done in his life is to endorse a check."

Tad gave me a solemn look. "He's awful smart, Mike."

"I know he is, but Tad, do you remember your pulled hamstring? And the sore arm? And the neck?"

"Sure."

"Do you remember how much you warmed up before those injuries?"

He thought for a moment. "I didn't."

"Right. Now think. Have you ever had a major injury after you *did* warm up a lot?"

"Yeah," he said righteously, "I sure did. That time Garrigan spiked me at the plate and cut my knee open. That was pretty major."

I shook my head. "I think you're missing the point, Tad."

"But my agent says—"

"Screw your agent!" Pepper whirled back over to us. "Your agent knows even less about this game than you do, you big dummy!"

"I'll tell him you said that." Tad seemed pained. Pepper leaned over to him and hissed into his startled face.

"I'll make it simple for you, kid. Either haul your ass out there and work out the kinks in that fat tub of lard you call a body, or you'll be playing in New Haven tomorrow night. You want to act like a minor leaguer, I'll be glad to make you one."

"Okay, okay. I'll go warm up," said Tad. Pepper spun on his heel and stormed out of the room. Tad winced. "He doesn't have to be so mean about it."

"I think he was just trying to make sure he was being clear. Say, I didn't know you were a mystery fan, Tad."

He seemed surprised. "Yeah, I am. I like a good mystery. Especially tough-guy stuff. I like tough guys."

"You ever read any Chandler, or Hammett?"

"Who're they?"

"They wrote some tough-guy mysteries once. You might like them. They're better than this one."

"Yeah? But they're old guys, right?"

"Dead and gone."

"So their stuff is a long time ago."

"It's still better," I assured him.

He shrugged. "Okay. I'll look into it. Chandler?"

"Yeah. Raymond Chandler."

"Okay. Thanks, Mike."

"Sure. You never know, you might even learn something."

"You think so?"

"Better go get loose now, okay?"

"Right. Yeah. Okay." But instead of rising, he settled back with his book.

"Tad," I asked, "what is it with you? Are you ignorant, or just apathetic?"

He shrugged. "Coach, I don't know and I don't care."

The Dome was brightly lit, and the temperature was a perfect seventy-two degrees. The Dome was always brightly lit every night we played, and the temperature was always a perfect seventy-two degrees. The man in charge of maintaining the temperature had once let it slide to seventy. Simon had heard about it somehow, and fired the guy on the spot.

It was a beautiful night for a game. It was always a beautiful night for a game in Buffalo, at least indoors. Big Jake Ellerbee was pitching for us tonight, so we had a fair shot at winning. Big Jake was a six-foot-six lefthander with a hard fastball, a nasty slider and an unusual approach to pitching. He was the only pitcher I'd ever known who claimed to ignore the batters entirely.

"I pitch to spots," he explained to me after he had finally decided that my interest was genuine and that I wasn't going to try to change his style. "As far as I'm concerned, the batter isn't there. Makes no difference who he is—I'm trying to make the perfect pitch. If he hits it, good for him. If I strike him out on a lousy pitch, I get very little satisfaction out of it."

I tried to explain this to Pepper once, but he just snorted in derision. "If the batter hits it for a double," he pointed out, "it ain't a perfect pitch."

Still, Big Jake was a terrific pitcher, and we were damn lucky to have him. He had been with Tacoma over in the American League, but they'd decided that his strange ways had a negative effect on their younger guys, and finally decided to get rid of him. So they dumped him on the worst team they could find in the other league—us—minimizing as much as they could the chance that he might come back to haunt them. That was our good fortune, but they needn't have worried. Big Jake was as indifferent to revenge or personal vendettas as he was to the identity of any hitter. Big Jake was, in fact, indifferent to most everything except his own personal vision of pitching and his belief in physical conditioning as a spiritual art.

In fact, he was one of the reasons I had my job. It was incredibly hard to get one of these coaching jobs at the big-league level, and I had tried for years to steel myself against the possibility that an opportunity might never come. It might never have, had it not been for Big Jake.

When Simon had fired Sailor Shoffey (whenever the pitching looked bad for a few weeks, which had been often enough, Simon dismissed the pitching coach, as if he were the one not getting the ball over the plate) I called Pepper and asked him to consider hiring me to replace the Sailor. Pepper agreed to do so not only because he knew I knew pitching and passionately wanted the opportunity, but also because he had played with my dad and loved him like a brother. He had to okay his choice with Mr. Lumpe, but Simon had liked the fact that I was only thirty-eight, figuring it would help rapport with the players if I was a sort of middleman between them and their considerably older manager; and he had also been intrigued by the idea of one of his coaches being better educated than he was himself. But he was wary for the same reasons, and his distrust showed when he asked me up to his office for an interview.

"Pepper told me about your graduate degree from Yale, Mike."

I just nodded.

"Although Pepper couldn't tell me what field it was in. I asked him, but he told me that you had told him that it didn't matter."

I nodded again. He hadn't, after all, asked me anything yet.

"That's good, Mike. I like a modest man. I see you got an undergraduate degree from Princeton, no less."

Another nod for the collection. He gave me a look that somehow combined defensive insecurity and aggressive belligerence in equal proportions.

"I didn't get in there when *I* applied. Did you know that?"

Now there was a question that called for an answer.

"No," I lied.

His jaw thrust out even farther than usual. "Their mistake."

"Well, having gone there," I told him, "I can honestly assure you that there are students they *did* accept of whom you are fully the equal."

He waved that off, but he was obviously pleased to hear it. "Well, we all make mistakes. They have to live with theirs—I have to live with mine, when I make them." He gave me a look that was clearly meant to be searching. "I don't want you to be one of my mistakes, Mike."

"I wouldn't want to be."

"I'm sure you wouldn't. So let's give it a trial run. You work with Pepper and we'll see how it goes. I'll let you know for sure one way or the other very soon. Fair enough?"

"Whatever you say. You're the boss."

"That's right. And I don't intend to let anyone forget it." He smiled, but it was clear to both of us that he wasn't kidding.

It was the very next day, my first trial day on the trial job, that I was following Pepper around when he stopped by the trainer's room. In a large private space in the corner, Big Jake stood in a tubful of raw white rice. He was buried up to the neck.

"Fuckin' martial arts exercises," Pepper muttered to me under his breath. "Man's a fuckin' lunatic."

"But a hell of a pitcher," I murmured.

Pepper walked over to introduce me. "Jake, this is Mike McGregor, our new pitching coach. I know he looks like a young pup, but he knows the game. Maybe you remember seeing his late dad, Halfway Harry McGregor. We call him Halfway because he gets so many check swings with those crazy pitches. Also because he always seems halfway here and halfway somewhere else. Old teammate of mine, one smart pitcher, screwball is his strikeout pitch. Kind of a wild man, but what do you want from a left-handed pitcher. No offense. Anyway, this is Mike. I'll let you two get acquainted."

Through all of this, Big Jake never looked at us. He never stopped breathing rhythmically, slashing his arms straight ahead and side to side through the tubful of rice. You couldn't see those powerful arms, of course, but you could see the rice at the top ripple slightly in whatever direction he extended them.

He displayed not the slightest interest in acknowledging our presence. Pepper shrugged and left us alone. I watched him for a few moments. He continued what he was doing as though I wasn't there.

"Interesting exercise," I said. Silence. "Does it strengthen the legs as well as the arms?"

He ignored me. His long, straight dark hair tossed as he worked. I looked away from him at the grains of shifting rice and asked casually, "Have you ever considered using brown rice instead? Might be healthier."

"I'm not eating it." He spoke though his teeth, still not looking at me.

"Rubs into your body, though. Every pore."

He didn't alter his movements or his breathing pattern at all; but for the first time, he gave me the briefest of glances, then turned away again and looked straight ahead.

"I'll consider it," he said.

I watched him for a few moments more, then left. Two days later I received a message to stop by Simon's office. I went.

Simon was a heavyset, thick-necked man with a round face and tiny little eyes that made him look piggy whenever he narrowed them with strong emotions, which was much of the time. When he paced, as he was doing now, he looked like a wild boar getting ready to hunt something. All you could do was to hope that it wasn't you.

He stopped pacing and looked at me. "Some days you eat the bear, and some days the bear eats you," he confided enigmatically.

"Yup," I agreed, not quite sure with what I was agreeing.

"I've had six pitching coaches in four years here, you know. None of them could handle it. The pitching stank, except for Ellerbee, and he wouldn't talk to any of them. Wouldn't say a single word. How the hell did you get through to him, huh? That's what I want to know."

"Me?"

"That's right; keep your little secrets." He looked at me with shrewdly calculating approval. "It's good business. Smart. You're a smart young man, Mike. Listen, just between you and me: why does a young man as smart as you are take a job as a baseball coach instead of becoming a success in some much better-paying field?"

"I love the game."

"Well, sure. But besides that?"

I let it go and simply asked: "How do you mean about getting through to Ellerbee?"

"Oh—I passed him earlier today, and I asked him how the arm felt. After all, I've got a lot of money invested in that arm. Now usually, when I ask him a question like that, he either grunts or nods without saying anything or, if he's in an especially good mood, he'll say 'fine.' But today, he actually stopped to say a whole entire sentence. Do you know what it was?"

"I wouldn't even guess."

"He said to me, 'That's the first pitching coach you've ever had here who's ever said anything that wasn't complete horseshit.'"

"I'm flattered."

"You're better than flattered, Mike." He winked at me and jovially stretched out a short, pudgy arm to reach up and clap my shoulder. "You're hired."

*   *   *

"That is so great, Dad," Jenna said enthusiastically that night at dinner. Everything our fifteen-year-old progeny did, she did full-bore; she was unmistakably her mother's child in that way as in so many others. Donna looked at our daughter with that expression that always managed to simultaneously blend approval and watchfulness. Seeing her piercing hazel eyes, I wondered, not for the first time, if I ever looked like that.

"Will you make a lot of money?" asked Laura. I don't know how she got so pragmatic at thirteen.

"Some, honey," I assured her.

"But he's not a ballplayer," Donna reminded her. "He's a coach. And coaches don't get as rich."

"Doesn't matter," said Jenna loyally. "Dad will be doing something he loves. That's what matters, right, Mom?"

"Right," said my smiling wife, her curly brown hair seeming to celebrate something as she held her head proudly regarding her eldest daughter.

"Mom makes money," Laura observed to no one in particular.

"Mom also does something she loves," said Mom.

"You love lawyering, Mom?"

"Of course she does," Jenna assured her. "Otherwise she wouldn't be doing it. Right, Dad?"

"Right," I emphatically agreed.

"I wonder," Laura wondered, "whether I'll get rich doing something I love, or love doing something that makes me rich. What do you think, Mom?"

Donna didn't even hesitate. "I think," she said firmly, "you should finish those carrots and worry about it later."

Squeezing

AS THE GAME PROGRESSED, I sat next to Pepper, as I usually did. It was easy to see he was distracted. It was also easy to see why. Every once in a while, he'd glance over at the phone on the wall. Not the black one that connected to the bullpen, but the red one Simon had installed that connected straight to the owner's box. Pepper knew—everyone in the dugout knew—that it might ring any time. And we all knew by now what those calls were like.

We were at bat trailing 2–1 in the fifth—Ellerbee had given up only one hit, but two guys had been on at the time because of an error by our third baseman, which was typical, and another by our shortstop, which wasn't, and both runners had scored—when the phone rang for the first time that night. I never knew if Simon had installed one with such a shrill, jumpy ring on purpose, but I wouldn't have been surprised if he had. He liked to keep his employees on their toes at all times.

Pepper stared at the instrument as though it were part of an alien invasion, but he picked it up. He had to. The players on the bench mostly pretended they weren't paying attention to the call; they all stared straight ahead at the field as if deeply engrossed in the game.

Pepper tried to keep his voice down, which was a challenge for him.

"Yeah." He listened for a moment. "Yeah, I know he's a right-hander and so is their pitcher. But the reason I don't send up a lefty to pinch hit is that if I do they bring in a lefty to pitch to him and their lefty in the bullpen is better than their righty on the mound who looks to me like he is just starting to tire now so maybe we can get to him before they figure it out and hook him, and I got my best left-handed lineup out there and if I make them bring in their lefty who is better anyway than this guy, I got their better pitcher pitching at an advantage over my lefty lineup, which I then have to leave in which hurts us the rest of the game, or pinch-hit for with righties in which case I got no lefties left on the bench and no righties either, and then the other team brings in their righty reliever who is their bullpen star and has got more saves than Jesus, and my lefty starters are now out of the game so I got to leave in my righties who are overmatched out there swinging against this smoke-throwing righty when they can hardly hit their southpaw grannies at a Sunday picnic, and now I got their ace fireman against my guys least likely to hit him and it's only the fifth inning here and all we need is a couple of stinkin' runs for Big Jake and that's why I'm not pinch-hitting."

He listened for a moment, then grunted something indecipherable and hung up quickly before he lost control and said what he really felt. He sat down next to me and regarded his gnarled hands.

"He says he still thinks his way is better, but if Johnson gets a hit all is forgiven," he muttered. "Can you believe that? Forgiven! Fucking fat stupid candy-assed shitheaded strawbrained bottle-peddling asshole. What the fuck have I got to be fucking forgiven for?"

"Johnson popped out to short," I told him. "While you were on the phone."

"What'd he do, swing at the first pitch?"

"Yeah."

"Fuck. So Zapata's up." He looked at the plate to confirm that the slim Dominican shortstop was indeed stepping in. "Shitfuck. That means the fat clown'll ring any second to tell me to hit for him, too. Fuckshit."

On cue, the red phone rang. Pepper looked at me. I wished there was something I could do, but there wasn't.

"Well," I said, "at least you knew it was coming."

The look in his eyes confirmed that my comment was no more help than I thought it would be. He picked up the phone and started talking without waiting to hear a word.

"I know his average stinks, and I know he's a singles hitter even when he's hitting them, which he isn't lately, but I'm not gonna hit for him. Yes, I'll be glad to tell you why. Because not only is he my only shortstop who can go to the hole and catch and throw whatever they hit at him and this is still only the fifth, but besides that they're gonna walk him no matter he wouldn't get a hit anyway, because my pitcher is up next and they'd always rather pitch to the pitcher who's less of a hitter automatically or pretty nearly though in this case I'm not so sure, but also because they're hoping I'll be dumb enough to hit for my pitcher to try to get a run in, which I won't pull

Big Jake when he's pitching like this with half the game to go even if he fans on three pitches, so you don't got to ask me next why I don't hit for Ellerbee when he comes up next which he will 'cause I guarantee you they're gonna walk Zapata."

We both glanced at the field where the intentional walk was under way. Pepper said to me, "Mr. Lumpe says that even as we speak, they're walking Zapata."

"Even as we speak," I agreed, watching the pitcher toss his fourth pitch intentionally far off the plate. The umpire waved Zapata to first, and he proceeded there at his usual gait, which looked like it would hurt him to appear as though he were making an effort. Angel was fast and quick diving for a ball in the field, but he put a great premium on looking cool—he had a habit of sauntering after pop flies just in time to barely catch them—so he always tried hard to look like he wasn't trying hard.

Pepper hung up the phone again and sat down. "I don't know how long I can take this," he whispered. His face had a sickly greenish tinge. "Hold the fort for a minute. I got to go to the fucking bathroom. My fucking stomach is acting up again." Teeth clenched, he glanced quickly at the field.

"Maybe Jake won't strike out. Redford's deuce is starting to hang like a peach on a tree, and he ain't got nothing else." He got up to go.

"Buck Thrasher," I said. Ordinarily, Pepper and I wouldn't trade old-timers' names during a game—no matter how much of what was happening on the field you absorbed, there was always more you were missing—but I was hoping a quick exchange might cheer him up, if only fleetingly.

He looked at me and mumbled, without enthusiasm, "Coaker Triplett."

"Van Lingle Mungo," I returned, playing an old ace. I knew that had to get at least the ghost of a smile from him. It did.

"Eppa Jephtha Rixey," he responded promptly. Then his face twisted in pain again and, his hand clutching his stomach, he turned to leave.

"Bill Wambsganss," I tossed after him.

He left the bench and went down the ramp towards the locker room. His voice floated back to me.

"Yeah, the old unassisted triple play. Funny thing to be remembered for, ain't it?" Then he was gone.

Pepper was right. Redford did hang a curve, and Big Jake, who didn't make contact too often but was strong enough to do something useful when he did, slapped the ball into right for a clean single. Since there were two down, Zapata was running on the pitch, and easily made it into third.

I gave the sign to Harry Brynan, our third-base coach. Harry had also played with Pepper and my dad; he was an old pro, and a smart one. He never hesitated or gave the slightest indication that anything unusual was up. He simply transferred the sign to the batter the same way he always did.

Willoughby stepped out when he saw the sign, which I'd figured he might. But he played it smart: he never looked at Harry a second time, which could have alerted the Jaguars that a play was on. Instead, he pretended to find something wrong with his bat, told the ump he was going to get a new one, and walked straight for the bat rack. I had already ambled over near it before the ump even called time.

When Willoughby got there, he picked up another bat and hefted it, talking to me without looking in my direction. I kept my gaze straight out at the field, not looking at him either. It was like we were both in some kind of spy movie.

"For real?" he asked, faking perusal of the bat.

"Yeah."

"There's two out."

"I can count to two, too."

"Where's Pepper, anyway?"

"Inside. It's my call." I spoke fast and low. "Terwilliger's playing way back and off the line because he's scared you'll slap it past him. If you drop the bunt fair down the third base line he'll never be in time, you'll catch him flatfooted, plus he still can't throw well since they cut him for elbow chips. Redford falls off the mound towards first and he takes forever to straighten up and he's a lousy fielder anyway. They'll never expect it. You're the fastest guy on the team, Marcus, and you know how to bunt, and Redford will put the first pitch in there. You're the only guy I can count on to put it down right and beat it out."

He liked that, all right. Out of the corner of my eye, I could see him smile. Sammy Kleh, the home-plate ump, headed our way to see what Marcus was doing.

"First pitch. After that, hit away," I added in a rush, then Sammy was upon us.

"Hey, Willoughby, I said you could pick out another bat, not cut down a tree and make one."

Then Marcus made his first mistake. He picked up his original bat and headed back to the plate. I hoped Kleh wouldn't notice; but Sammy doesn't miss much, and he didn't miss this. He stared at Willoughby's retreating back, then looked at me curiously.

"Where's Pepper?"

"In the head. His stomach was squeezing him."

He nodded, took one step away, then turned and looked at me sharply. I looked right back at him without changing expression. He turned his back to me and walked back behind the plate, putting his mask back on.

It worked just the way the squeeze play is supposed to and hardly ever does. Marcus, fired up at the challenge, waited till the last second before sliding the bat down and tapping the ball neatly towards third. It was actually a better bunt than was necessary; all he really had to do was get the ball down fair. Terwilliger lumbered in, but he never had a chance; Redford, who was actually closer, stared at the ball for a moment before even starting to chase it. The pitch was a fastball on the outside corner, a perfect pitch for Marcus to reach out and tap towards third (he was hitting lefty against the righty). What I hadn't told Willoughby was that the reason I figured he'd get a good pitch to hit was they sure as hell didn't want to walk him because then they'd have to pitch to Blasingame with the bases loaded, and they'd a lot rather pitch to Marcus, who's less of a threat to get on.

Zapata—who had been discreetly briefed on the play by Harry during my chat with Marcus—cruised across the plate before Redford even got his hand on the ball, and Marcus was so safe they didn't even throw to first. Sure enough, Kleh had picked up my hint about the squeeze coming, so he was thoroughly ready, in perfect position to see the play develop. The crowd roared—just the way it's supposed to when the home team works the squeeze play successfully, and for a base hit, no less—and the guys on our bench got excited and started whooping with glee (except for Strain, who seemed to be dozing, and Tambellini, who was combing his hair).

The Jag skipper slowly walked out to visit his pitcher. I hoped he'd leave him in so that Blasingame had a chance to take his cuts now that Redford was losing it and was rattled to boot.

The red phone rang. The guys on the bench looked at me. I picked it up.

"Great play, Pepper! Great!"

"Thanks," I said in a gruff voice I hoped sounded something like Pepper's, then hung up.

I was hoping they were willing to gamble that Redford could at least retire the side before they yanked him, when Pepper sat down next to me. He still looked greenish-yellow around the gills.

"What does he say?" he asked.

"He said 'great play, Pepper.'"

"That's 'cause it works. It's always a great play when it works. What'd you say back?"

"I said 'thanks.'"

"He thinks you are me?"

"I think so. I only said the one word."

He nodded. "I hear it on the clubhouse TV."

"Del Vecchio must've loved it."

"He does. He sounds as if he wins the lottery and the exacta on the same day. Screams 'holy tamale' maybe five, six times."

"He's excitable."

Pepper nodded in agreement. "Besides, he loves the bunt."

Blasingame grounded out and the inning ended. We watched our team take the field. Pepper looked at me.

"It is a good call, Mike."

"Hell, Pepper, you would have seen it before I did."

"If I am not distracted with this shit that is not really the game. If I am not busy defending my last move instead of making the next one which is my job down here."

I watched Big Jake wind up and pitch. It was a good pitch, a fastball high and in, but the batter fought it off and blooped it off the fists into left-center for a Texas League single. The next hitter managed to spin a decent outside curve off the end of his bat, slapping it the other way for another hit. Two on, none out. The red phone rang.

Pepper picked it up and listened for a moment before answering.

"They are two good pitches. He hasn't lost anything yet. Anyway, he is still better than anything I have in the pen. He stays out there until they hammer him like a two-by-four." He paused for another moment, grunted "Yeah," and hung up. Big Jake struck out the hitter for the first out.

Pepper shook his head. "This is insane," he said as softly as I'd ever heard him say anything. "This is not the way the game is meant to be managed."

"How's your stomach?"

"Lousy."

"Maybe you ought to have Doc Craig check it out."

"Yeah. Maybe I do that." He paused for a moment as we watched Ellerbee throw a low slider that the batter grounded on a nice, easy bounce to

Blasingame, who quickly threw to Zapata, who held the ball an extra second before throwing to Crockett just in time to complete the double play. Pepper shook his head.

"That fucking shortstop," he said. "One of these days he blows that play trying to make it look too fucking easy, and I bench him till he learns that you're allowed to throw the guy out by more than half a step."

The players came into the dugout, cheered by getting out of the inning without giving up a run. Pepper picked up the red phone on the first ring.

"Nice pitching," I said as Ellerbee passed me. He shook his head.

"That last pitch wasn't where I wanted it."

"But you were going for the double-play ball, not the strikeout."

"You noticed that." The hint of a smile touched his lips. "A few years ago, when I was younger, faster and dumber, I would have just tried to blow it past the next two guys, and thrown maybe nine, ten pitches and maybe one of them hits me anyway. This way, I get the two outs on one pitch, a nice simple ground ball."

"It's smart to make it easy on yourself."

"Yeah." The smile was gone now. "Funny, though, how long it can take you to learn that." He went to the far corner of the bench and sat there silently. I didn't hear him say another word to anyone for the rest of the game.

Pepper started to speak as soon as I sat down.

"Mr. Lumpe tells me again what a great play the squeeze is." I let him continue.

"He tells me how excited is Mr. Del Vecchio on the television."

"Del Vecchio would sound excited about an intentional walk."

"Dom is a fine ballplayer in his time, a .271 lifetime average and a quick second baseman who can really turn that double play. But you never know from his shilling on the television that he ever plays this game. I lose all respect for Dom when Garrett muffs the easiest ground ball you ever see one day at third and Del Vecchio yells, 'What a tough break—it hits him on the glove.'"

Tambellini doubled with two down in the eighth to drive in Blasingame with the winning run. Big Jake tired in the ninth, but Pepper brought in Garcia and Pablo shut them down with that off-speed junk of his, so we won 3–2. As soon as we got to the locker room Tambellini had his shirt off fast so that he could be bare-chested when the photogs came around. He claimed it helped the sales of his posters, but we all knew that Dante just liked to have everyone look at him with his shirt off.

It was a pretty relaxed clubhouse; it usually is when you win. It was mid–June and we were around .500 now, which didn't put us in contention exactly but which was a vast improvement on our cellar records of previous years. Best of all, we knew we would only get better. That is, if our owner would let us just play the game. But we also all knew that if that was a bet, you wouldn't take it.

Be Very Careful When
You Are Playing Anybody

THINGS STARTED TO UNRAVEL the next week when Philly came to town. It had nothing to do with Philly in particular—they just happened to be the team we were playing at the time—but Pepper immediately related it to baseball superstition.

"Philly is always my bad-luck team," he told me many months later. We were in MommaDaddy's Bar and Grille at the time; he had consumed what seemed like half a bottle of Jack Daniels, while I sipped a Blue (the Buffalonian nomenclature for Labatt's Blue Beer), and we both looked back at the whole strange season. "In my playing days, both my major injuries come against Philly, three years apart. And I can never hit even their worst pitcher to save my life. The year your dad and I win the pennant, Philly comes in dead last, but they are still the only team that has a winning record against us. That is the year your dad goes 17–5, and three of those five losses are against Philly. They are just my bad-luck team. Be very careful when you are playing Philly."

"It could have been any other team," I reminded him. "It had more to do with us than with them, after all."

"Be very careful when you are playing anybody," he amended.

In that Philly series, things started to go wrong from the very beginning of the first game when their leadoff man singled off Morgan Wyatt on the first pitch. Wyatt didn't like that. Morg was a burly, tough country boy who was pushing forty and had lost his good heater. The first game Wyatt ever threw for us, the Owls spent the entire game looking for his hard stuff while he one-hit them with off-speed junk, drawing this reaction from Pepper: "Either he's the greatest pitcher the world has ever seen, or he's lost his fastball." But Morg still knew how to pitch and was as vicious a competitor as you could wish out there on the mound. Pepper called Wyatt "a throwback," and he meant it as a compliment. So Wyatt did what you would expect a throwback to do. He threw a pitch right at the ear of the next batter, who barely managed to duck out of its way.

Now obviously no one gets much pleasure out of having a baseball thrown at his body; but people who haven't played this game have no conception what it's really like to stand up there at the plate. The pitcher, standing sixty feet six inches away (by the time he releases the ball, he's actually closer) hurls a hard, round missile which moves at about ninety miles an hour as it zooms towards your ear. It can injure or maim, and even if you want to hang tough in the batter's box your nerve centers scream out for you to go south pronto. It is a rare bird who is not affected by what the fraternity calls "purpose pitches." Some hitters get riled up and are even tougher: Joe DiMaggio and Frank Robinson would hit the ball even harder and farther off a pitcher who'd thrown at them. But many hitters are intimidated no matter how much they try not to be, and it makes them more vulnerable in the eternal struggle between the man on the mound and the man at the plate.

Morgan was doing what he had long ago learned to do—use the knockdown pitch as a warning and as a message. Mess with me, he was saying, and I'll make you pay for it. Wyatt had never been interested in being a nice guy; and as his natural skills had eroded, he was using the weapons he had left: guile and intimidation. To help the latter along, he didn't shave between starts, so that he always had a three or four days growth to make him look even uglier and meaner than he did already. He never spoke to anyone he was going to pitch against, and he always glowered whenever he looked at them. Unlike Ellerbee, Wyatt knew the batters were there—and he knew that they were the enemy.

The ump warned him, and the hitter gave him a hard look that Wyatt returned with contempt; but sure enough, the batter swung awkwardly at the next pitch—a curve that looked like it was heading for his ribs but then broke sharply over the plate—and grounded weakly to second. Blasingame flipped to second base; but instead of firing the ball to first, Zapata timed it as usual to get the hitter by a frustrating half-step—only this time, he miscalculated. The runner slid into him enough to make him take a little extra hop before releasing the ball, and the batter was a shade quicker down the line than Angel thought he'd be. It all took less than a second, and might not have even been noticeable to many fans; but it was enough to make all the difference. The batter, instead of being barely out, was barely safe. Instead of two out and nobody on, there was only one out and a man on first. In this game, that can be the difference between winning and losing.

Wyatt stood motionless a few feet off the mound and glared at his shortstop. Angel stood at second, kicking at the patch of dirt that always looked so lonely in the middle of all that fake green turf.

"Aw, shit," muttered Pepper. "Wyatt's pissed. Go calm him down—I don't want to waste a trip out there this early or make him think I think he's in any trouble."

I ambled out to the mound. Wyatt still stood there staring at Angel, who had returned to his position.

"Shake it off," I said as soon as I arrived. McCarter joined us, adjusting his catcher's equipment as he listened.

"That little fucker does that again and I'll knock his teeth out," Wyatt told me. He clearly meant it.

"Forget it."

"He's taking the bread out of my children's mouths."

"Both your kids are married. You don't support them any more," McCarter reminded him equably.

"I hate that kind of hot-dogging. I really hate it."

Crockett came over from first, but Zapata stayed at short, wise enough to keep away from Wyatt at this point. I didn't especially want Crockett there; his worrying wasn't going to help the situation. But he was just doing his job, coming over to try to help settle the pitcher.

"Don't worry, Morg. We'll just get the next guy."

"Shove it," snarled Wyatt.

"I know how you feel." Crockett was at his worst when he tried to be reassuring. "But there's no reason we should fall apart over this. It doesn't mean you have to give up back-to-back doubles or anything like that."

I shook my head at Crockett to try to get him to shut up, but Wyatt was already steaming. "Fuck you," he almost yelled.

Crockett blinked. "Hey, Morg. I'm your teammate. I'm only trying to help."

"And the horse you rode in on."

They glared at each other confrontationally. I could see Pepper looking on curiously from the dugout. Sandy Belcourt, the home plate ump, came out to the mound to see what was going on.

"Hey, fellas, we got a game to play here, remember?"

"Hey, ump," Wyatt asked him unexpectedly, "how's your wife?"

"Fine," answered a surprised Belcourt. "Why do you ask?"

"Cause she spread her legs so wide for all of us the other night I didn't know if they'd ever be able to get 'em closed again."

Sandy didn't really have a choice. He turned and made an elaborate thumbing gesture to indicate to those watching that he was throwing Wyatt out of the game. I give him credit for not saying anything to Wyatt at all while Morgan stalked off the mound and into the dugout.

Now Pepper did come out, disgusted when he heard what had happened. ("Take it out on the next hitter, not on the goddamn ump. Jesus, don't they teach you that in the Little League?") He brought in Donovan to take over; but Sam had nothing that day, and faced five men without retiring a single one. After the fifth straight hit, the red phone rang. Pepper held it just far enough from his ear that I could hear Simon's enraged bark.

"Get Donovan out of there. Have Dr. Craig examine him."

Pepper blinked. "Examine him for what? There's nothing wrong with him except nothing he throws is fooling anybody."

"He's endangering the fielders behind him. We have the contractual right to give him a physical examination any time we want. Well, I'm ordering Dr. Craig to give him one. Right now."

"You'll only embarrass him, Mr. Lumpe."

"Good. Maybe it'll help. His pitching couldn't get any worse, that's for sure. Meanwhile, bring in Sunderberg. Let's see what he's got."

"He just arrives from New Haven today. Maybe we should—"

"Let's see if he sinks or swims when the heat's on in the kitchen. If he's going to cut the mustard, he may as well start by going into the lion's den."

While I silently tried to visualize that, Pepper snapped tersely: "You want the kid, you got the kid."

Sunderberg got out of the inning with no further damage. He looked to be a control pitcher: ordinary fastball, decent curve, threw a forkball for his changeup. Location was obviously the key for him. The three guys he faced all made pretty good contact, but hit the ball right at somebody. The red phone rang after the third out.

"You see? The kid looks great, doesn't he? Three up, three down. I guess you don't have to be a so-called expert to know what moves to make in this game, no matter what you people say. Leave him in, no matter what."

"I intend to," said Pepper, and hung up.

The next inning Sunderberg retired the first man he faced. Four hits, three walks and a hit batsman later, the red phone rang again. Simon was screaming.

"Get him out of there! Now!"

"We're way behind and I already use up three pitchers in two innings. I need to let him eat up some innings for me."

"I said take him out. That's an order. He's disgracing the Buffalo Bears uniform. I don't care who you bring in, but get him out of there. Now!"

"All right," Pepper said resignedly.

"I'm sending Jay Greenberg down to the locker room to give Sunderberg a ticket to New Haven. I want him on a train back there tonight."

Pepper paled visibly. "You can't do that, Mr. Lumpe. You'll destroy the kid's confidence. He'll never be any good if he's afraid of making a mistake. He just got here today. Leave him up for another couple of outings anyway. Besides, I need the arm in the bullpen."

"I want the kid out of here. I will not have a pitcher on the Bears who spits the bit." This time, it was Simon who hung up first.

Pepper looked at me with real pain in his eyes. I couldn't tell for sure how much was his feeling sick, and how much was his empathizing with the poor kid on the mound who didn't yet know that this one bad inning would have him headed out of town within the next few hours. "I hate this," said Pepper softly, and went out to the mound to pull the kid and bring in Jack Lee.

Pepper told Sunderberg his fate before he left the mound. He could have pretended that he didn't know and passed the buck to Greenberg, but Pepper didn't play the game that way. The kid came off the mound and brushed past us blindly on his way to the locker room. There were tears in his eyes. I followed him into the room. He sat on a chair, crying openly. He saw me standing there and tried to stop weeping, but couldn't.

"I'm sorry," he sobbed.

"For what? You've got nothing to be sorry about. Some of the best pitchers around got clobbered in their first games. You'd be surprised."

"I shouldn't be crying," he said, crying. "There's no crying in baseball, right? Isn't that what that guy says in the movie?"

"Don't be a damn fool," I told him quietly. "There's nothing wrong with crying. It's a lot healthier than bottling it all up inside and pretending you don't care."

"I spit the bit," he told me sadly.

"You're not a horse, Curt. You're just a human being like the rest of us."

"Mr. Lumpe told me before the game that I had a great future if I had true grit and didn't spit the bit."

There were a number of things I felt very much like saying, but I fought them back and kept it to, "You had a bad day, Curt. Babe Ruth had bad days. We all do. Only God doesn't have bad days, and we're not even sure about that."

He looked at me wanly through the tears that streaked down his cheeks as if they were racing for some finish line in the general neighborhood of his jaw.

"It's just that I don't know if I'll get another chance," he said, clearly confessing his deepest fear.

"How old are you, Curt?"

"Twenty-one."

"You'll get another chance," I assured him. He smiled, which couldn't have been easy for him.

Jay Greenberg came in. The Bears PR man was in his usual spiffy suit—this one a three-piece navy-blue pinstripe—and was holding something that could only have been a ticket to New Haven. Normally Cole Boone, the General Manager, would give a player news of his demotion; but Cole was out of town scouting our Double-A team, so the unenviable task had fallen to Greenberg. Jay had his fake smile on, obviously prepared to have to tell Sunderberg the bad news.

"It's okay, Jay. Pepper already told him."

Greenberg visibly relaxed; the smile faded, and he looked more like a human being. "I'm sorry, Curt," he said, handing Sunderberg the ticket. "But Mr. Lumpe feels it's better for your development if you go back to New Haven. He feels you'll get more regular work there."

"But I just got here today."

Greenberg shrugged helplessly, trying unsuccessfully to look cheerful and reassuring. Sunderberg looked despondent.

"He'll probably trade me now," he said morbidly.

"It wouldn't be the worst thing that could happen to you if he did," I told him. They both looked at me oddly, but they both knew what I meant, even though the kid could admit it with his eyes and the PR man couldn't.

"New Haven's not such a bad town for a while," I reminded the kid. "It's just an experience to make the most of while you're there."

His smile was twisted. "It's no thrill for me."

"You won't be there long," I said, misunderstanding what he meant. He shook his head and enlightened me.

"I'm from Hartford," he explained.

We looked at each other and both started laughing. Our laughter got so prolonged and hysterical that even Greenberg joined in, glad and startled that this particular dirty job wasn't, for once, as unpleasant as the usual lying and pandering he was called upon to do. When we finally wound down, Sunderberg was still giggling with the absurdity of it all. I figured he'd be all right in time, if he didn't let it all get to him too much before he got out of this organization.

"Just hang in there, kid," said Greenberg impulsively. "Go get 'em."

"Right," I added. "When the going gets tough, the tough get going."

Jay joined the game with enthusiasm, gleeful at the chance to parody his normal line of horseradish.

"Winners never quit, and quitters never win."

"And let us not forget," I reminded him, "that old standby, every cloud has a silver lining."

"Even if it pisses rain on you anyway," added Jay, and we all three began laughing hysterically again.

When Sunderberg went to take a shower, he was actually smiling, and I felt better, even though I knew that the feeling wouldn't last. I thought of W.C. Fields' response when someone ugly accused Fields of being drunk. "That's right," agreed Fields. "But tomorrow, I'll be sober; and you'll be ugly for the rest of your life."

Jay actually had tears of laughter on his face. He shook his head at me.

"You guys," he said, smiling and shaking his head.

I just grinned at him, still feeling pretty good, and not wanting it to go away any faster than it had to.

"I like your Windsor knot, Jay," I said, eyeing the perfectly knotted blue-and-gold silk tie.

He smiled as if I had just paid him a bonus.

"Really?" he asked eagerly.

"Really."

"I really appreciate that. Most of the time nobody notices. You wouldn't believe how nobody notices. Thanks, Mike."

"Any time."

"Jesus," he confided to me, "I was sure this was going to be just another rotten job, you know? I never expected it would be all right like this. The kid is really taking it well, isn't he?"

"Yeah. But don't kid yourself, Jay. It *is* just another rotten job."

The smile left his face, but at least it took its time leaving.

"Yeah," he said quietly, and left.

The Unexpected Touch of Brass

WHEN I GOT BACK to the dugout, Pepper turned to me. "You're the pitching coach. Go talk to that crazy southpaw. If I got to pull him, I got nobody left but starters and my two short men."

"What do you want me to tell him?"

"Ask him why is he shaking off every single pitch the catcher is calling for."

I went to the mound to visit Jack Lee, an experience I often found equal parts entertaining and frustrating. Jack was a tall, lean lefty who had long hair, a beard, and a distant glitter in his meditative blue eyes. He was from Wyoming, adored the mountains, hated hunting, found big cities bizarre, and once told me if he hadn't loved baseball so much he'd have wanted to be a forest ranger. Jack was probably the most open-minded individual on the team. He'd discuss any subject at all with you—even if you only had the one you could talk about—with animated and genuine interest. That endeared him to some people, even though they did consider him flaky. Blasingame was still recovering from the time he had once asked Jack whether he preferred grass or turf, and Jack had answered that he didn't know, he had never smoked turf.

Of course, the flip side of that animated and genuine interest is that he always had an opinion about everything; and his opinions were sufficiently idiosyncratic to have earned him the nickname Pluto, as in the farthest planet (McCarter, our resident astronomer as well as film buff, literary and philosophy maven, refused to accept Pluto's demotion to the status of an ostentatious star). Lee and McCarter were the only teammates with whom Ellerbee would actually discuss his Zen exercises: Tom because he'd read about the concepts, but Jack because he'd explored them in his own way.

I went out to the mound briskly (giving the pitcher time to relax and settle down was irrelevant in Lee's case, since he was always in his own dimension anyway), but even so, McCarter was there before I was. I could see Tom's intelligence fighting with his frustration. He knew, liked, and appreciated Jack; but this was business out here, and Lee was driving him crazy. Still, Tom was the catcher and I was the coach, so he was smart enough to let me lead the conversation.

What I liked about Jack was what Pepper hated about him: that you never knew exactly what he was going to do or why he was going to do it. Most of the time that was because, as Jack cheerfully admitted, he had no idea himself until he found himself doing it. Unfortunately for Pepper, this extended to his approach to pitching. Lee was one of the toughest pitchers in the league for a hitter to outguess, because he never pitched according to any pattern that made sense to anyone else.

"Pepper wants to know," I told Jack, "why you are shaking off every single pitch your catcher is calling for."

"Pepper isn't the only one who wants to know that," added McCarter, his wryness not quite disguising his anger.

Jack pondered the question as though it were an abstract theory on which he had to make a thoughtful comment.

"They don't feel right," he finally said.

"Pluto," Tom explained patiently, "Kowalski is a low fastball hitter. He can't hit anything else. You threw him a low fastball."

"But I got him out on it."

"Only because he hit it so hard that Crockett couldn't get his glove out of the way."

"It was meant to be."

Tom sighed and tried again. "Gonzalez is a first-pitch, high-ball hitter. You threw him a high fastball on the first pitch."

"Really?"

"What do you mean, 'Really?'" Even Tom's cultivated patience was wearing out. "Yes, really. You threw him a high fastball on the first pitch."

"No, I mean was that really Gonzalez? I thought it was Fernandez."

Tom stared at him. Then, trying to stay controlled, he said softly, "Fernandez is a high-ball first-ball hitter, too."

"Yeah, but he can't hit it."

Tom's voice started to rise despite himself. "He hit it to the wall in right-center! Gonzalez can't reach the wall in right-center if you drive him there in a car!"

"I thought we were talking about Fernandez."

McCarter looked at Lee intensely, trying to get through to him with a searching look, since words obviously weren't doing it. I figured I might as well try.

"Jack, why don't you try it Tom's way for a couple of batters and see if it works? He does a good job of calling pitches, after all, and he does know the hitters. Why should you worry about it when he can do it?"

"I'm not worried about it," Lee assured me, scratching his beard reflectively.

"It's part of what I'm paid to do," Tom reminded him.

Jack looked at him seriously. "Money isn't everything, Tom."

McCarter couldn't take it any more. He slammed his mitt to the ground, but immediately pretended he'd just dropped it and bent down to pick it up.

"Oh, for God's sake," he muttered.

"Well, it isn't," said Lee passionately. "There's love and personal fulfillment, of course, not to mention art and family and baseball itself; but there's also the environment and our entire relationship to nature and the animal kingdom. Have you thought about that lately?"

"I like you, Pluto, I really do," said McCarter earnestly. "Don't make me kill you."

"What about strip-mining?" Lee was really getting warmed up now. "The whooping crane? The condor? Where have they all gone? How can we ever replace them?"

"We can replace *you*," I reminded him.

"That's true, of course," he agreed, suddenly calm and reasonable. "But there's nobody left to pitch but starters and the two short men, so I figured I was out here for a while; and since I'm just mopping up in a game we're so far behind it's unrealistic to expect us to be competitive—and even if we were to get competitive I'd be out of here in favor of Garcia or Hicks anyway—I figured as long as I was just here to get us through this thing as an exercise, I might as well try some interesting and exciting pitching motifs. You know, jazz it up a bit. The way you can jazz up a solid but unremarkable rock beat by adding the unexpected touch of brass to the predictable drum and guitar sections. It may be more effective or it may not, but it's at least different, and it keeps the senses alive, you know what I mean? Which reminds me: have either of you guys heard the new Eileen Rose CD? It incorporates this concept in a way that stirs the senses and makes the mind reconsider its own karma."

I waved Crockett back to first when I saw him start to come over, and I turned to McCarter. We exchanged a look.

"What do you think?" I asked him.

He relaxed, smiled and shrugged. "What the hell. What do I care, right?"

"That's the spirit," said Lee.

"Okay, Pluto, Modrzynski is up. How do you want to pitch him?"

"I have no idea," said Lee. "Let's just wing it."

McCarter held out his hands in acceptance. "Okay. I'll signal, you just let me know what you're going to throw."

"It'll be something unexpected, offbeat and interesting," Lee assured him.

"Okay," said McCarter, and started to go.

"Say, Tom," Lee called.

McCarter turned back impatiently. "What?" he barked.

Lee smiled at him. "It's only a game," he said.

We all looked at each other.

"Which we're losing in embarrassing fashion," McCarter reminded him.

Lee's smile became even warmer and more reassuring. "That's okay, Tiger. We'll get 'em tomorrow. Right?"

Despite himself, Tom grinned back. "Right," he said, and returned to the plate.

Lee looked at me cheerily. "Can I help you with anything else, Mike?"

"Just keep them off the bases, Jack."

He nodded in solemn assurance. "They're dogmeat, Mike. Don't give it another thought."

I started to walk off. Jack took a step after me.

"And tell Pepper not to worry. I'll get him to the eighth at least, and then he can always bring in Fast Eddie and let him practice throwing strikes."

I returned to the dugout. I could see that Pepper wanted to ask me what had been going on out there, but as I watched him I saw him decide that maybe he didn't really want to know.

"All straightened out with those two?" is what he asked.

I nodded. "Lee said to tell you not to worry, that he'll get you to the eighth at least, and then you can always bring in Hicks and let him practice throwing strikes."

"Wise guy," snarled Pepper. "If I don't need him on the team, I trade his ass out of here. Fucking wise guy."

"He is a left-handed pitcher, remember."

"True." He calmed down. "Southpaws are all crazy. No offense," he added quickly.

"None taken. I'm a righty, remember?"

"That's true," he said as if it were a discovery.

"My dad was the southpaw. And he'd be the first to agree with you."

Pepper grinned for the first time in a long while. "That he would," he said fondly.

The red phone rang. He stopped smiling. He picked it up, holding it close to his ear this time. He listened. "I don't," he said. He listened again. "Sure," he said and hung up. He looked over at me, shook his head and sat down.

"He wants to know what I think about Lee's beard. I say I don't. He asks me do I think it is suitable for the Bears' image. I say sure." He shook his head. "Jesus."

He looked at me. I could see he had to ask, even though the tone of his voice made it clear that he wasn't at all sure he really wanted to hear the answer.

"So what the hell is bothering Lee, anyway?"

"He was worried about the environment."

"What the hell for?" He shook his head dismissively. "We play in a goddamn dome. The environment is always perfect in this fucking place."

Samming

WE LOST THE GAME 15–4, so it wasn't surprising that Simon stormed into the clubhouse afterwards. He had done this before, but he generally picked his spots; he knew that browbeating lost its effectiveness if you did it too often. But sometimes when we took an unholy shellacking, he would charge into the locker room and scream bloody murder. Taking an unholy shellacking is something that happens to every team in baseball, including the very best, but Simon just wouldn't understand that. He thought that acknowledging the possibility of defeat was the same as resigning yourself to it. Custer probably thought the same thing.

Most of the times this happened, the guys pretty much controlled themselves—which wasn't easy, because they knew better than anyone when they'd played lousy, and they felt pretty bad about it without being harangued. But Simon truly believed that if he paid you enough, he had bought the right to humiliate you; and that if he humiliated you enough, you would be goaded into playing better and harder. As I already mentioned, he thought this was football.

"That's the sorriest exhibition I've ever seen in my life!" was his greeting to the players, who sat on stools or stood uncomfortably shifting their feet, hoping this wouldn't last too long. "If I were you, I'd be ashamed to face my family. You should be sneaking out of the dome with the peanut vendors. Garrett, you left six runners on base. Six!"

I couldn't believe he was picking on Joe Garrett. The biggest, strongest, most dignified man on the team, the unofficial team leader and the one most universally respected, he was also the one who could most easily rip any of us in half if he ever lost sight of his maturity and class. I was fervently hoping he wouldn't.

"I wasn't *trying* to leave 'em on base, Mr. Lumpe," he said softly in that deep voice that seemed to originate from Middle Earth.

"But you did!" screamed Simon, who always hated to be answered back. "You didn't drive them in, and that's what I pay you for!"

"I was trying my best," Joe said even more softly. I could see his powerful corded arms bunch up in tension (Joe never wore a sweatshirt under his uniform, no matter how cold the weather: he figured the sight of those massive biceps flexing at the plate would intimidate a lot of pitchers, and he was right), and I found myself hoping intensely that Simon would have either the brains or the luck to pick on someone else, and fast.

Donovan may have saved Simon's life. I don't know what possessed Sam to hurl his glove into his locker at that particular moment, but the resulting thud caught Simon's attention. His beady little eyes raced around the room to see who had dared make a noise. When he saw it was Sam, his face grew redder than the inside of an overripe watermelon, and he really exploded.

"Donovan!" he yelled. "I pay you all that money, and you pitch like that? Have you no shame? You disgrace that uniform, this team, the very nation itself! Have you no pride in yourself, man?"

Sam had had a brutal day. He was mad and frustrated; he was humiliated about Simon's spontaneous order that he be given a physical examination; and he didn't have Garrett's self-control even without the other factors. So it was a major effort for him to restrain himself; it was pretty clear that he was close to the breaking point.

"I don't need any goddamn physical," he managed between clenched teeth.

Simon couldn't have turned any redder, but his features did seem to deepen into a subtly darker shade. Before he could let loose with his next comment, though, McCarter's voice lilted calmly through the otherwise silent clubhouse.

"Sure you do, Sam. We all do. Got to be in top shape, right? Besides, maybe Doc Craig will give you some great drugs for what ails you."

It was a gutsy move on Tom's part; he knew Simon would have to turn on him now, but it was the only way to try to keep Sam from going over the edge. Simon cooled off enough to regard McCarter with suspicious, calculating eyes.

"You have something to say, McCarter?" he hissed.

"No, sir. Not really, sir. Sorry, sir."

"You stunk as bad as anyone else out there, you know."

"Yes, sir. And I know it, sir. I assure you I will endeavor to do better, sir."

"If that was a joke about drugs, McCarter, it was in damn poor taste."

"Yes, sir, it certainly was. I don't know what came over me."

"There is no drug abuse on the Buffalo Bears, am I right?"

"Oh, yes, you certainly are. And I can only apologize to my teammates for any sensibilities I may have offended. Guys," he stood up now, heady with the tightrope he was walking but confident he could maintain his balancing act, "I apologize to everyone for my joking about drugs, which as we all know none of us ever use, and which was in poor taste. Will you forgive me?"

Some of the guys nodded. No one said anything for fear of shifting attention to himself. The sooner this was over, the better, and we all knew it. Except, of course, for Simon. He glared around the room with the authority of a man who pays the bills, and knows that that single qualification gives him the power to abuse the people he pays.

"If you guys don't shape up, and fast," he said ominously, "there are going to be some changes made around here. And that goes for everyone in this room. Is that clear?"

More nodding, combined with some guarded relief at the hope that maybe it was over for now. It might have been, too, if Simon hadn't happened to glance at Donovan one more time before he went through the door.

"Jesus, Donovan," he said, deftly pouring some more salt on the wound and briskly rubbing it in, "I've seen little leaguers pitch better than you did today."

It wasn't especially insulting by Simon's standards; but timing is everything in life, and for Donovan, it was the proverbial straw that snapped the camel's hump. He simply exploded in a deluge of uncontrollable rage.

"Fuck you, Simon!" he screamed. "You've never played this fucking game, you fucking fat stupid bag of guts! You have absolutely no idea what goes on out there, asshole, you haven't got a clue, not one fucking clue, and then you come in here and tell us we were lousy, goddamn it, we *know* we were lousy, no one has to fucking tell us we were fucking lousy, and no one goes out on that field trying to be fucking lousy. This is a hard game, man, it's a fucking hard game, if it wasn't any asshole could be a major leaguer but you got to be able to really play this game to be in the bigs and you, you don't even know what it's all about. If you'd ever played this game for one fucking inning you'd know what a dumb ass thing it is to run off your mouth when you don't know what you're fucking talking about, you dumb fuck. We're trying, man. We're out there fucking trying. And all you can do is fucking sit back and criticize when you don't know what the fucking hell you're fucking criticizing, you fucking shithead!"

An utter, dead silence fell over the room. No one moved. Simon just stood there, his mouth hanging agape, motionless. Sam glared at him, his chest heaving, his harsh breathing as audible as rain on a tin roof.

Finally, Simon raised a trembling finger and pointed it at Sam. He was about to say something—probably "you're gone"—but when Sam saw the raised finger he snarled viciously and took a step towards the shorter man. Simon paled, turned quickly and exited the room without a word. Everyone left Donovan alone while, screaming obscenities, he rearranged the locker room until it resembled a tossed salad. I noticed McCarter discreetly taping the whole thing for posterity.

Tom had copies made up and gave one to every player on the team. As a coach—therefore implicitly a semi-member of management—I received mine only when I asked him for one. It remains one of my prized possessions. From that day on, we had two additions to our clubhouse vocabulary. Doing something that was likely to get you shipped out pronto was henceforth referred to as "pulling a Donovan"; and brutally assaulting someone with the unedited truth was called "Samming."

Missionary Man

DONOVAN WAS GONE, all right; traded the next day, with a couple of minor-leaguers, for Steve Armstrong—an announcement that drew audible groans from Willoughby and Blasingame, who had both played with Steve elsewhere. Armstrong was capable at third and first, okay in the outfield—though his arm wasn't much—and he was a strong, reliable line-drive hitter; but his team was willing to give him up because they didn't want to pay him what he would doubtless command as a free agent next year and because, according to the grapevine, so many of his teammates hated him. I wasn't worried about the former reason—whatever Simon's faults, he had amply demonstrated his willingness to overpay people if he decided they were players he wanted—but I was concerned about the latter.

"Why?" asked Pepper, who had enough to worry about already. "The guy can play this game, we all know that. So who cares about his goddamn personality?"

But that was wishful thinking. Some people can be hard for others to take, but they let you ignore them if you try hard enough. Armstrong, though, was a difficult man to ignore.

The day he joined the team, he walked from locker to locker introducing himself to his new teammates. A nice gesture, I thought, and asked Willoughby and Blasingame why they didn't at least make an effort to be friendly, considering that he was their teammate now, and that he might genuinely help the club.

"What you don't understand," Terry explained, "is that by ignoring him, I *am* making an effort to be friendly. It's only when I listen to him that he gets on my nerves."

When Armstrong came over to greet me, he was in uniform; but even in his baseball double-knits he somehow managed to look like a clothing advertisement in an especially slick fashion magazine. Every razor-cut hair on his smooth head was in place, as if none dared stray out of order. His teeth flashed so whitely that you had to repress an instinct to blink when he smiled at you. His handshake was firm enough to make a pair of pliers wince. The blue eyes regarded me earnestly from his square-jawed, perfectly even-featured face.

"Hello, Coach McGregor."

"Mike is fine."

"Okay, Coach Mike."

"Just plain Mike'll do."

"Okay, Mike. I'm Steve Armstrong."

"I know. Welcome to the Bears."

"Thank you, Mike. I'll certainly try to contribute to the team in any way I can. I've always been a team player. Individual goals shouldn't matter; it's the good of the team as a whole that counts. Right?"

"Right."

"Right. So if you have any suggestions or criticisms, I certainly hope you'll make them. I wouldn't want you to hesitate just because I have a .287 lifetime average and hit twenty-six homers the season before last. That doesn't mean I'm not open to constructive criticisms from my coaches and teammates. I'd really prefer it if I was treated as just one of the guys."

"You *are* just one of the guys."

His earnest look didn't waver; the blue eyes held mine steadily.

"Exactly. I really appreciate your taking that attitude, Mike."

"*De nada.*"

"Right. That's Spanish. I know what that means. And I gather that we have several Hispanic ballplayers on the club. I'm glad to hear that. It's the American way, recognizing talent regardless of race, creed, religion or national origin. I'm sure they're all fine, upstanding fellows."

"Zapata can get on your nerves sometimes."

"I'm sure that's just his ethnic way. One of the glories of our plural-istic society is appreciating the other fellow's point of view, don't you think?"

"Not me. I think anyone who disagrees with me is a horse's ass."

He nodded without missing a beat. "You're kidding, of course. I cer-tainly appreciate a sense of humor," he said solemnly. "It can be very important. I don't have much of one myself. It's one of my character flaws. But I'm working on it."

I nodded without saying anything. He regarded me with the same steadfast sincerity he had maintained throughout the conversation.

"Realizing how many areas there are in which I can still improve myself keeps me humble," he told me.

"I can see that."

"By the way. Speaking of humility. I asked around, and I gather there isn't an active Christian fellowship chapter on the team. So I thought I'd organize one. Just a short weekly get-together to thank the Lord for our blessings and maybe say a prayer or two for those worthy wishes closest to our hearts. Maybe you'd like to join us?"

"I don't think so."

"It wouldn't take long. Maybe half an hour or so. Just once a week."

"No thanks."

"I just thought it might help inspire some of the other fellows if the team's leadership was involved."

"I think I'll stay as I am."

"No man is an island."

"No continent is, either."

He pumped my hand again. "Well, thanks for this little chat, Mike. I enjoyed it." He moved away, looking around to see if there was anyone he hadn't met yet.

It wasn't long before the mere sight of Armstrong approaching made his teammates suddenly remember they should be in the trainer's room or warming up outside. In one sense, it helped the team's work habits: there were a lot more guys hustling out to the field so that they wouldn't have to talk to Armstrong in the locker room.

"Oh, Daddy, are you sure you're not *exaggerating?*" Laura asked me at the dinner table when I mentioned how desperately most of the team avoided Armstrong.

"No, honey, I'm not exaggerating."

"But is he really *that* bad?" Her slightly myopic but beautiful brown eyes always made me feel, whenever I looked into them, that they somehow contained my heart. She tossed her long, chestnut-brown mane as if she had just decided it was annoying her. "I mean, all he's doing is being friendly to people, right?"

"Don't be stupid," said Jenna.

"Don't talk to your sister that way." Donna's rebuke to Jenna was sharp and immediate.

"Well, she *was* being stupid."

"Was not," Laura protested.

"Was too."

"Was not."

Donna made a beeping sound twice, our signal to the girls that they were entering a danger zone and needed to cease hostilities immediately. Three beeps was red alert.

They both looked at their mother. Jenna's face, framed by her short strawberry-blond hair, seemed a bit sulky. Donna smiled at the intense, angular features of our all-too-soon-to-be sixteen year-old daughter, and reminded her:

"If you disagree with what Laura is saying, you can certainly explain why more effectively than just calling her stupid, can't you?"

Jenna's mouth stayed tight, the thin lips drawn tensely; but the clear gray eyes lit up with competitive challenge.

"Certainly," she said calmly. Her voice, so warm and emotional most of the time, became almost exaggeratedly precise the way it always did when she was making a conscious effort to be a grownup. She turned to her younger sister. Laura waited with the detached curiosity that always made me wonder what she was *really* thinking.

"You remember your dumb classmate you were telling me about?"

"Jenna." Donna regarded her sternly.

"Well, Laura herself called this guy dumb, didn't you, Laura?"

"How would I know?" asked Laura. "I don't even know who you mean."

"You know, your dumb classmate."

"I've got a lot of dumb classmates."

"You told me about this one."

"I told you about a lot of them."

"This one was obnoxious."

"A lot of them are obnoxious."

Donna couldn't keep her face straight. Jenna steadfastly refused to lose her grip. She kept the questions coming, knowing as we all did that Laura would make her earn every answer. I watched the two of them circle each other without ever moving from their respective chairs.

"The one who you said always wanted everyone to say Howdy Do every time they saw him."

"Oh. You mean Billy Kardensky."

"Yes."

"No."

"What do you mean, no?"

"He's not my classmate."

"What difference does it make?"

"You said he was my classmate. He's not my classmate."

"Okay. He's not your classmate."

"You said he was. He isn't. Billy Kardensky is only a year younger than you. I'm two years younger than you."

"I'm perfectly aware how old you are, Laura."

"Not if you think Billy Kardensky is my classmate, you're not."

I felt a surge of pride watching Jenna make the mighty effort to control herself. She didn't look at me, but I knew she was aware I was watching her. Laura's gaze remained locked onto her older sister, as if looking away would somehow give Jenna some sort of advantage.

Jenna took a couple of deep breaths, just the way I had taught her to do before shooting a foul shot. "Okay. You agree that Billy Kardensky wanted everybody to say Howdy Do whenever they saw him."

"Not whenever they saw him."

"Whenever they would have said hello. He wanted everyone to say Howdy Do to him instead of hello."

"That's right," agreed Laura with a trace of reluctance.

"And you told me that you thought that was really dumb and that Billy Kardensky was being a jerk."

"Billy Kardensky is an idiot."

"But he was only trying to be friendly, wasn't he? In his own stupid obnoxious way?"

"He's still an idiot."

"Of course he's an idiot. That's the whole point. If someone goes around trying to make you be friendly in exactly the way he wants you to be friendly, not the way *you* want to be, don't you think that person is obnoxious?"

"Yes."

"Well, that's all I mean. This new player on Daddy's team is doing the same thing."

"No he's not."

"Yes he is."

"He's not telling everyone to say Howdy Do instead of hello."

"Don't be stupid."

Laura smiled. Donna shot Jenna a look.

"She knows what I mean," Jenna said sullenly.

"Of course I know what you mean," agreed Laura. "All you had to do was say 'You know what I mean' instead of telling me not to be stupid."

"Eat your broccoli, Laura," Donna told her.

"I'd eat it quicker if it was a Beef on Weck. Can we go out for some later?"

"You can eat your broccoli now," Donna said in her overly reasonable lawyer voice, "or you can eat it in ten minutes. It's entirely up to you."

Laura considered for a moment, then reluctantly shoveled a piece of broccoli into her mouth and chewed it. After she swallowed, she looked at me.

"Daddy?"

"Hmmm?"

"Actually, I do see what Jenna means. If Mr. Armstrong is really like that, I don't blame the other players for not liking him very much. I mean, I wouldn't either. You'd have to lock him in a room with Billy Kardensky or something."

"Why don't you tell your sister that?" Donna looked at Laura with an intensity that made it seem as though she were scanning our daughter's vital signs.

"What? That you'd have to lock him in a..."

"That you do see what she means. After all the effort she took to explain it clearly to you, don't you think you should at least tell her that you know what she means?"

Laura looked at Donna, then at me, and finally at Jenna. Jenna sat straight in her chair, trying to look unconcerned. But her flushed face, and the unconsciously proud way she held her head back and slightly tilted to the right, made it more obvious than she knew that she felt a sense of accomplishment.

Laura carelessly flipped a piece of broccoli around her plate, regarding it as though it might attack her.

"Oh," she replied offhandedly, "she already knows that."

Chuga-chuga-chuga
Whoosh

WHEN I HEARD FROM Charlie Luposo, our equipment manager, that we had picked up Pete Cook on waivers, I figured I'd better have a talk with Cole Boone and find out what exactly he'd been thinking when he'd done it. As soon as I walked into his office, though, our General Manager held up his hands palms out.

"It wasn't my idea," he informed me before I had a chance to say a word. I sat in a chair opposite his desk and waited for him to continue.

"Simon says his record is too good to pass up. And the scouts say he throws as hard as ever."

I rolled my eyes as Cole spread his hands in empathy. He was a good baseball man, but we both knew that he was as helpless as the rest of us about decisions like this.

"Well," he said, "after we sent Sunderberg back down and traded Donovan, Pepper did say you had to have another arm in the pen."

"Not Captain Cook, Cole."

"He was on waivers."

"There's a reason for that."

He fidgeted. "Look, Mike, I argued against it. Simon really thinks it's a good idea. He thinks Cook will help the team and be good color for the local press."

"He's never been anything but trouble anywhere he's ever been."

"I know, I know," he said unhappily. He looked as miserable as I felt, and there didn't seem to be much point in discussing it further. There wasn't a lot either of us could do aside from telling Simon he was a damn fool, and both of us liked our jobs a bit too much to be doing that just yet.

So Cook joined the bullpen. Fortunately, most of the pitching staff had little to do with him. Ellerbee ignored everyone anyway, and Wyatt didn't listen to anyone. Danny Love was too smart and Van Vellis too experienced to have any truck with Pete. Jack Lee was on his own planet (for once, I was grateful for that) and I advised Garcia to pretend that he spoke only Spanish when Cook was around. But I was concerned about Hicks. I warned him to keep as much distance as possible from our newcomer, but Fast Eddie was a young, impressionable kid, and I worried; he was just Pete's type.

So one afternoon, when Cook was sprawled on the bench spitting tobacco at the pigeons and betting with Hicks on his aim, I waved him over to me. He hitched his pants and sauntered over. His seemingly permanent three day's growth, his unkempt dark hair, and his swaggering walk made it easy to see how he'd come by the nickname of Captain Cook. He went out of his way to cultivate the piratical image; he figured it was good for business, and it probably was. Trouble was, his business boded no good for anyone else's, and it was part of my job to keep him from wreaking havoc on the troops in my charge.

"Pete," I told him bluntly, "I don't want you messing up my pitching staff."

He grinned at me with more viciousness than amusement. "How could I mess up this bunch of pansy-assed pussy-whipped space cadets?"

"Stay away from Hicks."

He snickered. "Maybe you'd better tell the little punk to stay away from me."

"I did. I don't trust him to do it."

"Well, shit my britches, coach, if you can't trust the little fucker, I guess you'll just have to baby-sit him and make sure he doesn't do dirty in his diapers, huh?"

"Just don't give me an excuse to come down on you. If you do, I'll take it."

"I hear you're a college boy, coach," he said softly. He made sure that it sounded like an insult.

"I hear you're an asshole. I guess we both heard right."

I half-hoped he'd take a swing at me, but he just grinned with what seemed to be evident pleasure.

"You and me'll get along okay. At least you're not one of these fuckin' jerk-offs who pretends we all got to be lovey-dovey teammates and all that horseshit."

"Leave Hicks alone," I repeated.

"You do your job, coach," he told me evenly. "I'll do mine."

He grinned as though he thought he really was a buccaneer captain and strutted back to the bench, not even pausing as he aimed a gob of tobacco juice at Hicks' newly polished shoes. He didn't miss, as Fast Eddie's plaintive squeal attested.

A couple of days later, Pete was throwing in the bullpen, just loosening up in case he was called into the game. He tossed the ball with no great urgency while I watched to see how his stuff looked. Suddenly we heard a high, squeaky voice call:

"Captain Cook!"

The voice spoke in a tone of awed rapture. At first it seemed to be disembodied; but after a moment of glancing around, we all saw the speaker quite clearly. In fact, you couldn't have missed him. It was a little kid around nine years old. He was hanging onto the fence, his hands stretched to their limit as they gripped the wire that separated our bullpen from the nearby stands. He had apparently climbed from his seat to the edge of the fence, swung down and clambered his way to where he could actually see us moving around.

The boy had hung himself out there in flagrant disregard of his own life and limb; he was splayed across the fence in a position that made him look like one of those pictures of torture victims in a concentration camp. It was perfectly obvious which of us was his hero: I don't know if he even noticed any of the other guys. He just stared at Pete Cook with the look of a true believer who has just seen the face of his own personal God.

Cook paid no attention to the kid's adoring regard. He kept throwing to Cohen, who gestured towards the worshipful boy; but Pete ignored both the catcher and the kid. He just kept tossing those meaningless warm-up pitches.

"Captain Cook!" the boy called again, with the tentativeness of being scared and the determination of someone who has found Paradise and refuses to be expelled without a fight. "Captain Cook!" he repeated doggedly, hoping against hope that his hero would find him worthy of some slight acknowledgment.

"Jeez, Pete," said Cohen softly, "at least say hi or something."

"Fuck you," Cook answered him, throwing another pitch. Cohen caught it, then returned the ball with a purposefully wild toss. The ball sailed past Pete's glove and bounded to the fence where the boy still hung on, oblivious to the pain of his suspended arms and legs, conscious only of the fact that Pete was now actually facing his direction.

"Captain Cook," the boy breathed in awe, as if affirming the miraculous fact.

"Beat it, kid," snarled Pete. Then he picked up the ball and deliberately loosed a stream of tobacco juice in the kid's direction. Maybe he didn't actually mean to hit him, or maybe he did. Whichever, the tobacco juice splashed over the kid's face and shirt, the dirty brown globular spit dripping down his spread-eagled body.

Pete smirked slightly and threw the ball to Cohen. Dave caught it and stood up, holding the ball with his hands on his hips. Danny Love regarded Pete with a look of disbelief; Van Vellis' face showed his contempt. Garcia looked appalled, but then remembered he wasn't supposed to acknowledge that he knew English when Cook was around; so he just glanced over at me.

I walked over to the kid, who still hung there, pressed up against the fence. I would have wondered where he found the strength, but I knew what the sheer force of will could accomplish when you were a little boy who had a chance to see your baseball idols in the flesh. I had seen this kid a thousand times or more; I had *been* him once. Bullets wouldn't have stopped him from reaching that bullpen fence. I smiled at him. He smiled back through the dark spittle with which his hero had marked him.

"Hi, fella," I greeted him. "What do they call you?"

"Jimmy." His smile of happiness absolutely shone through his smeared face.

"Hi, Jimmy."

"That's Captain Cook," he confided.

"It sure is."

"He spoke to me." He said it a little fearfully, as if afraid that it was too wonderful to really be true. His look silently pleaded with me to confirm that it had truly happened.

"He sure did, Jimmy." I reaffirmed the miracle. "Go back to your seat now, okay?"

"Okay," he said, his grin exploding, his mission accomplished, his dream fulfilled. In that moment, I almost envied him. Not too many folks get spit on and find ecstasy in it.

I watched him clamber back to his seat. He looked as though he could fly if he'd wanted to. He made it easily back into the stands, unconcerned about the tobacco residue all over him, rapturous in having been paid attention to by his idol. I turned to face Cook.

"You're a prince among men, Pete."

He grinned. "Dumb little fucker gets spit on and doesn't know enough to mind."

"Well, Pete, with your help, someday maybe he'll learn to mind."

"You bleeding heart liberals kill me. You really do. If someone's stupid enough to take it, fuckin' let him have it. That's *my* motto." He spit on the ground in punctuation.

"Well, he's young yet. Give him time to achieve your mature wisdom."

Pete sneered in contempt, but the passion in his eyes and in his voice was real.

"Nobody gives you nothing in this life. I didn't make the world this fucked-up, but that's the way it is. Nobody ever gave me a break, and ain't nobody ever gonna give *him* one. The sooner the little prick learns that the better. I'm doing him a fucking favor."

"Why, Pete," said Danny dryly, "I didn't know you were a social philosopher."

"Ballplayers," he spat. "Imagine a kid being so stupid he has fucking ballplayers for heroes."

"A lot of kids feel that way, Pete," observed Cohen.

"A lot of kids are stupid."

"Who were *your* heroes?" Danny asked him.

"Outlaws," he answered immediately. "Guys who jerked around law and order and never got browbeat into no kind of respectability or religion. Guys who knew what life was for—grabbing all the highs and snatch and good times you can get your hands on, and to hell with everyone else."

"You must be fun to live with," said Cohen.

Cook grinned his pirate's grin. "I don't want no broad around full-time," he said. "Don't need one. Use 'em and lose 'em, that's my motto. When they start wanting to make a nice pretty package out of it and wrap it all up with pink ribbon, that's when it gets into big trouble for any man with balls."

"Thank you for those insights, Pete," I told him. "I'm sure we'll all give them the consideration they deserve."

When I recounted the incident to Donna later that evening, she literally ground her teeth and suggested that if some of the players used Cook's head for batting practice, it would not bother her in the least. "God, how I hate people who have no respect for other human beings," she said. "You have no idea how much male chauvinist misogynistic crap I have to wade through every day in the office, with crazy clients, with judges who are pompous political hacks and courtrooms that..."

"Sure I do." The moment I said it, I knew I shouldn't have. Interrupting Donna was never a good idea; interrupting her with a comment that you wouldn't be able to defend was borrowing trouble. She shot me a look that hit me fair and square.

"No, you don't. You spend your life playing a game. You have no clue what it's like out there in the real world when you can't just show people the scoreboard to prove you're right about something."

But within a week, we had occasion to remember Pete's comments on ballplayers and women. A feminist national magazine called *Athena* came out with an issue featuring, among other things, an "in-depth" interview with Pamela Armstrong, whom their magazine copy described as "the wife and partner of Buffalo Bear baseball star Steve Armstrong, who is undeniably cute (see photo) but who is definitely the kind of old-fashioned male that a lot of us wish they didn't make any more."

Donna wordlessly handed me the issue as soon as I walked through the door of our house. The tightness of her beautiful angular features telegraphed her tenseness. In the background, I heard Jenna bouncing her basketball outside as she practiced her moves driving to the hoop. We had worked on them together enough so that if I concentrated, I could visualize which moves she was trying just by listening to the rhythm and pace of the ball's syncopated thuds. Laura, I assumed, was upstairs tapping at the computer, mastering another byzantine program while listening to this week's favorite rock group on her headset. I read the interview carefully, then tossed the magazine down and gazed into space. Donna was looking at me as though she was a scientist and I was an experiment.

"Stupid," I finally said. "Really stupid."

"Don't say anything sexist," she warned, "or I'll throw this pillow at you. That *is* why they call it a throw pillow, right?"

"That wasn't sexist."

"No," she agreed with a trace of reluctance, "it wasn't. Actually, it *is* stupid. To say that to a reporter. But what she must have been going through all this time. Poor Pamela."

"Poor Steve."

"C'mon. You don't even like him."

"No, I don't. But this sure makes me feel sorry for the poor son-of-a-bitch."

"He doesn't merit our sympathy," she said firmly.

"Put it this way. He'll certainly pay for his sins now."

"Not enough."

"Enough," I assured her. I picked up the magazine again and read a few choice comments aloud.

"Being married to a ballplayer really isn't glamorous at all. He's on the road so much you're lonely most of the time and then when he's back you feel like you're just kind of there, like the furniture, only prettier and you can talk, though you're not supposed to do too much of that, either...."

"Sex? Exciting? Look, just because your guy's on a bubblegum card doesn't mean it's so great in bed unless you get off on bubblegum cards. I mean, athletes are sort of used to thinking of themselves a lot, you know? Chuga-chuga-chuga whoosh, and if the girl gets any pleasure out of it it's purely coincidence, let me tell you."

Donna's full lips were drawn tight, her light-brown curly hair seeming almost truculent as it framed her troubled features. She shook her head as if she would get both Armstrongs out of her hair if she could only toss it around with sufficient vigor.

"Chuga-chuga-chuga whoosh?" I repeated.

"Okay," she said defensively, "so she isn't all that articulate. But she makes her point, wouldn't you say?"

"I *would* say. And I'll have plenty of company in so saying."

"She even calls herself a girl," she muttered. "I mean the woman is *how* old? Twenty-seven?"

"Going on sixteen." She shot me a warning glance. I held up my palms peacefully.

"Look, I know what she means. The problem is, everyone else is going to know, too. How much fun do you think it's going to be for a straight-arrow old-fashioned male like Armstrong to have to put up with locker-room humor from his none-too-tactful peers in the daily environment of a locker room after they hear on TV that his wife thinks he's a boring chauvinist who runs for office in his own house and is lousy in bed?"

"*Fun?*" Donna spewed the word as if it were an obscenity. "A man that insensitive to his wife's misery—even if she is a dumb twinkie, she's still his wife—doesn't deserve fun. If he gets humiliated by this, it'll only be poetic justice."

"Well, I don't know if it's poetic or justice, but humiliated he is certainly likely to be."

"Good," she said with passionate satisfaction (whatever Donna did, she did passionately). "I hope it doesn't take long."

"It won't."

It didn't. Most of the guys had sense enough to avoid referring to the subject around Armstrong; and when Tad Strain did gigglingly ask Steve how the family was, he found himself suddenly lifted and moved a few feet away, where he beheld the large form of Joe Garrett regarding him.

"What you trying to do, Tad? Be clever?"

Tad nodded. Garrett shook his head.

"Forget it. Stick to what you know how to do." He paused. "*Is* there something you know how to do?"

"Sure," said Tad.

"Good," said Joe, and walked away. Tad looked a bit confused, but at least he left Armstrong alone for the moment.

Steve was actually on his way out of the locker room when Captain Cook came in. They both stopped to avoid running into each other. Cook moved aside, elaborately gesturing Steve towards the door.

"You going somewhere, preacher, don't let me stop you."

Maybe if Armstrong had just walked out without saying anything, nothing would have happened, at least not then and there. But I guess it was too hard for him to be referred to as "preacher" without feeling obliged to justify the name.

"I'm just going to the chapel, Pete," he said with aggressive amiability. "Maybe you'd like to come along?"

Cook's smile was so spectacularly unpleasant I wondered if he hadn't spent hours in front of a mirror practicing it.

"I'll leave prayer to you god-fearing pricks that feel the need of it. Me, I'll stick to good times and pussy."

"Hell, Pete," commented Tambellini from his locker where he was carefully combing his hair so that his cap, when he put it on, wouldn't crease the perfection of the manner in which his hair framed his head, "you won't find either of them in a goddamn locker room, will you?"

"I respect your skepticism, Pete," said Armstrong, continuing as if Dante hadn't said anything at all. "But if you just give it a chance, I'm sure you'll find that the strength of the Good Lord will be more help than you ever imagined."

The blazing sincerity that shone out of Armstrong's eyes, and the fervor with which he gripped his bible while his square jaw jutted out so firmly, seemed to offend Cook more than any insult could have.

"What would make me feel a whole lot better," said Pete with a mean grin, "is if you took that book you got there and shoved it up your evangelical ass so that you really were the holy shit you think you are."

Armstrong didn't even blink; he just held Cook's nasty look with his own earnest one and nodded understandingly.

"I know it's just your way of fighting grace. I know you don't really mean any of that."

"I mean fuckin' all of it," snarled Cook.

"I forgive you," said Steve serenely.

"I don't want you to fuckin' forgive me!" Pete yelled.

"That's all right," said Steve almost happily. "I do anyway." He started to walk past.

"Fuck yourself," growled Cook. Then he added viciously, "maybe you can manage that, since you can't manage to give your own bitch any fucking satisfaction."

Armstrong froze. He stood there motionless, his back to Cook, who continued to taunt him.

"It hurts my ego too, y'know. All the time the slut was screaming for more, I thought it was just that I was rodding her up so good. Now I find out that she was just hard up. Tough on a guy's self-image, I'll tell you."

Armstrong seemed even stiller, somehow. Garrett glided over to him with that deceptive quickness common to so many athletic big men.

"Just leave that trash, Steve."

"Oh, come on, Joe," said Cook. "You told me yourself how crazy Pamela was for black cock when the whore—"

He never finished the sentence, because Armstrong let loose a scream that still seemed to be echoing moments later when he and Cook were wildly tossing punches at each other while rolling and wrestling savagely around the room. The guys just jumped or moved out of the way; no one seemed inclined to risk interfering. Maybe they were just nervous about getting hurt themselves—it's uncanny how often peacemakers trying to break up a fight get hurt the worst—or maybe they just instinctively felt that it might be best to let them both get it out of their systems.

Cook was considerably the bigger of the two; he had height and weight on his side, and a far more sophisticated repertoire of dirty tricks. But Armstrong was in better shape, and was fueled by a fury that had been pent up who knew how long.

They pounded each other with noisy venom and vigor while we stood and watched. Blasingame, standing next to me, said in a voice too low for anyone else to hear:

"This is one of those fights where you hope they both lose."

In a way, they both did. Armstrong finally clobbered a gasping Cook into submission; only after Pete's eyes were thoroughly blackened, his lip cut and his nose bleeding profusely, did Garrett step in and haul Armstrong off. As it turned out, though, Armstrong had sprained his wrist, and could neither throw nor swing a bat for a couple of weeks. So he went on the disabled list, they both got fined, and to everyone's relief, they avoided each other and said little to anyone else for a while.

"Maybe we ought to make it a regular event," suggested Willoughby one day around the batting cage. "Keep 'em both off everyone else's back."

"We've got a lot of betting action for a rematch," said McCarter. "It's pick-em for next time. Consensus is it'll be a little tougher for Steve to get quite as fired up the second time around."

"The Holy Roller versus The Pirate King," suggested Willoughby.

"Be nice if we could just let the whole thing slide," I said.

"Forgive and forget?" Marcus gave me a gleeful grin. "That's what Armstrong thinks too, y'know. He says he's going to pray for Pete's soul."

"For God's sake, no one tell Cook." My alarm was real. "He'll get so mad we'll have another fight."

"Yeah," agreed Marcus dreamily. "Maybe we ought to make the next one to the death."

"Whose?" asked McCarter.

"Who cares?" replied Marcus equably. "Either way, it'd be a break for the rest of us."

Pressing Issues

THE REPORTERS WERE ALL over the place soon as word of the fight got out. It would have been a juicy story anyway, but Armstrong getting injured made it legitimate news as well. Fortunately, Cook just snarled obscenities at anyone asking him anything, so they got nothing from him they could either print or broadcast; and Steve just clenched his jaw firmly and insisted it was all a bit of ill-advised horseplay which had resulted, unfortunately, in this distressing injury. He assured the scribes that he and Cook had both shaken hands like the men they were, and he was looking forward eagerly to healing quickly so that he could once again contribute to the team.

Jay Greenberg did his best, but he would have looked uncomfortable even had he not been sweating heavily, which is what usually happened to him whenever he had to lie for any extended length of time.

"That's all there is to it, fellas," he assured them. "Just your basic accident which everyone regrets."

"But what was the fight about?" asked Willie Wolf. Willie, who covered the team for a local TV station, specialized in making his own opinion the story, so it didn't matter much what Jay answered as far as he was concerned. But there were others listening, so Jay just looked down at Willie—who couldn't have been more than five-four when you saw him off the TV screen—with his sincerest gaze.

"It wasn't really a fight at all, Willie. Just some good-natured kidding that got a little out of hand."

"Gee, Jay. I guess Captain Cook must have cut himself shaving. After he fell down in the shower and walked into the wall."

That was from Duncan Diggs, who always carried his own ax so he wouldn't have to look for one to grind. While Jay was figuring out how to respond, Wolf jumped in again, much to the PR man's relief.

"What does Simon have to say about all this?"

"Mr. Lumpe will be issuing a statement that says both players should have known better, and fines may be forthcoming since an injury was sustained that will hurt the team, but that boys will be boys."

Duncan's thin, mean features creased under the shock of grandfatherly white hair that so often made people assume he was more tolerant than he was.

"Come on, Jay. I'm not an idiot."

"Your secret is safe with me, Duncan," murmured Spencer Hirshberg. That drew an appreciative laugh from everyone except Diggs. Spencer was the best sportswriter in the city, a slight, quiet, perennially well-dressed man who never said anything he knew wasn't true and wrote as if he really cared about words.

Diggs flushed angrily, but he knew that Hirshberg was far and away the most respected person in their business, so he said nothing further. I could see his hard, beady little eyes register the supposed insult, though, and I knew Diggs was marking up yet another petty little grudge to hold against Spencer.

Hirshberg wandered over to where some of the players were dressing, then walked over to me.

"What do you think, Mike?"

"I think boys will be boys."

"When they won't be girls."

"You know how it is. Fighting spirit and all that."

"Oh. You mean they both wanted to win so badly that their competitive natures erupted, even though they both be valiant and valued teammates."

"I couldn't have said it better."

"You could have said it a lot more accurately."

"I wouldn't do that."

"No, I don't suppose you would." He smiled. "How are Donna and the girls?"

"Fine. Thanks."

"Laura still the city's finest schoolgirl computer whiz?"

"I sure don't know a better one. You've got a good memory, Spencer."

"Tool of the trade. And your girls are easy to remember. It's rare to find children who are that appealing *and* that gifted."

I couldn't have kept from grinning if I'd wanted to. "If you're angling for an invitation to dinner, you've got it."

"I'd love to. But I wouldn't do that to you during the season. I think your family should have you to themselves for at least the limited time they can. What you may do, though, if you insist, is buy me a drink at the nearby watering hole of your choice after tonight's contest of skill and newly exhibited determination."

"I do insist."

"You insist on what?" Diggs asked, coming up to us curiously in case he was missing something.

"Mike here insists on buying me a drink tonight."

"Good. You can buy me one too, Mike."

"No, I can't. I don't buy drinks for reporters. It's nothing personal, Duncan. It's just the principle of the thing."

"What are you talking about? Spencer's a reporter, too."

"I know, but he's an exception. He also qualifies as a human being."

Diggs wasn't amused, but he didn't say anything just then; Garcia was walking by, toweling off his wet head, and Duncan grabbed him as he passed.

"Hey, Pablo. What was the fight about, really?"

"*Que?*" Pablo asked blankly. I kept a straight face, but it wasn't easy. Pablo's English was better than Duncan's, and we all knew it.

"C'mon, Pablo, don't pull that stuff. What really happened?"

Pablo shook his head. "*No sabe,*" he murmured, and moved on.

Diggs looked after him disgustedly, then turned and called to Jack Lee, who was sprawled in a chair reading a book about bees.

"Hey, Jack."

"Yo." Jack looked up.

"What do you think about the fight?"

"What fight?" inquired Jack affably.

Diggs turned away from him and looked at me again with what he clearly felt was a probing stare.

"I'm going to ask you a question, Mike, and I'd appreciate a straight answer."

"I'm sure you would, Duncan."

"I mean it."

"I'm sure you do."

"I know none of you want to air private grievances, and maybe you're right not to talk about what those two were fighting about. But there's one thing I have to know, and all you have to do is give me a yes or no answer."

"What's the question?"

"Does any of this have anything, anything at all, to do with drugs?"

My surprise was genuine. "No," I assured him.

"You're sure?"

"Yes."

He nodded. "Okay."

"What makes you ask that?"

He gazed at me sternly. "Drugs are destroying the moral fabric of this country. If there's a ballplayer who even touches a drug, I want to know, so that I can crucify him in print until he's run out of this game. Every druggie on this planet should be locked up and the key thrown away, until we have a clean, healthy society again. Drugs are the ruination of civilization. Any of them. All of them."

"Say, Duncan," interjected Spencer.

"What?"

"I'll buy you a drink tonight. How's that?"

"That's fine. Okay."

"I'll buy you two drinks. Maybe even three."

Diggs looked at Hirshberg with surprise. "Thanks, Spencer. That's nice of you. I didn't know you felt the same way I do about all the scummy druggies."

"I don't."

Spencer patted him on the shoulder and moved away. Diggs watched him, confused. Then he turned right back to me.

"You have a lovely little girl, Mike, right?"

"Two, in fact."

"Two. That's right. And you love them, right?"

"Can't stand them. But they're useful around the house."

It took him a second. "Oh. You're kidding, right?"

"Right, Duncan. I'm kidding."

"What I'm driving at is, you'd be pretty damn upset if your daughters ever tried any drugs, right?"

"Sure. I wouldn't be too happy if they started drinking with any regularity, either."

"Drugs are illegal, Mike. Booze isn't."

"That makes all the difference, I guess."

"In my America, it does."

After the reporters had left, Homer Baker walked past, his brow as furrowed as a newly-plowed field. Homer was Del Vecchio's sidekick in the broadcasting booth. He had been a friendly, none-too-bright catcher in his playing days, and he was a friendly, none-too-bright broadcaster now, providing the play-by-play and feeding Dom straight lines so that Del Vecchio could do what was euphemistically referred to as "color," which is supposed to be expert analytical commentary but which in Dom's case tended to be irrelevant blather.

"Say, Homer," I called over to him. "What's wrong?"

He came over, keeping his husky voice low. "Well, the reporters are all over us to give them the inside scoop on this fight thing, but Simon says we shouldn't tell 'em anything."

"Then don't tell 'em anything."

"Yeah, I know," then added worriedly, "but I don't want 'em to, you know, stop liking us or anything."

"They don't sign your checks, Homer."

"Yeah. That's what Simon said, too." He glanced around, then lowered his voice still more.

"You'd think Cook and Armstrong would have more sense. I mean, in the old days, if two guys wanted to go at it, they'd do it outside in an alley. That way, if one of them was banged up afterwards, he could always say he got mugged or something, and he wouldn't have to drag his teammate into it."

"They weren't planning anything, Homer. It just happened."

"Yeah." He nodded sagely. "I guess they weren't thinking too good. You always get in trouble when you don't think too good. Still." He shook his head. "You'd think the reporters would be more loyal to the team than trying to throw dirt around."

"Can't blame them too much, I guess. After all, how often does a sportswriter get a story that has both sex and violence? How could they pass that up?"

"Yeah, I guess. But Dom says if they can't say something nice about someone, why say anything at all?"

"Saying nice things all the time doesn't sell papers or boost ratings. That's their job."

"I guess." He shook his head again, reminding me of a buffalo grazing on the plains, swinging his shaggy head back and forth to decide which patch of grass seemed more appealing. "Say, can you believe that dumb broad wife of Steve's saying all that stuff about him being a dud in bed and all? Jeez. Broads aren't supposed to talk like that about guys."

"Guys do it about broads."

"That's different. Broads aren't ballplayers."

"Not yet, anyway."

He stared at me in horror, then moved away as though he had just discovered that I had an infectious disease. I finished dressing, and found myself heading out to the field with Jack Lee.

"That's one thing about being a ballplayer," he observed as we ambled unhurriedly into the domelight. "It's a continuous series of exciting and often unpredictably messy events. You know what it reminds me of?"

"What?"

"Everything else," he said.

The Name Game

WHEN SIMON FIRST CALLED Pepper and me into his office to tell us about his new brainstorm, I thought he was kidding. I should have known better. Simon joked sometimes, but he never kidded. He regarded us expectantly, his pudgy face shining with pleasure, self-approval and excitement.

"Well?" he asked eagerly. "What do you think?"

I didn't even want to think about what I thought, much less express it, so I looked over at Pepper. I should have known better than to do that, too. Pepper looked like Danny Love had when a couple of the guys told the vegetarian pitcher that they had slipped rattlesnake meat into his tofu salad. Looking so sickly that I feared what he might do to Simon's new and embarrassingly expensive shag carpet, Pepper croaked: "I do not see why such an action as you describe is necessary."

Simon waved a dismissive hand at him impatiently. This was clearly not the response he wanted: and Simon was a man who did not like getting responses he did not want.

"You're a good baseball man, Pepper, but you lack real vision." He looked at the gnarled older man patronizingly and continued as though he were a teacher explaining multiplication to a favorite but momentarily recalcitrant third-grader.

"A man in my position—a leader, a father-figure, an example to us all—has to look at the big picture. And that's what I'm talking about here, boys. The big picture. This will attract media attention. Boost the box-office. Give us character and color."

"We wouldn't need any of that," I heard myself saying, "if we were winning enough to be contenders."

It was true, of course, but I knew before I finished the sentence that I was borrowing trouble by saying it. Simon's hot little eyes glittered at me as he spoke, his voice for once muted and measured.

"That may be so, Mike," he said deliberately, "but we're *not* winning enough. That's all going to change. A lot of things are going to change around here." He frowned at Pepper, whose head was bowed as he gazed miserably at the carpet. I reproached myself silently but sternly for not keeping my mouth shut. But suddenly, Simon brightened and addressed us again, sure that we would share his enthusiasm if only we understood what he was trying to explain.

"I'm surprised you don't see what a great idea I have here. After all, it was the two of you who made me think of it in the first place."

"Us?" Pepper almost yelped.

"Sure." Simon was beaming. "I've heard you two playing your little game of trading old-time ballplayers' names with each other."

"We do that for fun," I said. It sounded better than saying "for refuge."

"Of course you do. And that's what baseball is about, boys—fun. Sometimes you fellows get a little too close to the game and lose sight of that a bit. But giving all our players colorful nicknames for our fans to latch onto and enjoy will bring some of the fun back into this great game of ours. That's clear to me. Is it clear to you?"

Pepper had a choice: nod in agreement or be fired. He nodded.

"Good," said Simon. He turned to me. "I'm expecting your help on this, Mike. With your education, and knowledge of all that great traditional baseball lore, you're just the man to help with any naming issues. So I'm telling the players if any of them have a problem with their assigned nicknames, they should see you." He smiled in the way a shark must smile at the passing fish which is to be that day's lunch. "You'll be responsible for every player adopting a nickname that they—and I—will be satisfied with." His smile widened slightly, making his teeth seem somehow sharper.

Clearly, I was expected to say something. "Sure. If you think I can handle it."

"I don't think. I *know* you can handle it." He leaned forward slightly, and I saw those teeth come closer. "I don't hire people who can't handle what I give them."

He leaned back again, expansive now. "You'll do an A-okay job, Mike, I'm sure of that. A-okay."

He stretched, yawned, patted his ample stomach and shifted to his crisp, efficiently businesslike voice.

"I've given Charlie Luposo instructions to sew the new nicknames onto the uniforms, so they'll be ready for tonight's game; and I've gone over the names with Dom so that he'll be able to refer to them over the air." He suddenly clapped his hands together enthusiastically. "It'll be tremendous, you'll see. Tremendous."

Walking back to the clubhouse, I was as silent as Pepper. There didn't seem to be a whole lot to say. Before we got there, though, he stopped and turned to me.

"Use my office if you want. I'm going to find Harry, and until game time me and him are going to shoot some pool and get very, very drunk."

So I went into his office, closed the door and waited for the guys to arrive, notice the new nicknames sewn onto their game uniforms, and come charging in. I had taped a note to the door that read "One at a time, please," and as I sat there in the calm that I knew would soon be shattered, I wondered who would be the first one in.

It was Danny Love, which was a break for me, because Danny wasn't a screamer. His father was half-Chinese, half-Israeli, his mother half-French, half-Swedish; he had dark good looks with a hint of the exotic to them. Danny was the kind of pitcher most clubs didn't draft high, despite his impressive college record, because he had three perceived strikes against him. To begin with, he was considered "too small" at a slender five-eight. He could mow down hitters as though they were a lawn, but he didn't *look* overpowering—and it is truly amazing how many people in this business overrate physical specimens and underrate guys who do it on guile and intelligence and skill and heart instead of raw strength and power.

The second strike against Danny was that he was an Ivy Leaguer (the only one on the team, unless you counted me) and because of his Harvard degree he was often perceived as "thinking too much," a habit that makes a lot of baseball folks distinctly uneasy. The third and final strike was that, partly as a result of his education, he was suspected of being a smartass wiseguy, the kind of lippy (i.e., outspoken) egghead (i.e., intelligent) intellectual (i.e., articulate) punk (i.e., younger than you are) that managements tend to hate to have around.

Though only a rookie, he had gained this reputation before he'd pitched a single game as a pro, when—after he'd thrown two no-hitters for Harvard—one of the other teams in our league had sent a scout to check him out, with instructions to interview him for intelligence and attitude if his stuff looked good enough. The first question the scout asked him, reading off a prepared list, was whether eleven o'clock was before or after midnight.

Danny looked at him for a moment. "I can't commit myself on that."

"What d'you mean?" asked the nonplussed scout.

"It's before one day's midnight, and after another's," explained Danny. "I'm afraid I can't give you a definitive answer unless you rephrase the question so as to make it more specific."

The scout stared at him, then wrote in his notebook: "wrong answer."

"If you've pitched nine innings," he continued, going on to his next question, "and the score's only 1–1 but you've given up ten hits and six walks and the opposing pitcher has given up only two hits and no walks, how would you characterize the game you've pitched?"

Danny considered the question, then replied, "Tied."

Well, word got around about his "attitude problem," and when added to his being "too small," there he was, still available when we drafted. Fortunately for us, Cole Boone was too smart a general manager to ignore the fact that the kid kept getting people out. Rookie or not, I expected Danny to be one of our biggest winners this season.

Much as I appreciated his pitching ability, though, what I was most grateful for at the moment was the pride he took in approaching life calmly and logically. Danny was nothing if not rational, and I knew that whatever he had to say, we could discuss it quietly. Which turned out to be a lucky thing, considering what he had come into the office to say.

"Mr. Lumpe," he began without preamble, "has offered me five grand as a bonus if I agree to legally change my first name to True."

I regarded him with disbelief. He raised an eyebrow slightly, but remained otherwise impassive.

"Really," he affirmed.

I sighed and toyed with the old baseball that Pepper kept on his desk, the one that had been signed by every one of his teammates, including my dad, the year they'd won it all.

"True Love," continued Danny. "Get it?"

"I get it. What did you say?"

"I said no."

"What was Mr. Lumpe's response?"

"He increased his offer to ten grand."

"What did you say to that?"

"I said no."

I said nothing while Danny continued his calm recounting.

"He said it was as high as he could go. I wondered aloud whether it wasn't as low as he could go. He misunderstood me. He thought I was talking about money. He assured me that he could go a hell of a lot lower. I told him that I had no trouble believing that." He paused. "We did not, as they say, have a meeting of the minds."

"How was it left?"

"He told me to work something out with you."

I shook my head, though I wasn't sure at what.

"Okay, Danny. We're supposed to find you a nickname..."

"You mean like Butch or Chip or Buzz or Biff or Scooter or..."

"...one that Simon thinks is catchy but that you can live with."

He leaned back in the chair and gazed meditatively at the ceiling. "I'm not sure," he mused, "that there is any such animal."

"How about Doctor?"

He looked at me curiously. "You mean like Doctor J or Doctor K or..." He stopped. "I get it. Doctor Love. A lover, not a fighter. The doctor of desire. All that kind of nonsense. Yeah. I can live with that. Okay."

"Of course, I'll still call you Danny."

"I would hope everyone would."

We were silent a moment. "Doctor Love," he repeated, and shook his head, amused. "My family will think I finally got that doctorate they always wanted me to have."

I thought of Tambellini, his bare-chested poster and the teenyboppers who called themselves Dante's Darlings. "Dante may be jealous of your nickname."

"Nah. He *likes* his."

"He does?"

"Yeah. He told me he thought it captured his power and temperament."

"No kidding?"

"Nope."

"What *is* his nickname?"

"The Inferno."

After we had both stopped laughing, Danny got up and went to the door.

"Thanks, Mike. You do good work." He paused. "For a Princetonian."

"Listen, Harvard, you're lucky we're not calling you *Crimson Love*."

He grinned. "Have you seen *your* new nickname yet?"

I hadn't. My stomach sank to somewhere around my knees.

"Simon is obviously impressed with your alma mater," Danny continued, unable to keep the grin off his face. "Speaking of Old Nassau."

"All right. What *is* my nickname?"

"Tiger," he told me.

McCarter was next. He was half-amused, but the half that wasn't was furious. "C'mon, Mike," he said as soon as he walked in. "Being arbitrarily given a silly nickname is bad enough; but must it be as inappropriate as it is insulting?"

"What is it?"

Instead of answering verbally, he held up the uniform jersey he carried in his hand. There, sewn over his uniform number, were the words: "Mad Dog."

"Mad Dog McCarter?" he waved his hand in disgust. "I mean, really. Even guys who don't like me could do better than that."

I couldn't help but agree. It could hardly have been more inappropriate for the well-read, articulate, reasonable catcher.

"What made him pick that?"

"He must like alliteration." He pulled a piece of paper from his pocket. "And to make my rejection of this tacky appellation more palatable, I have prepared for you and the powers that be an alternative list of nicknames more acceptable to me."

He handed me the list. It only took me a moment to look it over. "Mephistopheles?" I glanced at the next one. "Messiah?"

"They're just as alliterative as Mad Dog."

"You must be kidding."

"*I* must be kidding?"

"What about," I said slowly, "if we settled for what we actually *were* calling you when we went on that hamburger binge on the last road trip?"

He considered. "I don't know," he finally replied, "that I much care for being named after a fast-food hamburger."

"You could do worse," I reminded him.

He glanced forlornly at his uniform shirt. "I already have," he observed sadly. He rose, then spoke as decisively as he did to pitchers when he went out to the mound to reassure or rebuke them.

"Okay. We'll go with Big Mac. It's cheesy, but..."

He left, allowing Zapata to come storming in. It was an extraordinary sight, dedicated as Angel always was to the religion of being cool. After all, this was a man who rolled antiperspirant over his entire body before every game so that no one would see him break a sweat. But now he entered like a wild man, screaming a torrent of non-stop abuse in Spanish. I let him flood the room with curses; whenever one of the Hispanic players around the league really got rolling with native obscenities, it provided me an opportunity to enhance the limited vocabulary of the semi-fluent Spanish I had learned at Princeton and Yale.

Angel was really giving me a semester's worth; I actually took notes as he stormed around the room. Later on, I'd have to consult Garcia or Fortunado on what some of these words actually meant, since there were so many I'd never heard before, not even on the night in Phoenix when their shortstop Ibanez spiked Fortunado at second and the two of them put on a verbal fireworks show of Spanish insults, each as a matter of pride trying to out-curse the other. But I had to admit that Zapata was putting them both to shame at the moment. Every oath, imprecation and blasphemy that he'd held in check all the years that he'd been keeping so zealously blasé came pouring out in this one torrential deluge.

I was so impressed that I was genuinely sorry when, after about four minutes, he began to wind down, then finally regained control of himself. He stood there, still furious but also ashamed at all the emotion he'd shown. I glanced at my notes.

"So, Angel," I said to him, "I gather that you're unhappy with the nickname, and not if they tie you to a stake in the middle of the desert on the year's hottest day and sixteen mothers of dogs—I think I may have lost something in translation there—set ten thousand red ants on your slashed belly and they devour your intestines and make you eat your own tongue will you wear such a uniform for any Yankee excrement of a diseased whore who—well, anyway, I gather that the general idea is that you don't like your nice new uniform. Am I correct in this assumption?"

"Never," he hissed through clenched teeth. "Never will I put on my back such a stinking insult."

I gestured for him to show me the uniform shirt. Instead of handing it to me, he flung it to the floor with an oath and a gesture of contempt. I picked it up and spread it on the desk. It was hard not to laugh, but with a mighty effort I managed—just barely—to control myself. Angel was volatile enough already; if I so much as giggled, he might take it as an affront and break every stick of furniture in the office.

The uniform read: "Viva Zapata."

I looked up at him. "Well, I know it's pretty silly," I said, "but is it really that much of an insult? It just says hooray for you. And I thought Brando was pretty good in the movie."

"He means me to use this as a first name." The hiss was even more sibilant than before. "And as a first name, the word is feminine. It is a *woman's* name."

Now I understood. "Listen, forget it," I told him. "We'll come up with another nickname. You have any suggestions?"

"Jose," he offered.

"I don't think—"

"Raul," he said.

"Never mind," I told him.

"Emiliano?"

"Just go back to Charlie and tell him to sew Angel back on. We'll just make Angel your nickname, you know, call you the Angel of Buffalo or something."

He looked at me gravely. "You are my friend, Mike. You are a true *hombre*." He seemed his old self-possessed self once more. "You understand that a man must do what a man must do."

"Absolutely. Who's next out there?"

It was Crockett, even more edgy than usual. "It's confusing," he complained. "I mean, what the hell kind of a nickname is Davey when my name is Jim? People will think I'm some other guy named Davey, that Jim got traded or sent to the minors or something. This is just the sort of thing my analyst says promotes schizophrenic tendencies. I mean, what's more schizophrenic than wearing Davey on your back when your name is Jim?"

"Davey Crockett was a great American hero," I reminded him.

"Well, fuck him. I mean, that's great for him, but I'm still trying to really come to terms with my own identity, you know what I mean? I'm trying to cope, and it's hard enough to get to deal with who you really are deep down as a defined understood human being capable of self-love, without suddenly having to be identified as some historical figure who's completely unknown to you, I mean psychically. Hell, the guy's been dead for what, a hundred and fifty years or something like that? I mean, who needs this? When my wife left me last year, she said I didn't know who I really was, and I told her I did too. What's she going to think if she knows I'm playing first base with fuckin' Davey on my back when my name is Jim?"

"You ever go fishing?"

He looked at me quizzically. "Sure."

"What do you fish for?"

"Depends. Brook trout, catfish..."

"Okay. Let's call you Catfish."

"Why?"

"Because you used to race off after playing baseball to catch some catfish, so your friends back home called you Catfish, since you were always fishing for them."

"But I wasn't. And they didn't."

"Who knows that? Who cares?"

"I know it. All my friends know it."

"But they don't pay your salary. Simon does. And he'll love it. It's colorful and homespun, and it echoes a great player of the past."

"Catfish Crockett?" he tried it aloud. "Well, at least it sounds like a nickname and not another identity or a completely different human being," he said dubiously. "But speaking of Catfish Hunter, what if people compare us and think I'm offending his memory or something?"

"He was a pitcher. You're not. Besides, he wasn't the first. There was a Catfish Metkovich played for Boston in the forties."

"Yeah?" He brightened, then looked suddenly worried again. "What position did he play?"

"Some first base, some outfield," I told him reluctantly. Sure enough, his brow furrowed and he began to speak plaintively again.

"That's what I play, dammit. What if people think that I just—"

I never found out what Crockett was afraid people might think, because just then, the office door was flung open. McCarter and Blasingame stood in the doorway looking at me.

"You'd better come out here, Mike," said Tom.

"Yeah," added Terry. "You don't want to miss this."

We emerged into the locker room where the guys were gathered around Joe Garrett, who was ripping off the letters of his new nickname, one by one, with his bare hands. Garrett was big and strong and could do that. Garrett was also African-American—and the nickname Simon had given him, I realized as I watched the individual letters flutter to the carpet, was "King Kong."

Charlie Luposo shuffled his feet nearby, looking even older and more shriveled than usual. "It wasn't my idea, Joe," he mumbled softly.

"I know that," said Garrett as he continued methodically ripping. The other players said nothing as they watched, except to applaud or cheer when another cloth letter fell to the floor.

Del Vecchio's first mistake was to enter the room at that particular moment. "Say," he asked cheerily, noting the crowd around Joe's locker, "what's up?"

The sixtiesh but spry infielder-turned-announcer joined the guys and then made his second, and worst, mistake. He saw Garrett ripping letters off his uniform and greeted the large third baseman with: "Hey, what'cha doing, King Kong?"

Garrett's huge, chocolate-brown arms paused in their assault on the shirt, and he slowly turned and advanced on the slight, gray-haired broadcaster. The players parted to make way for him as if Joe were Moses and they the waves of the Red Sea.

Dom's smiling expression transformed into one of dawning terror as Joe reached down, grabbed him by the lapels of his garish plaid jacket, and with one hand, effortlessly lifted him high into the air. Dom opened his mouth to speak, but before he could say a word Joe casually slammed him against the wall.

"Help!" squealed Dom. "Someone help!"

Joe regarded him as though Dom were a cockroach and Garrett was idly deciding whether or not to crush him.

"Don't call me that," said Joe quietly, his calm more frightening than any shout could have been. "Don't ever call me that."

"But that's your new nickname! Simon says!"

"Simon says?" repeated Joe with odd detachment.

"That's how I'm supposed to refer to you on the air. Simon says."

"You will not refer to me that way. Not on or off the air. Not tonight, and not ever. Is that clear?"

He lifted Dom higher against the wall as if he were a raised flag. His huge hand gently closed around the smaller man's skinny, wizened throat.

"Is that clear?" Joe repeated.

His eyes bugging, Del Vecchio frantically nodded yes.

"Because if you do," Garrett continued in his deceptively calm rumble, "you will live only long enough to regret it." He released his grip on Dom's throat and gently lowered the gasping Del Vecchio to the floor.

"But what do I call you?" he asked desperately. "Simon says everybody's got to have a nickname. You too, Joe."

"My name is Joseph Edward Garrett. Joe *is* my nickname. Call me Joe." He smiled pleasantly.

Dom's eyes darted to me. Joe followed his gaze and looked at me to see what I would say.

"Sounds good to me," I said. Del Vecchio scurried wildly out of the clubhouse to the safety of the broadcast booth and the comfort of the Chivas Regal bottle he kept tucked away there.

Most of the rest of the team was no problem. Blasingame just laughed at Terry the Pirate, Marcus liked being called Whip Willoughby, and Armstrong okayed Ace—once we reassured him it meant something other than a playing card, which he was afraid might hurt him in a future campaign he planned for the U.S. Senate from his home state of Utah, where his fellow Mormons didn't exactly approve of gambling. Fortunado had no objection to the nickname Lucky and Wyatt didn't give a damn if Dom referred to him as "The Marshal." Big Jake, Fast Eddie, Pluto and Captain Cook already had legitimate nicknames.

Pablo was, he told me in his elegant Spanish, a bit embarrassed at being called "Gunsmoke" Garcia, considering that all he threw was off-speed junk; but if it made *Señor* Lumpe happy and helped the team in some obscure way he did not understand, then it was all right with him. Tad wasn't so sure he liked being called "Muscles" Strain (Danny Love suggested we change it to "Mental" Strain), but he *was* sure he didn't want to get into a confrontation about it; and when his agent told him he might be able to parlay the nickname into some sort of endorsement deal for a breakfast cereal, Tad relaxed about the whole thing.

A few others did have problems they discussed with me. Ray Rademacher, an easy-going, mild-mannered country boy from Georgia who was a useful if unremarkable utility infielder, was uncomfortable with being called "Sugar Ray."

"For one thing, it's a black guy's name," he confided to me awkwardly. "I got nothing against black guys—I get along with Marcus and Bo Johnson just fine, you ask 'em if I don't, and I admire Joe more than anyone else here, and Denny Savage is a real fine gentleman. But it don't feel right for a white boy like me to be calling himself a name like Sugar Ray that no white boy like me ever carried and that's a name tied to two proud black boxing champions, and it just don't seem right, is all. And there's something else, too, that kinda bothers me about it, to tell you the truth."

I waited for him to continue. He shifted uncomfortably, then did.

"Mr. Lumpe explained to me that he picked it because it was a great fighter's name, and that it would help make my image a lot tougher. He kinda made it clear he'd really like it if I got in a couple of fights or something— you know, sort of make people think I'm a real tough S.O.B., and like that."

He hesitated. "I don't want to pick fights, Mike. I hate brawling. I been around brawlers all my life back home in Georgia, and I always hated it. Always seemed dumb to me to go looking for a fight for no good reason. Always seemed to me there must be a better way to settle arguments."

There was a quiet pleading evident in his gentle brown eyes. I felt like patting him on the head, but of course I didn't. I just kept my voice as relaxed and easygoing as I could when I answered him.

"What color hair do you have, Ray?"

He looked utterly bewildered. "Gee, Mike, you're looking right at it. Can't you tell?"

"I'm asking *you*."

Puzzled, he replied, "Brown, I guess."

"Looks a bit reddish to me."

"Not really. Just plain old dirt-brown, far as I know."

"But with reddish highlights. Enough to call you Rusty if we felt like it."

He slowly smiled, reached out a hand to mine and shook it firmly.

"We feel like it," he said.

Denny Savage's problem, on the other hand, was more related to Joe Garrett's, but he didn't have Joe's stature, job security, temper or temperament. The reserve outfielder, a light-hitting defensive specialist who knew he could be readily replaced, was aware that the slightest aura of trouble-making could prompt his departure. So he waited until everyone else had left the locker room before looking me up and asking that our conversation be kept confidential.

Denny was a slim, graceful African American with a shy disposition and a diffident manner. He was a terrific cook, and occasionally delighted some of the bachelors on the team by inviting them over to dinner (he had invited Donna and me over one evening, too, and she still insists it's the best dinner anyone's ever made for her). He was also gay. Some of the players knew it, most didn't; those who did never mentioned it. Denny knew Simon well enough to know that if the owner ever suspected anything like that, he'd get rid of Savage immediately, afraid his sexual preference was an infectious disease that would contaminate the entire team.

For all of these reasons, Denny was anxious to keep a low profile as a pleasant, reliable player always ready to do whatever was asked without even the suggestion of complaint. It was difficult for him to bring himself to come see me, and he did it with obvious reluctance; but he did it.

"I don't want to make trouble, Mike," he confided. "You know me. But I just feel badly about this nickname business. You understand why, don't you?"

"Yeah, I do," I said, and I did. Simon had nicknamed him "Noble" Savage.

"But," he said unhappily, "I'm not sure what to do about it."

"Well, your name's Dennis. How about Dennis the Menace?"

He smiled a shy, secretive smile. "I've been called that," he said dreamily, the pleasure of the memory evident in his liquid dark eyes. Then his expression clouded. "But will Mr. Lumpe okay that?"

"He'll go for The Menace part. He'll like that. It sounds tough."

Denny giggled. "It *is* tough. Thanks, Mike."

"You bet. You think any of us want to go around calling you Noble?"

It seemed odd, but somehow fitting, that the Johnson boys came to see me together. Fitting because they were our right-field platoon: Bo, a big black lefty with power who swung at too many bad pitches and struck out too much; and Bob, a slim white righty who lacked Bo's power, speed and raw athletic ability, but who made contact more often and didn't make the mistakes Bo did both at bat and in the field.

"We got a problem," announced Bo.

"And maybe a solution," added Bob.

"Well, don't leave me in suspense," I said.

"The nickname Mr. Lumpe has given me," explained the muscular black man, "is Buck."

I tried to suppress a groan, but didn't quite. They both grinned at me.

"The thing is," explained Bob, running a hand through his thinning blond hair, "is that I always wanted to be called Buck. And Bo here hates it, I guess you can see why. And the name they gave me, I guess 'cause I'm just a country boy, is Bubba."

"And I *like* that," said Bo.

"So we were wondering...," said Bob.

"Whether we could switch," finished Bo.

"If that's okay," added Bob.

"Do it," I told them. "I only wish all our problems were that simple."

Bob smiled with relief, but Bo shrugged. "Won't make any real difference," he said. "They always think either of us is the other one, anyway."

The final nickname problem came up a couple of weeks later when Cohen came over to me after a game had ended. The reserve catcher was in his civilian uniform: a camel's hair sports jacket over a pale blue Sea Island cotton shirt with a tan and blue patterned tie, impeccably pressed navy blue trousers, and brown penny loafers. He looked, as he usually did, like an ad for *Yuppie Quarterly*.

"Hi, David," I greeted him. "What's up?"

"I've got a bit of a problem with this nickname business."

"Why," I wondered aloud, "would anyone have a problem being called Chainsaw?"

"Well, I know how cute they think it sounds with Cohen, and that's okay; I don't even mind that idiocy Del Vecchio made up and said on the air about my getting mad when my car broke down and cutting it in half with a chainsaw. I mean, I never did anything remotely like that in my whole life, but I realize it's just hype, and PR is PR. Got to sell the product—I understand that. Even if it is all complete horseshit."

"So what's the problem?"

"Well, you know I'm a stockbroker in the off-season."

"Of course I know. You're the one who gave me the tip to buy that Reynolds Pharmaceutical stock when it was down to four and a half. And it's at eleven and a half now."

"Eleven and three-quarters," he corrected automatically. "But I wouldn't hold onto it for too much longer if I were you."

"You think it'll go down?"

"If I had to venture a guess, that's the guess I'd venture."

"Thanks."

"You're welcome. Anyway, the thing is, ever since Dom started pushing this 'Chainsaw' nonsense, I've noticed it's had a subtle but definite effect on my professional dealings. And it isn't a favorable one."

"How do you mean?"

"It's hurting my image, Mike. I can't allow my on-field job to hurt my image as a skilled evaluator of current market trends, and I notice that some of my clients address me in a slightly different manner since I was tagged with this nickname. I'm frankly concerned that this will lead to my not being taken as seriously, which in turn will lead to my not being taken at all. It's bad for business—I can feel it. Call it a hunch, but I know I'm right. People feel secure with the financial investment counsel of a stockbroker named David; but they may not entrust their trading options to a ballplayer called Chainsaw. It doesn't contribute much to the conservative, sober image, you know? I mean, how cautious is the advice going to sound if it's coming from someone named Chainsaw?"

I saw his point; so we discussed it for a while and finally settled on Chip. Simon would buy it, and it was evocative enough of blue-chip to make David feel more secure about his image in the investment portfolio business.

That about took care of the name game, except for the fallout from the Garrett incident. Simon was furious about Joe manhandling Dom until I assured him that Joe had only been horsing around, which of course he hadn't, but I knew that both Joe and Dom, for their own reasons, would want to agree that he had. Simon also couldn't see why Joe was so offended at being called King Kong. I tried to explain, but I don't think Simon completely understood, because after I'd finished explaining he suggested, as an alternative nickname, "Godzilla."

I almost said "Why not 'Gorilla'?" but I was afraid that if I did he'd like the idea. Finally, in desperation, I suggested that Dom refer to him on the air as Joseph Edward. After all, how many players had their own full names as nicknames?

"Too formal," frowned Simon. "Too stuck-up. Not common man-of-the-people enough."

"Well then, how about Joe Ed?"

He considered, then nodded. "Better. Yes. I like that much better. Joe Ed Garrett. It even sounds like a nickname."

"It *is* a nickname. It just happens to be his real name as well."

"That's okay. As long as it sounds good. A nickname by any other name, or something like that. Right?"

Some Days the Bear Eats You

IT WAS SOON APPARENT that the what's-in-a-name-game was only the beginning. Full-blown brainstorms began arriving from Simon like so many Athenas springing fully armed from the head of Zeus, most of them just about as relevant to baseball.

First came the colored baseballs.

"What's wrong with them?" Simon asked us aggrievedly, looking back and forth between my face and Pepper's bowed head. "I think it's a terrific idea. It's not even my own idea, if you want to know, and I still think it's great. So that shows you how objective I am."

"Whose idea is it?" I wondered aloud.

"Junior's," he told me proudly.

"I haven't seen him around much lately."

Simon frowned. "He's in India studying with some kind of guru. I think it's just a phase. It had better be."

"Really? Who's the guru?"

"I don't know. Some hairless Indian. But that's not the point. I was talking to him before he left, just spitballing ideas about how to improve the game, make it a little jazzier, keep it from being so damn boring..."

I hoped he would think the choking gargle coming from Pepper was just something caught in his throat. I didn't have to worry about it, though; Simon was so caught up in his own vision that he wasn't paying that much attention to us.

"...and Junior reminded me that when he was a kid he had a multicolored ball, and I thought, of course! Just like the old ABA had, you remember the basketball league?"

"Sure. The one that went out of business."

"Right," he agreed enthusiastically, then stopped and looked at me. "Well, they didn't go out of business because they used a multicolored ball. That was an idea whose time hadn't yet come."

"Still hasn't. As far as pro basketball goes. Or football. Or hockey. Or..."

"The point is we're going to be innovative. Exciting. After all, wouldn't you agree that a plain white ball is just too dull, too conventional?"

Pepper finally raised his head. "What color," he managed, "did you have in mind?"

Simon leaned back with a pleased smile. "I thought orange and blue. They *are* our state colors. Attractive combination, don't you agree?"

I spoke quickly to distract his attention from Pepper's reaction.

"Be kind of hard to see an orange and blue baseball," I observed as calmly as I could, reminding myself to approach this as though it were a reasonable discussion. The man was our boss, after all. Not only did he sign our checks—and both Jenna and Laura, as well as their mother, were vehemently in favor of food and shelter—but he also gave Pepper and me the chance to make a living enjoying the game we loved so much we could hardly do without it, and about which he understood so little.

Simon looked quizzical, as if that thought hadn't really occurred to him. "You think so?" he finally asked.

"Tough enough to see a white one."

He frowned for a moment, then brightened perceptibly. "Well then. An orange ball. We can make it fluorescent! That'll add an exciting dimension to night games, right? A ball that glows in the dark."

We couldn't talk him out of it. But the Commissioner's office, which could always be counted on to take the most craven, expedient course in the face of any crisis, decided that Simon's displeasure was preferable to the expressed hostility of almost all the other owners, few of whom expressed the slightest interest in the idea ("It'll cost more money," said Calvin Barber, owner of the Jaguars, as if that simple observation made the entire idea not worth another moment's consideration). Simon was disappointed, but not for long: only until he came up with the idea for a twenty-second buzzer.

The genesis for that inspiration came from a game in which we were completely shut down by Alberto Antonio Jesus Juantamoreno, a pudgy, crafty Venezuelan righty part of whose technique was to break the hitter's rhythm by frequently stalling. He would stare at the sky as if trying to predict the weather, or take a long time kicking dirt from his cleats, or regard the ball with curiosity as if examining an ancient Egyptian scroll; anything, in fact, to annoy the batter and thus destroy his concentration. He could be hell to hit against, and also to play behind: his own fielders frequently had trouble staying alert, and that sometimes backfired against him. But on this particular night, Simon had watched Alberto make our hitters look like high school freshmen seeing their first breaking ball, and Simon became furious and decided to strike back against any and all such offending pitchers who would treat his club in such an unseemly manner.

"We've got 'em," he told us triumphantly after calling Pepper and me into his office to unveil his new plan. "We'll teach them they can't get cute with the Buffalo Bears."

We looked at him, puzzled. He grinned happily.

"I checked with the TV people and they agreed with me that any pitcher who takes more than twenty seconds between pitches is taking too long. Cuts into commercial time, or it might anyway. Checked with the commissioner's office too, and the Commish told me that whatever the TV people said would increase our revenue is what we should do."

I knew I should just keep my mouth shut, but I didn't. "What if TV says we should start all our games at daybreak so as not to interfere with college football?"

"Then we'll start them at dawn. Most people sleep too damn late anyway. Anyhow, I'm installing a twenty-second buzzer on the scoreboard. It'll be automatic. Every time a pitcher takes more than his allotted twenty seconds, a buzzer will go off. You'll be able to hear it through the whole dome, and the scoreboard will flash, 'PITCHING VIOLATION!' over and over. That'll speed up the game, you bet! And the Commish will force the umps to award the batter a ball on the count whenever some clown like Juantamoreno takes enough time between pitches to have a three-course dinner. It'll work. You'll see."

It worked, all right. Against us. The only person to set off the buzzer was Morgan Wyatt, who pitched for us on the second night after the mechanism had been installed. Wyatt always worked at a deliberate pace so as to keep control of the proceedings. The grating wail of the buzzer so rattled poor Morg that, after glaring at the offending scoreboard with helpless venom, he faced six successive batters without retiring a single one. When he finally got out of the inning, he left the dugout and walked all the way up to the booth where sat the middle-aged, bored-looking man who ran the scoreboard mechanism.

"Which one of these gizmos is the buzzer?" inquired Wyatt.

The man gestured towards one of the switches.

"Turn it off."

"I can't do that," replied the man apologetically. "I've got a job just like you do. Mr. Lumpe has ordered me to leave it on."

The burly pitcher reached over and, without another word, ripped the buzzer switch and its wires away from their connections. The man looked stunned as Wyatt tossed the electronic debris into a wastebasket with a practiced flick of his wrist.

"All right. Leave it on. See if I care."

Simon later ordered Pepper to fine Wyatt for the incident, then he told the press that all fines were completely the manager's decision and that he, the owner, would never interfere with his manager's running of the club. But he left the buzzer disconnected, not wanting the embarrassment of having it again sound off against one of his own pitchers. He did hook it back up once more, on the next occasion that Juantamoreno pitched against us in the dome; but this time, Alberto worked so quickly and efficiently that he completely threw off our hitters' timing, and shut us out on five hits. He never came close to using up even fifteen seconds between pitches. Our pitchers, on the other hand, racked up eight violations between the three of them. Sammy Kleh, umping behind the plate, promptly called a ball on each shriek of the buzzer. After that, the buzzer disappeared, and none of us ever mentioned it again. At least not in front of Simon.

Then Simon started announcing a series of promotional stunts. Most of the players snickered or groaned, but when Blasingame commented, "Well, at least we can play the game itself without having to deal with any of that shit," there was a chorus of appreciative agreement in the clubhouse. As it turned out, though, Terry couldn't have been more wrong. Ironically, literal shit was exactly what the players had to deal with. During the Milking Contest pre-game promotion—which Simon had decided would appeal to all the local farmers, while showing our appreciation for the national plight of the small farmer in America—one of the cows, being milked in shallow right-center field, started dropping turds on the artificial turf. She must have thought it was grass. The grounds crew noticed it, all right, but so did the players. Even though Donelli's crew cleaned it all up prior to the game, Blasingame kept sneaking glances at the spot, convinced some of the dung still lingered ("the stink sure as hell does," he swore). And when he slipped and fell while chasing a pop fly to short right, he blamed the mishap, in no uncertain terms, on "that goddamn shit-slick spot out there. It's not enough we got to put up with all the general shit around here; now we got to fall on our face in the real stuff, too. Shit."

"Well," said McCarter, "I guess it's a classic illustration of the difference between the abstract concept and the tangible reality. You know, between taking shit and actually falling into it."

"Fuck you too," mumbled Blasingame morosely.

The ballgirl incident backfired in equally flashy fashion. Simon hired the two young women who had been the most recent winners of the annual "Miss Buffalo" contest to be ballgirls for the team. Shawna would field foul grounders on the right field line while Fawn patrolled the left field area. They were both pretty, of course, but there was a definite difference. Fawn was a slim, athletic brunette who took her job with surprising seriousness, actually taking grounders whenever someone would hit some to her so as to improve her fielding; whereas Shawna—proud possessor of an undeniably voluptuous blonde figure which was, as Marcus delicately put it, "more stacked than a deck of cards when Vellis is dealing"—particularly enjoyed playing to her appreciative audience. She was prone to discernibly wiggle as she prepared to catch a foul grounder, and she was fond of prancing around triumphantly, jiggling as she leaped up and down, after she had made even the most routine recovery of the ball.

Donna was so incensed at what she referred to with characteristic objectivity as "that disgusting sexist display of revolting bimbo-ism" that she refused to bring the girls to games any more. Only when Jenna pleaded did she relent; and then only after Jenna agreed that Shawna's displays were "really gross," and in fact were a perfect example of what she and her friends were most interested in avoiding. "Any guy who really wants *that*," she told her relieved and pleased mother, "is an unmitigated dork." Though when Shawna seemed at one point to be, as my wife put it, "pole-dancing without the pole," Donna was appalled to hear her daughter mutter, "Buttana."

"Where does she learn words like that?" my wife wondered when she described all this to me.

"Buffalo," I reminded her. "It's local dialect. And the fact that you're upset about her using it means you know what it means too."

On July Fourth, Simon ordered the two girls to perform in red, white and blue bikinis, and as a promotion declared it "American Bikini Day" and gave tri-colored bikinis to women who bought tickets to the game. Fawn wasn't too thrilled, but didn't protest too audibly, since she wanted to keep the job; but Shawna, predictably, was pleased as a pitcher going four-for-four at the plate. As it turned out, though, Shawna's ambitions went beyond parading for her fans in the Dome. When a nude spread of her appeared in *Playboy*—"This Girl Has Balls"—Simon was appalled.

"This is totally inconsistent with our family image!" he sputtered. He was particularly incensed over one photo in which Shawna was spread-eagled in the air in what was supposed to be an attempt to snare a line drive, a photograph in which she wore nothing except a Buffalo Bears cap.

So that was the end of both ballgirls. To avoid any similar incident, Simon fired both women.

"It's not fair!" Fawn insisted unhappily in the locker room, which we allowed her to enter to say goodbye to the players. "I would *never* have done that. Why should *I* have to lose my job, too? I was getting better at it, too, really. Wasn't I, guys?" We all agreed she was. "It's just not fair," she repeated through her unbidden tears. "To be replaced by a boy just because of that goddamn stupid exhibitionist little twat."

Fawn was right; it didn't seem particularly fair. But she was at least partly wrong about her replacement. Simon did have to put a couple of ball-boys on the lines to shag fouls; but that job no longer included, as it once had, handing new balls to the home-plate umpire. In yet another inspiration, Simon had a device built into the ground a few feet behind home plate so that, at the press of a button, a mechanical bear popped up holding a new batch of balls that the embarrassed umpire had to take from the basket which hung from the bear's proffered metal paw.

"With that dumb-ass shit-eating grin that bear's got, and all those buck teeth, he looks a lot like Junior," observed McCarter; but he was careful to whom he made the observation. The resemblance was persuasive enough, though, that everyone on the team soon took to referring to the bear as Junior except when they were within earshot of Simon.

"I don't know how long I can take this," Pepper reiterated. We were at Frank and Teressa's Anchor Bar on Main Street, where chicken wings—called Buffalo wings by outsiders—had originated, but where Pepper was at the time ignoring the local delicacy in favor of drowning his frustrations with Jack. Trouble was, the more he drank, the more melancholy he became.

"I don't so much mind the dumb fuck being such a stupid moron. I don't even mind the fact that he knows less about baseball than my dog does. I don't mind that he's such an ignorant son of a bitch. What I do mind is that he's such an ignorant son of a bitch at the top of his fucking voice."

"Well, you know what they say. What goes up, must come down."

"And vice-a-versa." He took another drink and glared at the glass as if it had insulted him by finding itself empty. Then he suddenly grinned.

"You remember that story?"

"The one about Bill Guthrie? Sure."

"Yeah." His face was suffused in delighted nostalgia. "When that rookie hitter strikes out and gets so pissed off that he throws his bat way the hell up in the air, and Guthrie, calling balls and strikes that day, looks up at the sky, and the rookie looks up with him, and they both watch this bat climbing higher and higher, and the umpire says to the rook..."

We recited in unison: "Son, if that bat comes down, you're out of the game."

Pepper roared in amusement, then quieted down and switched drinks, ordering a Genny. He stared at the ale, looking more relaxed, but somber again.

"Mike," he said, "I cannot take this lunacy much longer."

As it turned out, he didn't have to. We had no idea, as we sat there drinking that night, how soon it would be that Pepper wouldn't have to put up with Simon any more. We didn't know it yet, but the bat was already on its way down.

Crackerjack

MAYBE IT WAS SHAKESPEARE who said that the most harrowing of hurricanes begins with the slightest breeze. Or maybe it was Sophocles. Or Yogi Berra. Or maybe no one actually ever said it at all. But I'll tell you this: it's true enough no matter who said it or didn't.

It all started innocently enough (then again, The Flood probably started with a few raindrops). We were playing the Owls in a game that was as routine as baseball ever gets to those of us who are fascinated by any baseball game. The pitching was mediocre and the hitting mostly sluggish, the score was tied at 5–5 in the sixth, and Tambellini had just surrounded a fly ball as though it were an elusive butterfly, yet somehow managed to catch it. After he tossed the ball into the infield, Pepper kept looking at him as Dante aimlessly toured a section of left field. When I followed Pepper's gaze I saw what he was staring at—and wished I hadn't.

Our left fielder was eating candy. Out of a box. In the middle of a game. While waiting for the next pitch to be thrown.

If the Pope had opened fire on the Vatican with an AK-47, Pepper could not have expressed greater disbelief. He stepped out of the dugout, called time and started a deliberate walk towards left field. I followed him out at an angle, passing our third-base coach and staying in foul territory. I was going to leave what was coming to Pepper's discretion; but since he didn't have much of that, I also wanted to be nearby if anything got out of hand. As it happened, when Dante saw Pepper coming out he sort of drifted towards the foul line, so by the time Pepper actually reached him they were both maybe fifteen feet away from where I stood.

"Hey. Skip. What's up?"

Tambellini's affable greeting was, to Pepper, more goading than a mad rant would have been. I could see that Pepper was at the edge of his self-control before he even started to speak.

"You're *eating*," he hissed.

Dante looked at him blankly.

Pepper shook his head slowly, almost robotically, as if trying to communicate with a Martian. "You don't eat in the middle of a game," he snarled. "You don't stuff your fat face with food while you're on the field playing this game. You're a bum, kid. I don't care how much talent you got, if you got no respect for this game, you got no business playing it. Get off this field. Now."

"Huh?" Tambellini sounded as bewildered as he looked.

"Off. The field. Now."

"Come on, Skip. I'll put it away if you want." He waved the candy box in front of Pepper. It was sort of like waving a red cape at a bull, only the bull would have had a milder reaction.

"Get off the fucking field!" Pepper screamed, jumping up and down like an Olympic gymnast warming up. "You don't deserve to be in left field! You don't deserve to be in *any* field! You don't deserve to fucking *live!*"

"Hey!" said Dante, and put his arm straight out. I couldn't tell, either then or on the video replays I watched countless times afterwards, what he thought he was doing. Maybe mindlessly waving his hand, maybe just trying to keep Pepper away, maybe even attempting to hold him up because Pepper was leaning so far into him that he thought the older man was falling forward. Maybe he wasn't thinking of anything at all, which would certainly be consistent with his other behavior. In any case, the next thing we knew the two of them were tangled up rolling on the outfield grass in what appeared to be a fight.

The rest of our team poured out to swarm around the combatants. In most baseball fights, that's what happens. You go out to support your teammates, but at the same time what you're *really* trying to do is mill around looking pugnacious while actually avoiding injury to yourself or anyone else. But this wasn't most baseball fights. For one thing, it was just our team. The Owls stayed respectfully in their dugout, mesmerized by something they'd never seen—a team fighting with itself—but at the same time knowing instinctively that the more complete their non-involvement in the proceedings the better off they were likely to be.

When Captain Cook took the occasion to look around and—upon locating him—to sucker-punch Armstrong simply because the opportunity had unexpectedly presented itself, we suddenly had another bout to referee. Eventually, what with ballplayers tripping all over themselves and sprawling around looking for all the world as though they were competing in a mud-wrestling competition without any visible mud, Pepper and Dante were both ejected from the game. As were Captain Cook and Armstrong. As was I.

We all trudged into the locker room together. Armstrong stalked towards the showers to avoid any further contact with the steaming Cook, who slammed his locker open and started to toss around whatever he found in there.

Tambellini stopped and, for reasons I will never comprehend, waved the candy box at Pepper.

"It was just popcorn, Pepper."

Pepper looked at him as if Dante had just stepped from an alien spacecraft. "What?" he sputtered.

"You said I shouldn't be eating food. But it's not food. It was just Peanuts and Crackerjacks."

"I don't care if it is steak and potatoes!" Pepper screamed into his face. "You don't eat fucking anything when you are playing the game! How fucking stupid can you fucking be! Even in the Little League they know enough not to eat in the middle of the game! What are you, a fucking moron?"

"That's exactly what he is," Cook offered his unsolicited contribution. "Fucking moron who can't even read."

"Hey! I can read." Dante protested in a manner that seemed intent on justifying the "Inferno" nickname Simon had assigned him.

"Look at the box, genius. It says crackerjack. Peanuts and crackerjack. Not crackerjacks. It's singular, not plural, idiot."

"I never knew you were a grammarian, Pete," I said.

"Fuck you too."

"That don't make sense," said Dante. "There's so many of them. How can it be crackerjack when there's so many of them? Gotta be cracker*jacks*, right? Like peanuts. No one says peanut and crackerjack, 'cause then it'd be just one of each, and what's the point of having one peanut and one crackerjack? I mean, who'd do something like that? And why? No one eats just one of each. You know anyone who eats just one of each? And they sure as hell wouldn't sell you a box that had one peanut and one crackerjack. Not for four bucks they wouldn't. Hell, not for a quarter. Well, maybe for a quarter, if it was in one of those cute little packages, you know? But no one would fuckin' buy it if they did. So maybe they left the 's' off crackerjacks 'cause they're stupid. Or maybe *they* can't spell. Or maybe they figured there wasn't enough room on the box. But there really is, see? Lookit this box. There's room. If you just put the 's' back in crackerjacks..."

It wasn't Pepper's scream that brought the reporters into the locker room. I know that because I had just noticed, as Tambellini waxed grammatical, that they were gathering around us already. But if they hadn't been, it was certainly likely that the holler Pepper loosed would have brought them in quicker than a Sandy Koufax fastball.

Pepper told me later that he was just reaching for the Crackerjack box that Dante was waving around as he spoke. But all anybody saw was his hand shoot up just as Dante's drew back, with the result that Pepper's palm landed abruptly on Tambellini's chin. Dante was twice his size and half his age, but he was off-balance; and as any hitter will tell you, balance is everything. Dante staggered backwards, his heel caught a stool, and he fell crashing to the floor.

Anything that happens right in front of a roomful of reporters, photographers and cameramen is not going to stay secret for more than maybe two seconds. The expression on Pepper's face as he watched Dante sprawl to the floor, cameras aiming quickly at both of them, told me clearly that he knew not only what had just happened but what it meant. At that moment, his position on the team became untenable. Most owners would regard their manager engaging in a physical brawl with one of their players as anathema; and though owners of baseball teams were as a group famously judgmental, hypocritical and unforgiving, Simon probably ranked at the top of each of those categories even among his peers. With reporters screaming questions at him, Pepper walked past them into his office without saying a word. I was only a step behind him, closing the door on the ravenous newspack and locking it. Pepper stationed himself behind his desk while I commandeered the easy chair. We just stayed silent for a while as people howled questions through the door as though they could will it to be nonexistent. Eventually, they quieted some. I figured they were eliciting some dumb comment from Dante that would somehow manage to make things sound even worse than they were. But things were more than bad enough already, and we both knew it. Pepper finally spoke, his normal raspy growl oddly calm, almost relieved.

"It has to happen."

"No, it didn't."

"Yeah, it does. Maybe not this, but something, sooner or later. It is all crazy now, Mike. These kids, Simon ... there is just altogether too much that happens that is not baseball. You know how I love this game. But some-times—more than sometimes these days—this is just not the game you and me grow up to play."

"Maybe he won't...," I had difficulty finishing the sentence, but he picked it up where I'd left off.

"Sure he fires me. He kinda has to. *I* fire me if I'm him. You know, get-ting fired is not such a bad thing sometimes when you need to take a break from what you are being fired from because it is not what you sign up to not be fired from."

He shook his head. "I am sorry to do this to *you*, though."

"Don't be silly. I'm only here because of you."

"You have a future in this game, Mike. I got a past. You're good at this. And you're a young guy who is one of us old guys who are not here anymore to try to teach these kids who don't know yet the right way to play this game. I play a whole lot of innings already in my time. You ain't reached your peak yet. You got to reach your peak in this life, Mike. Because if you don't, you'll never know what it feels like when you do."

He stood up and, to my astonishment, reached out to shake my hand. When he had, he said, "Good luck to you, Mike," and walked calmly through the door. As he went through the locker room, I heard reporters screaming simultaneous questions at him every step of the way. He responded to each and every one of them with the same unchanging sentence. No matter what they asked, he answered:

"Baseball is a beautiful game."

Eventually, the piranhas of the press went elsewhere, and so did most everyone else. I took a long, hot shower, and took my sweet time getting dressed, so I figured I might be the last member of the team still there. But I wasn't. Dante, fully dressed, had not yet left. He was sprawled on a bench in front of his locker, seemingly lost in thought, though thought was not where many of us would ever have expected Dante to be lost.

"Dante." He didn't seem to hear me, so I moved directly in front of him. "Dante," I repeated.

"Yo."

"Can I ask you something?"

"Sure, coach."

"Why in the name of all that's holy were you eating Crackerjack in left field during a game?"

"I still think it should be Cracker*jacks*, coach."

"Why, Dante? Just tell me what made you do it."

He thought about it for a long moment as if searching his soul for the answer. Then he seemed to find it.

"I was hungry," he said.

Anyone Can Field the Good Ones

PEPPER DESCRIBED IT TO me the next night. We were at MommaDaddy's Bar and Grille drinking Screamers (though I also liked calling Genesee Cream Ale by another of its local nicknames, Green Death).

"I never see anything like it," he said.

"Few people have."

"Simon is standing there in his office yelling at me. Nothing new there. He tells me that he has already fired me and informed everyone in management and my lawyer. It is all on paper and everything. A done deal. He says he has no idea yet who will replace me but he is damn sure it will be someone who will refrain from socking his left fielder. He tells me a manager does not punch out his left fielder no matter how much of a stupid fucking brainless dupa the left fielder happens to be. Simon says he agrees with me that a player cannot disrespect the game but he tells me since the video makes it look like I am trying to hit the guy, he cannot resort to plausible deniability. That is what he actually says."

"Plausible deniability?"

"Yeah. I think it means lying. Anyway, he says we are stuck with the consequence of my action."

"What did you say?"

"I told him we were stuck with a hell of a lot more than that. But I also tell him I do not blame him for doing it. I tell him that *I* fire me if I am him. I figure that calms him down."

"It doesn't?"

"He goes haywire. All I am doing is agreeing with him, but his face turns redder than a tomato in August and he starts yelling like he is in some kind of screaming contest he really needs to win."

"What was he screaming?"

"Don't really know. Something about the image of the Bears and how his father would spin in his grave if Simon doesn't decide to cremate him so he has no grave to spin in but he would if he did. Not sure. Something like that. Then it happens. Right out of—"

"Left field," I finished the sentence. He looked at me and grinned. I can't begin to tell you how much I admired his ability to do that after all he had just been through, what with Dante first and now Simon.

"Yeah. One second he's standing there yelling to beat the band and the next second, he just stops. Looks like he's never seen me in his life, then just pitches forward like one of Wyatt's sinkers on a good day. Falls flat on his face. At first I think he is maybe joking, but he is not joking. Then I am sure he must be dead. So I ask his secretary to come in and take a look. She does and she starts yelling almost as loud as him. I tell her maybe it will do more good if she gets on the phone and screams for an ambulance. So she does, and they come, and it turns out he is not dead. He is resting peacefully, they say. In a fucking coma. Any word on how he is?"

"I spoke with the doctor. No way to tell. He says Simon is stable. He could wake up any minute, or stay like this for twenty years. The Doc says there's no way to know for sure. Told me anticipation invites medical error."

"If you *don't* anticipate, that's how you *get* an error. Ball goes right past you if you don't anticipate that it's coming your way."

I signaled for some more Gennys. "So what happens now?"

"Well, I'm fired. No two ways about it. I'm out of here. Normally Cole would just go out and hire Leahy, who is free now that Detroit is dumb enough to fire him, or Carney, who is still unemployed 'cause Philly is too stupid to hire him, or Clement, who by this time is probably sick of living in Arizona, or someone else who actually knows what he's doing during a baseball game. But Cole can't hire anyone yet. 'Cause now that Simon is doing his impersonation of a vegetable—though even in a coma he's probably still smarter than Tambellini—you know who Cole's got to go to now for an okay on everything, right? You know who is now in charge of the whole circus?"

I knew. We both knew. We looked at each other, wondering who would say the name first. I did, finally.

"Junior."

"Junior," he agreed. "Who apparently is just back from India doing whatever you do with gurus in India. Team's got a kid space cadet as a fucking owner. Can you believe that?"

"Problem is, at this point, I can believe most anything."

"Yeah. Me too. That's what I can't believe. So what do you think happens now with Junior in charge?"

"Who knows? Guess everyone should be ready for anything."

"Yeah." Pepper knocked back his Pounder. "Like the man said, do not alibi on bad hops. Anyone can field the good ones."

Chief Buffalo

"Mike, do you remember when I was young?"

"You're twenty-four, Junior."

I had been surprised, when I came home earlier, to see Jenna suddenly stop the crossover dribble she was relentlessly practicing in front of the basket we had hung over the garage door (she was already better at it than I'd ever been) and greet me with a wave. Normally, nothing short of a hurricane would break her concentration when she had a ball in her hand.

"Hey, Dad. You have a message. You're supposed to go to The Egg and see Junior."

"Mr. Lumpe, Jenna. Mr. Lumpe the younger, anyway."

"He called himself Junior when I answered the phone. I just figured it would be more polite to honor the name he chose to call himself than to call him Mr. Lumpe just because that's what conventional society thinks is appropriate. The more I learn about conventional society the less sense it makes to me anyway. Does it make sense to you?" Instead of waiting for a reply, she spun back to the basket and practiced reverse layups, being sure to alternate hands so that she could drive from either side. I reached for the door.

Her voice sailed past my ear like a message pitch. "He said as soon as you can."

So here I was in Simon's office, adjusting to the unfamiliar vision of Junior behind the desk instead of Simon. Although Junior was inches taller than his father, he somehow didn't fill out the chair as much; his skinny body seemed almost surrounded by the huge, plush red leather chair Simon always felt added authority to his interviews. Although he was three years out of college, Junior still looked closer to Jenna's age, and the jug ears framing his round baby face made him appear like a high school Buddha.

He waved away my observation about his age with a dismissive motion of one soft hand. "I realize I'm young chronologically. But I've been given a great gift. Do you know what it is?"

"I wouldn't even guess."

"Wisdom beyond my years. I was as a child when I went to sit at the feet of my guru Mashinamdev. Now I am still a child, yes, but a wiser child. Wiser because I am so much more deeply aware of my own ignorance. So many people are unaware of the depth of their own unawareness, wouldn't you agree, Mike?"

"I sure would."

"I knew you would. Do you know how I knew?"

"You were aware of it?"

"When I was young—before I left to learn from Mashinamdev—you once gave me a book. Do you remember?"

"Sure. It's nice *you* do, though."

"It changed my life."

"It just struck me as something you might like."

"Like. Such a seemingly simple word, yet how opaque it always is. What seems simple is so often complex, don't you think? What is 'like,' really? Is all not love? Except of course that which isn't?"

"I wouldn't argue with that."

"That's because you too have a well of wisdom within you, Mike. And I admire that. I more than admire it. I respond to it. Mashinamdev says that to admire is to realize that your image in the pool reflects back at you the projection of your own values, but to actively enter the stream is to express your full self in a way that makes you one with the water."

"Gets you pretty wet, too."

"Yes. Part of the experience. And what is life if not the sum total of our experience as we pass through this dimension of reality? And you have the experience, Mike."

"I have *what* experience?"

"With the Buffalo."

"The city?"

"No, the team. I'm changing our name from the Bears to the Buffalo so that we can be the Buffalo Buffalo. The resonance is pleasing, don't you find? If you say it aloud, it rolls off the tongue. Buffalo Buffalo. I always found it somewhat odd that we represent a city named for one creature and yet adopt another beast as our mascot. We all need to be proud to be Buffalo, Mike. Which is why I need you to be Chief Buffalo. The leader of our great herd."

"Chief Buffalo?"

"My new manager. You're the only one who is familiar with our team, with our strengths and weaknesses, who also understands what I'm talking about."

"I have to tell you, Junior, I'm not sure I *do* understand everything you're talking about."

"But you speak my language, Mike. You're the one who gave me *The Supreme Adventure*. And when I read the words of Peter Hayes, I felt the thunderbolt he himself felt. Only *you* would have given me that book, because only you *gave* me that book. It's karma. You may not be completely enlightened—I'm not either, far as that goes—but we both *seek* enlightenment, don't we? And how many people in professional baseball can say that and be speaking the truth?"

As I tried to figure out the best answer to that, he continued. "Do you happen to remember Peter Hayes's story about the boy with the glasses that he taunted until he put them on as a joke and suddenly realized that for the very first time he himself could see clearly? That is my own metaphor, Mike. I can see clearly now, or at least more so than I ever could when I was young. Younger. And you are what I see. You leading the enlightened charge of the Buffalo Buffalo. As chief of all buffalo."

He paused for dramatic effect, and in that moment he suddenly resembled Simon. "You're my manager, Mike. Please accept. I need you to. The team needs you. The karmic universe needs you. That's why you're here, now. If you were not the man for the job, you would not be here, now. That you are is a manifestation of our needs. It would be disrespectful to those needs to not honor them."

It was my lifelong dream and I wanted to shout "YES!" into the air. But the image of Pepper being chased out the door by a throng of reporters kept gnawing at me—I wouldn't even be a part of this team were it not for him—and I also reminded myself that this had to be a family discussion, not a unilateral decision. And deep down, I wondered if I was ready yet to really take charge.

So it was off to MommaDaddy's to drink some more with Pepper, who got good and mad when I expressed my reservations about taking the job even though it was, along with my family, what I most wanted in the world.

"Are you fucking nuts? Do you know how few of these jobs are ever out there? Do you know how often you get the chance to have one? Try almost never. Now you suddenly have an owner who is the only one likely to ever be crazy enough to give *you* the job instead of all these baseball lifers who if you don't mind my saying so have earned the shot a hell of a lot more than you have. But does he want Clement or Carney or Leahy? No. He wants you, with your Princeton books and your southpaw logic even if you are right-handed. Lord knows why it's you he wants. But who are you to argue with the Lord?"

"That's pretty much what Junior said. In so many words."

"So what's the fucking problem? Don't you *want* a shot at the title?"

"Well, sure. But I also..."

"What? Want to be loyal to me or some crap like that? Look, I'm not managing this team no matter what happens. And I am a hell of a lot happier if it is you than someone else. I am fucking thrilled to see you get the shot. And I am bitterly disappointed in you for the rest of my days if you do not take it. So you got a choice. You can be happier and richer and have the dream of a baseball lifer's lifetime and make your family proud and an old man thrilled, or you can be a fucking moron. I know it's a tough decision, but tough decisions are what being a manager is all about."

The family conference over dinner was less profane but otherwise went much the same way. "I can't believe you're even hesitating over this," said Donna, disregarding her food to regard me as if we hadn't yet been introduced.

"That's what Pepper said."

"He has the advantage of not having read *Hamlet*. Or trying to *be* Hamlet."

"Who'd want to be Hamlet?" asked Jenna between forkfuls of linguini primavera. "Hamlet died young."

"How young?" inquired Laura.

"You'll find out when you read it," her sister informed her.

"Older than me?"

"Of course older than you."

"Then he wasn't all *that* young, was he?"

"He was *young*, Laura. Older than you can still be young."

"Not to me."

"Laura, *I'm* older than you."

Laura smiled wickedly at Jenna. I could see her consider saying "Exactly" then decide not to. She attacked her linguini while Donna examined me as if I were a new legal brief.

"It's an opportunity you could hardly have even dreamed of. That you've always secretly wanted."

"Not so secretly," interjected my older daughter.

Donna beeped once at Jenna, then returned her attention to me. "And for more money, even. And if you don't take it that won't do Pepper any good at all, and in fact he *wants* you to take it. And if you turn it down you'll just end up working for someone else who isn't Pepper and you'll be miserable."

"No, he won't," said Jenna.

"Of course he will."

"If he turns it down, he'll probably get fired," Jenna offered helpfully.

"But he'd still be miserable," Laura observed brightly.

I held up my hand to halt the skirmishes, if only temporarily. "I just wanted your opinions. You know I'm not going to do something like this unless this family is in agreement about it."

"When are we ever in agreement about anything?" asked Laura.

"I think we are now," came Jenna's prompt reply. "Aren't we?"

"Are you asking me what I think?" Laura was incredulous.

"Obviously."

"Wow."

"Laura." I only said the one word. My younger daughter looked at me, suddenly serious.

"I absolutely think you should do it, Daddy. If you want to," she added quickly. I smiled at her for adding that caveat and turned to Jenna, who didn't even wait for me to ask.

"I think you'd be out of your mind to say anything but yes," she stated with an unshakeable conviction that reminded me how much she was her mother's daughter. I turned my attention to Donna, whose hazel eyes glittered above those high cheekbones as she shook her head at me.

"You know what I think."

"That's never stopped you from saying it anyway," I observed. She almost smiled, but suppressed it easily enough.

"But," I said, "as far as Hamlet goes—"

"Hamlet didn't have a wife and two wonderful daughters."

"You don't have to suck up to us, Mom," said Laura.

"Oh, stop it, Lor," Jenna told her. "Can't you tell when she really means it?"

Donna ignored both girls and kept my eyes locked with hers. "And Hamlet didn't love baseball. Not this much, anyway."

"Well, he lived in Denmark," Laura said.

"I'll bet there are even Danish people who love baseball," Jenna said loyally.

"I'll bet there aren't."

I held up my hand again and for a brief fleeting moment, quiet reigned. I looked around the table.

"So we're agreed? We take the job?"

Jenna's hand shot up with conviction. Laura raised hers more languidly but without the slightest hesitation. Donna gave me a look that reminded me one more time why I had been so lucky to marry her, and raised both her hands high.

"Hey, Mom," protested Jenna, "you can't vote twice."

"Maybe she's just voting twice as hard," suggested Laura.

"No," I told both of them. "She's voting for me, too."

Skip

So I told Junior I would gratefully take on the task at hand, but I had one request that was important to me. It gave him pause.

"That may not be a good idea."

"Then again, it may be a *great* idea."

"There's got to be some other old baseball guy who could be your bench coach. Besides Pepper. I mean, we just fired him. What'll it look like?"

"It'll look like we don't care what it looks like. You know, make us look bold and independent. Our own man. Men. People."

"What'll my dad say? If he ever wakes up from that coma. It'll send him right back into another one. Dad's not real big on forgiveness."

"But he's big on demotions, right?"

"He loves demotions. It's one of his favorite things to do besides firing people, to demote them."

"Well, this is a demotion, isn't it? It's not as if you're hiring Pepper to take back his old job. Your dad laid down the law about that. No more managing this team for Pepper. But this way he's still with the Bears. I mean the Buffalo. Loyal to the team and to the Lumpe family. You now have this great opportunity to be generous and give him a second chance at the same time you're demoting him. It would be kind of a two-fer, wouldn't it?"

"I don't know," he said as if he didn't.

"And he'd be a bigger help to me than anyone else possibly could. Pepper has forgotten more about this game than most of us will ever know. It's been his whole life. And without the pressure of managing, he would be free to just watch things on the field and tell me what he notices. And of course we trust each other."

"I still don't know."

Whenever you try to convince anyone of anything, I reminded myself, give him *his* reason for agreeing, not yours. So I took a deep breath, hoped there was water in the pool, and dived in.

"Let me ask you something. Did Mashinamdev ever say anything about rocks?"

He almost spun in the chair. "How did you know that?" He seemed genuinely stunned.

I hadn't, of course, but I reckoned there was a reasonable possibility. Rocks tend to lend themselves well to metaphors and similes, and I had already heard enough about Mashinamdev to know those were among the guru's tools. If Junior had said no in answer to my question, I would have tried something else. The sea or the moon. Maybe grains of sand. I was pretty sure one of them would be a winner.

"I just sensed it," I half-lied. "What did he say?"

"He said that when you throw a rock into the water, it makes a splash, but then sinks. Whereas if you skip a rock across the water, each time it touches the surface, instead of sinking it leaves ripples that meet each other and slowly extend until they become gentle waves in a faraway sea, leaving a legacy instead of a fleeting splash."

Perfect. Thank you, Mashinamdev. You're my kind of guru.

"That's exactly what I'm trying to say. Why let Pepper sink with this noisy splash when we can let him continue making waves?"

Whoops. Disaster. Not what I meant at all.

"Gentle waves?" I desperately amended, hoping I hadn't blown it. I tried frantically to figure out how I could possibly blend a buffalo and water into the same image. Maybe a water buffalo? No, no... Then I noticed that Junior was hardly even listening to me. His eyes were aglow.

"Genius," he breathed in awe.

"Well," I replied tentatively, "that's awfully nice of you, but it does seem overly generous..."

"Genius," he repeated to himself, apparently not having heard a word I had said. "That's what it is." He turned to me. "I've got it. Thanks to you. What a team we make, huh?"

"You've got what?" I asked, genuinely confused.

"We'll have both of them. As bench coaches."

"Both of who?"

"Pepper. And Mashinamdev. They'll both be on the bench with you.

It'll be fantastic. Don't you see? Yin and Yang. Each with an utterly different perspective. It'll be unprecedented."

"That's for sure," I managed.

"Give you two extremes to balance."

"I can hardly wait."

"For a little while, anyway. We'll be lucky if I can convince Mashinamdev to stay more than a week or so. He loves new experiences, and I'll make another contribution to the temple, so I'm pretty sure he'll agree to try it. But he won't leave India for too long. Says the mountains always help clear his mind and sooth his spirit. Not too many mountains in Buffalo, unfortunately."

"Maybe we can buy some."

"You're kidding, right?"

"I'm not sure any more," I told him honestly.

He thought for a second. "I'll e-mail him. Mashinamdev has no phone, but he checks his e-mail every night. Says it's better than a sleeping pill. So you'll have them both. Pepper can give you baseball advice and Mashinamdev will help with spiritual insights before, during and after the game. You'll love him, Mike. He's a kindred spirit. One of us."

I wasn't quite sure what that meant but figured it would be wise to just let it go and accept things as they apparently were. And I had the feeling that I needed to be as wise as possible, because I was getting the distinct sense that, no matter how much that managed to be, it was unlikely to be even close to wise enough.

Pepper was so grateful to still be breathing major-league baseball that he didn't even flinch when I told him that Junior had made it a requirement of his new employment that he apologize to Tambellini.

"Sure," he said without hesitation. I looked at him and started to repeat it, certain that he couldn't have understood me correctly if he was agreeing so affably. But he waved my next sentence away before I could finish it.

"I got it. I apologize to the lunkhead. No problem."

And he did. In front of me, when I called Dante into the office and asked him if he was man enough not to have any problem with Pepper helping me on the bench if Pepper apologized to him for their fight. Dante drew himself up in manly fashion as soon as I phrased it that way.

"I'm fine with it, coach. I mean, Skipper. I can forgive like a good Christian. Not like Armstrong, I don't go to church like he does, but he just creeps everyone out anyway and I don't do that, do I? I probably got my flaws too, and truth is, Pepper, I oughta apologize to you for eating the Crackerjacks during the game. You're right, I shoulda waited till after. What if I was still holding the box and had to throw the ball after I caught it? Coulda been embarrassing."

"Pepper?" I looked at him. "You have anything to say to Dante?"

"Yeah." he took a deep breath. "First thing is, Dante, I wish I have your muscles. Those are some pecs you got there."

Dante swelled with pride. "Thanks, Pepper."

"I have those muscles, with my knowledge of the game, I am probably still playing baseball when I am seventy-six, which by the way I am not yet, nowhere near, well, not very. Also, I am very sorry what happened in the locker room. I am sorry because I lose my job, true, but I am also sorry because I never mean to hit you at all, you are much bigger, stronger and younger than me, why would I hit you, I am only trying to grab the stupid Crackerjack box. So it is true that at this time we are speaking of I am more than somewhat upset with you because you are giving me the impression you are a hopeless fucking moron with no respect for the game which we should all have because it is a beautiful game that we love and it feeds ourselves and our families besides ... you got a family, Dante?"

"I got a hot date tonight. Miss August. Year before last. But still in great shape. As good as me, almost."

"A family is a wonderful thing."

"Yeah. I got a mother. And a father, 'course. I do love my mother, Pepper. She's always been real good to me and stood by me even when I was a total jerk, which believe it or not, I sometimes am."

"Well, that's what a mother's for, Dante. So if you thought I was trying to hit you, well, I wasn't, and I apologize if it seemed that way. And if it seemed to you that I was being unfair, well, if you thought that, I'm really sorry for you."

"Aw, thanks, Pepper." Dante stuck out a large hand. "Let bygones be history, huh?"

They shook hands, and Dante, after promising to play hard for me, left. I looked over at Pepper.

"That was some apology."

"You like it?"

I waved him to his chair, but he shook his head adamantly. "That's your chair now, Mike. You're the skipper."

Pepper made sure that he was nowhere visible when I went into the locker room to greet the guys. Some players came up to wish me well, others just seemed nervous trying to remember if when I was just a coach they'd said anything to me they might now regret. The conversation I appreciated most was the one with McCarter, who asked if we could have a quick private word. I said sure, and we moved away from all the others.

"It occurs to me," he began, "that it would be good for the team, and especially for you as the new manager, to win your first game."

"Not a requisite for survival, I hope, but yes, it certainly would be very nice."

"It further occurs to me," he continued with a barely suppressed grin, "that there is a way I just might be able to facilitate such a result."

"Really."

"It's possible."

"By all means, tell me how."

"Well, I noticed they're pitching this rookie against us today. Wilmer Guadalacra. Who has quite a fine fastball. His curve needs work and his changeup is still a rumor, but he can bring it."

"I hear it sits at 94–96."

"He's touched 97–98, actually."

"You've seen him?"

"Played against him. In the minors. When I was rehabbing the shoulder injury and he was in the St. Louis system."

"And?"

"And he tips his pitches, Skip."

Tom was grinning ear to ear, and I was thinking what a hell of a manager he was going to make someday, and marveled at how so many players wasted the opportunities they were being given to learn so much more about the game they played every day just by watching it.

"How?"

"Whenever he's going to throw the fastball," Tom now resembled a Cheshire Cat in a baseball uniform, "he smiles."

"Smiles."

"Yup."

"You're kidding."

"Nope."

"And he's unaware of this?"

"Nobody seemed to notice. It was Single-A. The kids down there didn't know you could study the game. They thought you just went out there and played."

I nodded slowly. "You want to tell the team? You're the one who saw it."

"I think it'll make you look really good, if he still does it. I don't need the credit for noticing it. You can use some; it's your first game managing, and the jury's still out with some guys whether you have what it takes. So just regard it as a gift from me to you."

"Thanks, Tom. A lot."

"That's okay. Just remember it in the dog days to come. And in the future, when you speak of me—and you will—be kind."

I gathered the team together before the game to tell them what I expected of them—show up on time, play hard, run out everything no matter how hopeless, and I would understand physical errors but I wouldn't appreciate mental ones. Then I paused for a moment, and told them I had a private scouting report on the rookie pitcher. When they heard what it was, a couple of snorts of derision rapidly escalated into a shared, loud laugh that rolled over the room. Tom looked at his teammates and warned, "Before we get too cocky about it, fellas, bear in mind that even if you know it's coming, it'll be there in the high 90's. Still tough to hit."

"Hell," Garrett's deep voice rumbled mellifluously, "I can hit a jet plane, you show it to me three times."

In the event, Joe only had to see it once. He let the first pitch, an outside curve, go by for ball one. Then the kid smiled and threw the fastball. It went out quicker than it had come in, sailing majestically over the left-field fence. It was a three-run homer when he hit it because Marcus, knowing he wasn't getting the heat, singled to center on the first pitch, and Terry, after missing the first fastball he knew was coming and fouling off the second, waited patiently for the next one and then drilled it for another hit. In fact, the only one of our first six hitters who did not reach safely was Dante, who was way behind the fastball when it blew by him. When he returned to the dugout, he looked sheepish.

"Sorry, Skip. Shoulda hit that."

"You knew it was coming, right?"

"Not really sure," he confessed.

Crockett, McCarter and Cohen all turned to join me in looking at him. "Why the hell not?" I inquired.

"I wasn't sure he was smiling."

Crockett shook his head in disbelief. "I could see him from here. Hell, Dante, he looked like he'd won the fucking lottery."

"Couldn't be sure. Thought he might be, you know, just happy or something."

"Happy?" Cohen's disbelief permeated the dugout.

"Which might have meant a cut fastball. Or maybe even a sinker. Just couldn't tell for sure."

Maybe we should have held something back, because after we knocked out the kid with four runs in the first, they went to the bullpen for Rick Blessing, a savvy veteran who shut us down for the next six frames. By that time they had tied the game. When Bo Johnson doubled in the eighth with two outs, they brought in Adly Salamanga, their closer whom normally they would save for a lead in the ninth. But Langer, their manager, was smart enough to realize they wouldn't *have* a lead in the ninth unless they shut us down before we got there. So he brought in his fireman to kill the rally. Heads swiveled on the bench when I ignored Cohen, Armstrong, Rademacher, and Strain and instead turned to Fortunado.

"Bring us home, Hilario," I encouraged him. Fortunado, the all-purpose utility man who was so happy to be in the league that he celebrated every day as though it was his birthday, grinned ear to ear and grabbed a bat. As he approached the plate, I could hear the silent speculation raging around me. Okay, Rademacher and Cohen are righties and Hilario is a switch hitter. But in Hilario's case that just meant he was equally ineffective from both sides of the plate. And anyway Strain was a lefty bat and Armstrong, though a righty, was a far better hitter than Fortunado, so what in the name of Hank Greenberg could I be thinking?

When Fortunado singled up the middle to score Bo and get us back the lead, I could feel the atmosphere palpably change. I had done something that seemed peculiar and it had worked. Therefore I maybe understood something they didn't. Which meant that as far as they were concerned, I had, at least for the moment, established my qualifications to be Manager. They now trusted me—at least until the next game—to be their field general.

No one actually asked me afterwards why I had rolled those particular dice, though McCarter, when he passed me, gave me a mock salute. But when I arrived home, both girls were waiting. Jenna was, as usual, pacing restlessly around as if her lean, athletic body needed to move, while Laura sat on the couch, pondering her thoughts and occasionally writing something down in a notebook.

"We were arguing about why you did that, Dad," Jenna greeted me.

"Not really arguing. It was a civilized discussion," Laura clarified.

"You were yelling at me, Laura."

"Well, you were yelling at me, too, but I was at least being civilized about it."

"So why did you use Fortunado, Dad?" Jenna refused to take Laura's bait.

"Because Salamanga is tough."

"Uh-huh." Jenna waited and Laura, seeing her older sister being patient, bit back whatever she was going to say and waited as well.

"And I figured sooner or later if the game was tight we'd see him in there. So before the game I checked everyone's career stats against him to see how they'd done."

"You don't know how to do that on a computer, Daddy," Laura pointed out.

"I know. The team does it for me. Joey runs them."

"Who's Joey?" inquired Laura.

"The Stats intern in the team's office," Jenna informed her. "He's just out of Princeton, and he's kind of cute."

"He's a lot cuter today than he was yesterday," I said.

"I could probably do that as well as he can. Better, probably," asserted Laura confidently.

"I don't doubt it," I assured her. "But you were in school and I was in the stadium and I needed them as quickly as I could get them and he works for the team and you've got your own homework to do so I looked at the numbers and lo and behold, most of our guys make Adly seem like Christy Mathewson at his peak. But Fortunado, of all people, owns him."

"Owns him?" asked Laura, not sure if she was supposed to understand but quite sure that she didn't.

"It just means he always does really really well against him," Jenna explained.

"In this case," I added, "he was hitting a career 5 for 9 against him. After today that means he's hitting a cool .600 against one of the toughest relievers out there. Problem is of course that he doesn't hit his weight against anyone else, and Hilario doesn't weigh much. So I just took the chance. Figured Fortunado would have confidence against Salamanga that the others wouldn't. Funny how that works in baseball. Tom Seaver was one of the greatest pitchers of his era, a no-doubt-at-all Hall of Famer, but there was a journeyman bench player named Tommy Hutton who always hit him like Seaver was his country cousin. This is a strange game sometimes."

"So you were playing the percentages," Jenna mused.

"And doing his research," Laura added. "That was really smart, Daddy. You're smart sometimes."

"I try to be."

"We know that. It's just that sometimes you succeed at it."

"I don't think that came out quite the way you meant it, Laura," her sister told her.

"That's all right," I assured them both. "I realize that was meant as a legitimate compliment."

"I still think I can do better than Joey. I can take an intern. Even one from Princeton."

"You're just starting high school," Jenna reminded her.

"I could have taken him when I was in junior high."

"That was, like, two months ago."

"Exactly. And I'm even better now than I was then."

Laura left with an aura of assured confidence. Jenna regarded me appraisingly.

"Dad, can I ask your advice on a completely different subject entirely?"

"Of course, sweetie. Baseball isn't everything."

"Oh. For a minute there, I thought maybe it was. Anyway—you know I'm in this play at school."

"Sure. James McLure's *Drive-In Dreams*. I'm looking forward to seeing it."

"That's just it. Mrs. Craft—she's our drama teacher and she's directing the play—doesn't like what I'm doing. She wants me to indicate the emotions more. She keeps saying, 'You've got to let them know it's comedy, dear.' But I feel stupid indicating anything. I know she knows more about how to do this than I do, but I know I'm terrible when I do anything that feels fake. I mean, if *I* feel fake, how can anyone watching me believe a thing I'm saying, if I don't myself? I just don't see the point of playing a character if you don't actually feel like that character. But then again, she's the director and I'm supposed to do it the way she directs me to, right? I mean, you tell us how aggravated you get when one of the guys on the team doesn't do what you tell him to do."

"I don't get aggravated," I protested.

"Sure you do, Dad. You just try to pretend you're amused. That's how we can tell how aggravated you are. Anyway, what should I do, do you think?"

"I don't know. It's your decision."

"That's a big help."

"But I can tell you what you *shouldn't* do. You shouldn't do anything that makes you feel phony. You're right—no one is going to believe in any reality you don't believe in yourself."

"But what do I tell Mrs. Craft?"

"Tell her about Al Simmons."

"What *about* Al Simmons?"

"He hit stepping into the bucket."

"Doing what?"

"When the pitch came in, he stepped *backwards*. The first thing they teach you is to not hit that way. You're moving all your weight away from the ball instead of stepping into it. It's almost impossible to hit doing that. Except for Al Simmons. He played twenty seasons and ended up with a career batting average of .334."

"So?"

"So when his manager with the Philadelphia A's had this player whose batting stance was all wrong, what do you think he did about it?"

"What did he do?"

"Nothing. He left him alone. His manager figured that if it wasn't broke, why fix it? What difference did it make how ridiculous his style was if the guy hit .390 twice and .380 twice? And what are the chances he would have hit anything close to what he did if he was forced to change his natural way of doing it?"

"So you think I should step into the bucket?"

"If that's the way your acting feels the most truthful, yes. Not because it guarantees it will work that way, but because it's a safe bet it won't work as well any other way."

She held up her hand and then reversed it downwards to receive the low-five we exchanged. "Thanks, dad," she said happily. "I knew that if we really tried, we could have a conversation that had nothing to do with baseball."

Guru

I KNEW WHO HE was, of course, when I saw him on the floor of my office. Even if he hadn't been sitting cross-legged, I would have recognized him immediately, since we had no one else on the team from India. But I had been expecting a wizened old sage, not this smiling, smooth-complected young man who greeted me with a friendly tilt of his shaven head.

"You must be Mike."

I bowed to him.

"I always liked the origin of the bow," he continued as though we were old friends resuming a lifelong conversation, "the notion that one is acknowledging the godhead in each and every one of us. Is that why you did it?"

"Nah. I just mistook you for Japanese."

His expression never changed, but laughter spun around a dance floor in his eyes. "You wouldn't be the first, believe it or not. Does that surprise you?"

"Nothing surprises me," I told him. "Though everything is unexpected."

Now he did smile, and rose so smoothly and effortlessly to a straight standing position that had I blinked I would have missed the movement.

"You and I," he said with certainty, "are going to get along."

Actually, as the days went by he got along easily with pretty much everyone, much to my relief. Jack Lee cornered him whenever possible to ask him questions about Zen, and sometimes Tom or others hung around listening; and, unexpectedly, I once saw the guru gesturing to an obviously interested Ellerbee in what seemed to be an exchange about physical exercise. Most of the others just live and let live, and so did he.

One exception was Pepper, who always found something else to do whenever Mashinamdev was around. One day a couple of hours before a

116

game with the Owls, Pepper and I were discussing the opposition lineup in my office when there was a gently insistent knock on the door.

"Come on in," I said. The door opened and the guru glided in. Pepper started to stiffen and then looked at his watch only to remember that he didn't wear one—the scoreboard had a huge clock built into it and anyway Pepper never cared about what time it was during a game. Before he had a chance to improvise another urgent task, Mashinamdev addressed him directly.

"Pepper," he asked, "is there a reason you are so reluctant to speak to me? I was just wondering."

Pepper looked at him. I could see him decide to just bull honestly ahead.

"I am not reluctant to speak with you," he told him. "I just got nothing to fuckin' say."

"You have a great deal to say, much of it worthwhile," our visitor gently disagreed. "But there may be nothing you wish to share with me."

"That's the fuckin' truth."

"I hope that you will consider reconsidering. There is so much that I might learn from you, I would be saddened to lose such a rare and valuable opportunity. I would consider that a great loss."

"You makin' fun of me?"

"Quite the opposite. I simply wish you to teach me."

"Me? I'm not the guru here."

"But you are," came the calm remonstrance. "You are a master of your own faith, the religion of baseball. Though I have long regarded your game with fascination, I can only imagine how much of it you may understand that I do not."

"Long regarded? You just get here."

"Yes, but the tireless efforts of the great American lady Muriel Peters, who loves both India and baseball, have brought baseball coaches from your major leagues to Delhi, Mumbai, Chennai, Calcutta and Manipur. I have watched the instruction, and even a blind man could see the joy of the young players and the pleasure the American coaches take in imparting the rituals of their religion. This is one faith that does not seek enemies to kill; it feels only pity, not condemnation, for those who are not among its acolytes. It spreads pleasure over an entire season, reconciles its faithful to loss and— what is the word you use for a player's difficulty in maintaining his personal standards?"

"Slumps. Everyone gets 'em. Except Ted Williams, maybe. But he's dead now. And even when he is playing, he isn't like anyone else."

"Slumps, yes. Perhaps no aspect of the game seems to me more fascinating than its realization that success in one's efforts must be defined by one's failures, since failure is the norm and success is not."

"How do you mean?" Pepper seemed genuinely interested.

"Well," the guru measured his words meditatively, "to hit for an average of .300 is considered outstanding, yes? Yet this represents hitting safely in only three of ten attempts. If the batter fails seven times out of ten, he is revered. If he fails six times out of ten, he is considered immortal, as was the great Ted of whom you speak. Yet even *he* is still failing most of the time, is this not so?"

"I guess it is. Yeah. Unless you just go by on-base percentage."

"Pepper, tell me: how long does any game last?"

"It varies, I guess."

"But it doesn't, does it? Isn't it always the same?"

"I don't see ... oh, yeah, I see what you mean. It lasts until the last man makes the last out."

"So the time in normal measurement has no meaning. In theory a game could last forever."

"I am in some that feel like they do."

"Your game has no clock. No artificial end. It ends when it is over, not a moment before. I find this charming. May I ask you something else?"

"Yeah, go ahead, guru."

"I hear that you and Mike have a pastime of exchanging names of former players of the game. No explanations or identifications, only the simple exchange of names. May I ask why you do this?"

Pepper looked at me, not sure how to answer that, so I did it for both of us. "It makes us feel better."

"Lifts your spirits?"

"You could say that."

"Yes. And why? Is it not that to evoke those cheerful ghosts, those spirits of the past, enables you to feel your connection to those who walked this path before yourselves?"

"More or less," I agreed.

"Though they ain't all that fuckin' cheerful," observed Pepper. "The Georgia Peach will sooner spike you or spit on you than smile at you. But I get your meaning."

"You do?"

"Sure. Football's just a war game where oversized thugs slam into each other, basketball's the world's greatest celebration of glandular freaks outside a Hollywood, hockey's a bunch of guys fightin' on skates, and no one gives a hoot what happens six years ago much less sixty. But baseball, every time a guy throws a no-hitter we all remember Johnny Vander Meer and his two in a row. Every guy who hits in, say, more than thirty games straight reminds us how unbelievable it is that DiMaggio has that 56-game streak. And do you know, guru, that in the game The Clipper is stopped Ken Keltner, the Cleveland third sacker, makes a pair of circus catches either one of which is normally a clean hit and that after that game DiMaggio hits in another sixteen games? So that streak is 72 if Kenny does not play that day like he is campaigning for the Hall of Fame. And even the 56-game streak, no one yet even really comes close to it to this day and that is in 1941, which by the way is the same year Teddy Ballgame, the one and only Mr. Williams, hits .406 and that is the last time anyone ever touches .400 either, so that is some year."

"And you remember it as though it were yesterday."

"Well, yeah. Because it kind of is."

"Exactly. Yesterday and tomorrow are both today. All is connected, and we are all one."

"Jam yesterday and jam tomorrow," I offered, "but never jam today."

He smiled. "*Alice in Wonderland* is a great book. Perhaps too profound for many adults, but that is no fault of the author."

Pepper started to say something but then stopped, not sure of the words to use. Mashinamdev just stood at ease as though time had no relevance. Pepper finally reached up to slap the taller man approvingly on the shoulder, waved to me and exited the office.

"That was pretty slick." I meant it as a compliment, but he regarded me gravely.

"No, it was not slick. It was simply simple."

"Well, you've got him on your side now, anyway."

"I only showed him that *I* was on *his* side. I honor wisdom in any form, Mike. In his world, he is wise and I am the most novice of ... what is the correct term I seek?"

"Rookies."

"Yes, the most novice of rookies." He considered me thoughtfully. "Tell me, Mike. When you first meet someone, what should they need to do to gain your respect?"

"I don't know. What?"

"Nothing," he informed me softly. "Everyone should have our respect until they do something to lose it."

I thought about that comment a few days later on Mashinamdev's last day with us before his return to India. He had thanked me and especially Pepper for all he claimed to have learned from us, and by this time Pepper was treating him as though he were Yogi Berra himself. Now he was sitting cross-legged on the carpet in front of Jack Lee's locker, and Lee was saying farewell in his own fashion, which in Jack's case meant speculating on the parallel shortcomings of comparative faiths. From a few lockers away, Captain Cook decided to inject himself into the discussion.

"I just want to tell you, guru-man, that I'm glad you're leaving town."

"No one asked you, Pete," observed Jack.

"Because," Cook ignored Lee completely, "every word you say is utter and complete bullshit."

The guru regarded him calmly. "There are so many who agree with you that had I ever bothered to keep count, I would have lost it by now."

"You think you're smart, don't you."

"A smart man is one who knows how to get out of a situation that a wise man would never have gotten into in the first place. So no, Pete, I don't consider myself especially smart."

"You hang around and talk to all these guys like you're something special."

"*They* are something special," he corrected gently. "You all are. That is why I am so pleased that you all speak with me."

"Well, *I'm* not fucking speaking with you."

"No?"

"No."

"Then how would you describe what you and I are doing at this very moment?"

Cook shot him a venomous glare. "You think you've got all the fucking answers to everything."

"Of course not," said Mashinamdev. "Asking questions is an indication of intelligence. Knowing all the answers suggests the lack of it. You may be confusing me with—how would Pepper say it? Oh, yes. You may be confusing me with a pitcher who loses with his third-best pitch."

Pete shoved off his stool and loomed threateningly over the much smaller man, who remained unmoved both literally and figuratively. "You trying to make me look like a fool?"

"I'd say you're doing that pretty well without his help," said Jack.

Quietly and quickly, several players suddenly stood right by Mashinamdev's relaxed figure. Garrett was one of them. Cook took a look at the powerful, unsmiling third baseman and stepped back, deciding maybe it wasn't worth it.

"Peter?"

Cook, startled to be addressed by the guru, turned back to him belligerently.

"What?"

"If you think I'm a fool, or a fake..."

"I know you're both," snarled Cook.

"Well, I'd more likely be one or the other. But let's say you're right. My question to you is: why do you care?"

"I don't."

"Then why bring it up with such force?"

Cook started to give a response, but seemed to have difficulty finding one. By this time a collection of his teammates were silently watching him, waiting to see what he'd say.

"I just don't like you pulling the wool over everyone's eyes like you do."

"You are deeply concerned, then, about the psychological state of your teammates?"

"I don't give a flying fuck about anyone but myself, pal. And you don't fool this boy."

"Then why do you care?"

Pete started to speak, stopped, then stomped away in frustration. Mashinamdev tossed Jack a puzzled look.

"Pulling the wool?" he mused wonderingly. "Why would anyone wish to pull wool over another's eyes? Why not a smooth silk? Or a nice Egyptian cotton?" The tension defused, Mashinamdev completed his farewells to everyone, and I went with him towards the limo that Junior had sent to whisk him to the airport for his flight. As he walked, we passed Armstrong on his way in.

"So long," Armstrong clapped a friendly hand on his shoulder. "I wish you a safe journey, Mashinamdev, and I hope that you eventually find Jesus."

"Oh, I've already found him," replied the guru placidly. "I just decided to leave him where he was."

Laura's Lineup

THE WAY OUR HOUSE is designed, you pass through the living room before you either enter the kitchen or go upstairs. As a rule, Donna was either in the kitchen or in her office upstairs, because she was always doing something. So it surprised me somewhat to see her lying on the couch, one blue-jeaned leg dangling from it, her work-shirted arm thrown over her eyes. She moved the arm so she could see me.

"I believe in the law," she informed me as though I had asked. "Hey, I'm a lawyer. So I don't really want to kill people. But sometimes there are people I just really want to kill."

I sat down in the leather chair and waited for her to continue, which she immediately did.

"Lisa Lopez is eighteen and she's got this abdominal condition—that chronic cramping pain I told you about. So she buys this drug Relieviate over the counter—over the counter!—that guarantees it will relieve her pain. Which it does. What Denniston-Canada Pharmaceuticals neglected to mention was the risk that it might also make you sterile for the rest of your natural life. So there I am, suing them on her behalf, and this slimy corporate lawyer of theirs asks me for a meeting at which he smugly tells me the amount for which they are prepared to settle. I ask him why we should settle at all considering how strong our case is, and he tells me that if we don't, the company will just tie us up in endless expensive litigation and appeals forever which they can afford but neither I nor Lisa Lopez have the resources to endure. So I ask him out of curiosity how they reached that particular figure. He says Denniston-Canada did a cost/benefit analysis which estimated how many women were likely to become sterile as a result of taking the product, and how much they could afford to spend on that number of estimated lawsuits while still making more profit than they would with a recall of the product. Which prompts me to ask why in hell he is telling me this. And this Austin Benedict creep gives me the smuggest look you've ever seen and says to me, 'Because there's not a goddamn thing you can do about it.' And the worst of it is, he's right. There really isn't. But I swear, I wouldn't have put him on the floor if he hadn't looked so unbearably smug."

"You *hit* him?"

"Just kicked out the leg of his chair when I stood up. I tried to make it look accidental. Then when he fell I stepped on his hand with my heel. Accidentally, of course. He was screaming he was going to ruin my life and sue me. But he won't."

"You're sure?"

"Yes. I told him I knew about his arrest for trying to pick up an underage boy in a Syracuse Airport men's room. He got apoplectic and screamed that those records were sealed. I just laughed at him. He's a degenerate evil pervert, but he's not a complete fool. He knows if I got to those sealed records, I could also arrange to have them leaked to his employers."

"You talk to Chris?" Her brother was in C.I.A. intelligence—though we had been instructed to always refer to him as an employee of the State Department—and could pretty much find out any information he really wanted to.

"Let's just say you're not the only one who knows how to do research. Anyway, he calmed down. Realized that it wasn't worth ruining his career to avenge minor humiliation and fleeting pain. Shrewd move on his part, actually. But it gets me so mad. Too mad, sometimes. When I think of Jenna and Laura having to live in a world where young women are exploited and ruined by primordial slime like Austin Benedict and the Denniston-Canada machine, it just makes me want to blow them up somehow."

"Well...," I stopped because I didn't really know what to say.

"Well, what? I know I can't. I even know I shouldn't, even though I should. When I was in law school, I just wanted to leave the world a better place—however slightly—for the kids I would eventually have. You remember I said that when we started going out?"

"I remember on our second date you told me how much you hated injustice and most of all people who thought money was more important than human dignity."

"That was our third date," she corrected me.

"You sure?" I knew as soon as I said it that I shouldn't have. I knew better than to question Donna when she was certain about something and I wasn't.

"Of course I'm sure." She tossed me a look that brushed me back from the plate. "Don't you remember? Our second date was when you took me to that ballgame to see if I liked it enough for you to consider marrying me."

"I guess you did, huh?"

"Well, it was a good game. 2–1. I prefer a pitcher's duel. Everything matters."

We were both silent for a moment. I moved over to the couch and held her. She let me.

"I wish there was more I could do," I confessed.

"I know," she said. "I wish there was more *I* could do, too."

"At least we're both doing what we love," I reminded her.

"True. But do we both love what we're doing?"

"Don't we?"

"I guess." She moved her curls away from her face, where some of them were threatening to cover one eye. "By the way, Laura wants to see you."

"Okay," I said.

"In her room."

"Okay."

"Whenever you have a minute."

"Okay."

"Now might be good."

"Want to tell me why?"

"Let *her* tell you."

I walked up the stairs feeling a bit insecure. Whenever I heard that one of the girls wanted to talk to me, I found myself hoping I hadn't somehow disappointed her. I knocked at Laura's door and heard her voice invite me to come in. She sounded calm enough. I decided to interpret that as a good sign. I entered and closed the door.

"Hi, Daddy."

"Hi." She swiveled away from the computer at which she was sitting and started to say something, then visibly hesitated. I just waited. Finally she said, as if dipping a verbal toe into the conversational water, "I've been thinking."

"Glad to hear that."

"About the team."

"My team?"

"Yes."

"What about them?"

"Well ... I've been reading Bill James. You know, sabremetrics. All those statistics that challenge conventional assumptions about baseball."

"I'm pretty familiar with the concept of sabremetrics."

"I know you are, Daddy. A lot of what he says seems logical."

"I agree with you, honey."

"I don't know much about baseball the way you do, but numbers make sense to me."

"You're better at them than I ever was. And I'm proud of you."

"Well," she said tentatively, then plunged in recklessly. "It's about your lineup."

"What *about* my lineup?" I asked with a sudden sense of where this was going.

"It may not be your best one, Dad."

I stood there silent for a moment while she watched me. But I wasn't stunned, as she seemed to think, by her challenge to my baseball logic. I was absorbing that for the first time I could remember, she was calling me Dad instead of Daddy. Some sort of line had been abruptly crossed; she had exchanged her little girl blanket for a young woman cloak, and while that struck me as endearing, I suddenly felt a profound sense of loss. Her look took on a patina of concern.

"I don't mean to be critical, Dad."

"Sure you do. But that's okay. Criticism is an ingredient in the recipe; things can get pretty bland without any. Let's hear your theory."

"Well ... I know that Marcus is faster than Terry and is more of a threat to steal, but Terry always has a higher on-base percentage, and you want your leadoff man to be on base as much as possible, right?"

"Sure you do."

"And Bill James has all these statistics that demonstrate that stealing bases is hardly ever worth even trying, because..."

"I know he does."

She went absolutely silent, and in my mind I rebuked the impatient ministers of my interior. Shut up, I reminded them. Let her finish. Whatever she wants to say. Just let her finish.

"Sorry, honey," I said, likely sounding as abashed as I felt. "I didn't mean to interrupt you."

"That's okay."

"No, it's not." It came out more sharply than I meant it to. She looked at me with a mixture of surprise and curiosity.

"So," I continued, "you're asking why I don't lead off with Terry?"

"You don't have to agree with any of this. I know that."

"I agree about the importance of on-base percentage," I assured her. "But to say that stealing bases is meaningless..."

"Statistically," she ventured carefully.

"We played the Cougars yesterday," I said. She regarded me like a big cat tracking a trail, silent but focused. "When Marcus walked to lead off, their pitcher threw over to first base four times to keep him from taking a big lead. Right?"

She nodded.

"So Reynolds, their pitcher, was worried Marcus would steal second and put himself in scoring position with no one out. Which maybe he might have if I was sure it was worth his trying it, which I wasn't. But Reynolds was thinking about it."

"You mean he was letting himself get distracted."

"Exactly. Plus, because Marcus led off and was standing on first, now Reynolds is a lot less likely to throw Terry a breaking ball that might go into the dirt and even if it didn't would still be a tougher pitch for the catcher to handle which might make it easier for Marcus to steal. Which means Terry is going to see maybe an extra fastball or two instead of a curve or slider which means he has a better shot of getting a hit which may be one reason his on-base percentage is what it is. You see what I mean?"

"I think so," she said thoughtfully.

"Bill James hates the sacrifice bunt, right?"

"Yes."

"I'm not crazy about it either, because I hate to give up an out. He's got a point about that. But like everything else, it depends on the circumstances. If I've got a fast runner on first with nobody out and the pitcher's up and he can't hit and even if he could he's slower than a snail on vacation of course I'm bunting with him. If I don't he'll either strike out or even worse, hit a grounder that's an easy double play. I'd rather have the runner on second in scoring position with the top of my order coming up when a clean single will score him from there."

"That makes sense," she admitted. "But statistically..."

This time I didn't interrupt, but she didn't continue right away. Finally she concluded, "Numbers don't lie, Dad."

"No, they don't." I was still trying to get used to Dad. "But they're like people, Laura. What they're telling you isn't necessarily the whole truth, either. You know how some people can tell you something that seems true but is at the same time kind of misleading?"

"Sure. My friend Rebecca does that all the time. She says all politicians do it too."

"Well, not *all* of them. Some of them just stand there and outright lie. But it's like ... remember you were telling me how tricky it can be doing research on the internet?"

"Sure."

"Remember why?"

"Of course. There's tons of information, lots of it wrong anyway, and it takes forever-and-a-half to figure out what you really need and what you don't."

"Right. It's raw data, not knowledge. It's just information, right? Not truth. I love all the new statistical information sabremetrics gives us. Statistics are the lifeblood of the game, we all know that. But it's a tool, not gospel."

"But..." It was easy to see that she wasn't at all sure she wanted to complete whatever sentence was in her head.

"What, honey?"

"Well..." She paused, then bravely plunged in. "Isn't it at least possible that Mr. James is right and you're wrong?"

I smiled. She seemed not to have expected that, and she visibly relaxed.

"Sure. Bill James is brilliant. He's pioneered this entire field. He even invented it in a sense. He's the best there is at what he does. But isn't it possible that his personal conclusions are still just one man's opinion?"

"Sure," she said slowly. "I guess."

"Look, Bill James listed his all-time team and you'd have to be crazy to argue with Ruth or Gehrig or Ted Williams or Honus Wagner. But his all-time second baseman was Joe Morgan. Now come on, who would seriously choose Morgan over Rogers Hornsby?"

"I never saw either of them." She sounded wistful.

"Let's stick to the statistics, then. Numbers don't lie, you say. Well, Joe Morgan's lifetime batting average was .271. Pretty underwhelming, right? And certainly a far, far cry from .358, which was Hornsby's career average. For *five* consecutive seasons, Hornsby *averaged* .402! Joe Morgan couldn't come *close* to hitting .400 even in his dreams."

"Didn't Joe Morgan play for, like, twenty years?"

"Twenty-two."

"Okay. So maybe playing when he got older pulled his average down or something?"

"Hornsby played for twenty-*three* years."

"Oh." She thought about it. "Was Morgan's On Base Percentage really good?"

"Excellent. .392, in fact."

"Then wouldn't Bill James's thing about On Base Percentage explain why he prefers Morgan?"

"It would if he could explain why a .392 OBP is preferable to a .427, which is what Hornsby had."

"Wow. That sounds really high."

"It's beyond high. It's absurd. He was on base close to half the time. Though that was an era when the batting averages were higher and the E.R.A.s were lower."

"That sounds like a paradox."

I hadn't thought of that. "It is, isn't it?"

"Maybe power?"

I was taken aback, and it probably showed. "You're so smart it scares me sometimes," I confessed.

"Then Morgan did have more power?"

"No, he didn't. His lifetime slugging percentage was .434. Hornsby's was .577, which again is *way* higher."

"Then why do you say I'm so smart?"

"Because it was such a smart question to ask," I told her.

"So why does he think Morgan is the best of all time?"

"Because he's wrong. And he's entitled to be. He's welcome to his opinion. But that's all it is, an opinion. It's not fact, it's not science, and it ain't necessarily so."

I could see her working on the problem as though it were a complicated computer program in her head. "Was Morgan a lot better defensively?"

"That's harder because none of us, not you or me or Bill James, ever saw the Rajah play defense. From what I gather, Morgan was better. But not enough to make up for Hornsby being a vastly better hitter."

"Maybe Mr. James just has this thing for Joe Morgan."

"Maybe. Okay, here's another. As the single greatest pitcher of all time, Bill James chose Roger Clemens. Great pitcher, even before the steroids. But most baseball players I know who saw them both pitch would rather have Sandy Koufax at his peak than Clemens at his. Sure, Clemens was dominant for more total seasons. But for half a dozen years there, Koufax was almost unhittable. If you scored a run off him you'd celebrate. Take them both at their peak, and for a single game you had to win, or a World Series ... well, you might want to consider that Clemens has a postseason E.R.A. of 3.66. Koufax has one of, believe it or not, 0.95."

She looked up at me, despondent. "I was just trying to help," she told me as though she had broken a priceless ancient vase.

"I know. And you do. You have no idea how much."

"It's just ... I know I can't play basketball, or *any* kind of ball really, the way Jenna can—I mean, she's really *good*—and I can't skate like she can either..."

"I can't skate at all."

"Yeah, we all know that, Dad," she assured me. "And the only thing I'm really lots better at is computers, and I just thought that maybe if I could figure out some way to help you..." Her voice trailed off and she stared longingly at her computer keyboard as if waiting for it to whisper some secret into her ear.

"What was the rest of your lineup like?"

"Pretty much the same. You could make a real good case for flipping Mr. Crockett and Tom at five and six..."

"You could," I agreed. Donna had drilled into both of our daughters the need for them to preface the names of the team's players with "Mister" unless they knew someone well enough to have been invited to be on a first-name basis.

"...but I know you're doing that to split up your lefties and righties so that it's harder for the other team to bring in a relief pitcher for more than one hitter at a time."

"I am."

"I did have one question about the bullpen."

"Go ahead."

"I know Mr. Hicks throws really hard, but he doesn't get people out nearly as often as Pablo does, so I keep wondering why anyone would bring him in instead of Pablo."

"Because he throws really hard. So you hope he gets better at where he throws it, because if he does, he'll be *a lot* better."

"Mr. James calls that a high ceiling."

"So do the rest of us."

"But isn't it sort of true what Mr. McCarthy says, that a pitcher who hasn't control hasn't anything?"

"Mr. McCarthy?"

"Joe McCarthy, the manager of all those great old Yankee teams? He had a bunch of sayings like that. I looked them up online."

"I'd really love to see them. Any chance you could find them again and print them out for me sometime?"

Her eyes shone in a way that, for me at least, justified the creation of human life on earth. "Sure, Dad. I can do that."

She immediately turned back to the computer as though I had already left the room. I did, but not until I'd taken advantage of the opportunity to kiss her bowed head as she clicked away at her computer as passionately and precisely as Christy Mathewson's pitches had constantly nicked the outside corner.

New Life in Old Mexico

IT STARTED WITH HOME runs and somewhere along the way became about racial tolerance. Baseball is a strange game, with a tendency to be its own, constantly adapting metaphor.

Billy Bronson had not hit a home run that night against us, which qualified as news because Bronson was in the process of threatening the single-season home run record. The slugging first baseman of the Titans was a left-handed monster of a power hitter; but Garcia's sidearm southpaw junk had whiffed him twice, much to the absolute delight of our fans in the dome, and Pablo—whom I had called on for long relief and left in the game because he was painting the corners like a Dutch Master—had helped us win the contest.

The statistical breakdown that Laura had given me a couple of days earlier had displayed an unanticipated effectiveness that Garcia seemed to have had over Bronson for most of Billy's career—though not so much lately—which had in fact been one of several factors I considered when I brought him into the game. But the Titans played out west and this was the first time we had seen them this season, so I was guessing. I didn't know the full history until the post-game press interview with Bronson, when Duncan Diggs—whose disinterest in tact was surpassed only by his obsession with the subject of drugs in sports—startled the congregation of his fellow journalists by inquiring somewhat pugnaciously:

"Billy, isn't your home-run total this year simply the result of the designer steroids that are threatening to ruin major-league baseball?"

Bronson looked at Duncan's neck as though he were yearning to rip it from his torso. "Don't know what the hell you mean, man. I don't use nothing illegal."

"But Billy, you look like you've been drinking helium. Are you saying that your body adding massive bulk in your late thirties is natural?"

"Of course it's natural," snarled the slugger. "I do this killer workout routine. You wouldn't last five minutes doing it with me, little man. I do it every day, twice a week."

"Some of your teammates have said you use substances, too," said Diggs.

"Who? Who said that? I'll rip their..." He paused and smiled. "Substances. Sure I do. Use special vitamins."

"What about Growth Hormone cream?"

"Don't know nothing about that. Rub in some flaxseed oil sometimes. Makes me limber. You want some flaxseed oil? Good for what ails you."

"If it makes you limber, Billy," inquired Spencer affably, "how come you seem so muscle-bound this year?"

"What you talking about, man. I'm strong. Powerful. Why you call me muscle-bound?"

"Well, you looked like you couldn't get around on Garcia's pitches."

"If I was muscle-bound he'd be throwing fastballs by me. He be throwing nothing but junk out there. Throw me real pitches I'll hit 'em out. Garcia always give me trouble with that slop of his, even back in little league. Throws off my timing. But that ain't nothing. I'll get him next time. Give me a second, third at bat with him, I'm gonna hit it all the way back to California."

I wasn't sure if anyone else had noticed, but I saw Spencer stop taking notes and his head yank up as if he'd just gotten whiplash in a car collision, so I knew right away that he and I, at least, had heard the same thing. I went back to the Buffalo locker room, looked for Pablo, and asked him to come into my office. When he did, I repeated what Bronson had said. Garcia gave me a long, slow look before saying, in his Spanish-accented but graceful English, "So?"

"Between the steroid mess and the home-run record, Billy's had a thousand stories written about him this season. Even I know that he grew up around Atlanta, Georgia, and I don't even give a damn."

"So?"

"So if he never left Georgia as a kid and you were a penniless child in a tiny village somewhere in the south of Mexico, then would you mind telling me how in the name of Martin Dihigo you could have played against each other in the same Little League?"

He took a lengthy pause before he spoke. "Ah. Dihigo, yes. What an *hombre*. They say he played all nine positions, most of them better than anyone else. If the Major Leagues had only been willing in those days to let a black Cuban into their games, or if he had been born thirty years later..." There was something he seemed conflicted about telling me, so I waited patiently for him to decide what he was going to say. When he finally continued, it was with careful deliberation.

"*Tue tienes que saber esto*, Mike?"

"Yeah, I do need to know, Pablo. At least I think it's better if I do. I don't know who else caught it, but Spencer Hirshberg sure as hell did, and he's as good a reporter as I know. Whatever there is to find out, he's going to find out. I didn't call you in here because I wanted to make waves, Pablo. I did it so I could see if there was any way to keep them from knocking us over when they hit us. Because hit us they will, *amigo*."

"*Si. Comprendo.*" He nodded a bit sadly; but the great sigh that emerged from him seemed more one of relief than discomfort.

"I guess I always knew some day this might happen. And if I have to speak about this to someone, I am glad it is you, Mike. You are an *amigo*. So I will tell you what Billy knows that others don't." He took a deep breath. "I am from Atlanta. Well, a suburb near there. A community called Serenbe."

"How did you get there from Mexico?"

"I didn't. I am not from Mexico, Mike."

"Okay," I said slowly, still not getting it. "So you're originally from Georgia, not Mexico. So what's the big secret, Pablo?"

He watched me warily as he told me. "The big secret," he confessed, "is that I am not Pablo."

"You're not Pablo, Garcia?"

"No. I am not Pablo. Neither am I Garcia. I am not Pablo, Garcia, or Pablo Garcia."

"Then who are you?"

"Morris Goldberg." Then he added, for whatever reason, "My family called me Moe."

"Moe Goldberg."

"Yes." There was another pause which neither of us rushed to fill, then he leaned back and said: "Maybe I'd better explain."

"Maybe you'd better."

So Pablo—Moe—explained to me that he'd never been all that remarkable as a young player. Hell, even now he hardly threw hard enough to break a pane of glass; it was all location and guile for Pablo. Moe. Cunning and changing speeds. Which he was certainly doing now. And how his education-obsessed Jewish parents, while progressive enough to let him play baseball throughout his school days, nonetheless insisted on his getting a college degree. So he had gone to a local college where he had learned, among other interesting things, fluent Spanish ("easier to get a handle on than superstring theory," he assured me). And when he'd graduated and gone with some hard-partying classmates for a wild weekend of carousing in Mexico, he had met at their hotel a scout for Nogales of the Mexican league. The two of them ended up in a passionate discussion concerning the finer points of the great and noble pastime of baseball, and Miguel had confided to young Moe that the teams in the Mexican League were under enormous pressure at the moment to stop importing so many gringos and to instead find more local talent.

Moe had long dreamed of making it to the major leagues, but slight as he was, with his unremarkable arsenal of pitches, he had never convinced even a minor league team to sign him; he simply didn't have the natural gifts to be a legitimate high-ceiling prospect. And there he was, about to leave college. Free to go wherever he wanted. With his olive complexion and fluent Spanish. Miguel was skeptical of the idea, but Miguel was also desperate, and Miguel was impressed by the kid's pinpoint control when he threw to him. So Miguel accompanied Moe to Nogales and introduced the local community to their new left-handed hurler, their homeboy Pablo Garcia. Pablo then proceeded to pitch so effectively in the Mexican League, especially after he discovered the joys of switching to a sidearm delivery that had lefty hitters waving helplessly at his pitches, that when Buffalo was scrambling around seeking any effective middle relief—and the Bears at the time were so short of left-handed pitching the team was willing to give a try-out to virtually any southpaw pitcher who was still breathing—Cole Boone took a flyer on a cheap, incentive-laden contract for the little Mexican lefty.

"It would have been awkward at that point to replace Pablo with Moe," he said. "For one thing, it would have made them feel like fools, and no one will keep a marginal player who makes them feel like a fool. Anyway, it was Pablo they wanted, and I got along fine with Pablo. It's not as if I have any prejudice against Mexicans, especially when I am being one. It would have been easier at the time for me to be anti–Semitic than anti–Hispanic. Not that I'm either one. I just wanted to pitch."

"And Bronson never said anything."

"No. Billy and I always got along. I have my secrets, and he has his."

"You mean like the steroids and the growth hormones and all the other chemical junk he pumps into his body."

"He has his secrets and I have mine."

"You ever hear of a 37-year-old's body going through any kind of normal alteration that makes his hat size two sizes bigger between seasons? That seem natural to you, Pablo?"

"No, but maybe it's a miracle."

"Or should I call you Moe now?"

"Any chance we can keep Pablo around? You know as well as I do that it's borrowing trouble, one way or another, to trade him for Moe."

I did know that, but I also knew that Spencer would find out the story sooner rather than later. So—having first ascertained as well as I could that no one else seemed to have either noticed or cared about Bronson's boyhood connection to Garcia—I asked Spencer a couple of days later if he'd join me in my office for a moment. When he did, I didn't try to be cute about it, but just asked him bluntly:

"You heard what Bronson said the other day, didn't you?"

Hirshberg saved us both a lot of time by not pretending that he wondered to what I might be referring.

"I don't really credit anything Billy says—a man who cheats as shamelessly as he does, and probably has who knows what kind of side effects from all those drugs he uses. Frankly, I wouldn't believe him if he told me the game began in the first inning. So I don't really listen to him. But I do *hear* him. And yes, I heard the Little League comment."

"Anyone else pay attention to it?"

"Not that I know of. Not sure, though."

"You follow up on it?"

His hesitation was brief. "Yes."

"Find anything yet?"

"Got a colleague in Atlanta working up a list of all the lefty pitchers Billy ever faced in Little League. When I get it I'll see if any of the names on it used a Mexican passport at any time after they played each other."

"All that'll take you some time."

"Some," he observed cautiously.

"You ask Pablo yet?"

"Sure. He said *no sabe*. Then he asked me in perfect English if I knew what that meant."

I sat back while he just waited for me to say something.

"There *is* a story," I finally said. "And a good one." He looked pleased. I continued, "but it's not news. It's more of a feature."

"You're not the best judge of that, Mike," he reminded me with a mildness that didn't fool me in the least.

"I can give you the whole story. Today."

"If?" he prompted, knowing the word was implicit in what I hadn't yet said.

"If you hold off on it. For just a little while."

"Why? Whoever he really is, it'll come out eventually."

"I prefer eventually to now."

"Why?" he inquired. It was a reasonable enough question, and I suddenly realized that any answer I had to that query wasn't much of one. Spencer was right; it would come out, and when it did, it would come out as a "gotcha!" exposé. The only way to really get through this with any dignity was for Pablo to tell the story of his own accord—to come out of the multi-ethnic closet, in a manner of speaking. To present it as his own choice to tell the truth, the whole truth, and nothing but...

So that's how we handled it. Pablo sat down with Spencer for an exclusive interview. Spencer got his story and scooped all his colleagues, and Pablo got to frame all his actions in the light he wanted them portrayed. The story came out as a charming and engagingly funny human interest story, and people mostly joked about it as opposed to being upset. Except, unsurprisingly, for Duncan Diggs, who wrote a column raging about the dishonesty of our southpaw reliever.

"Duncan's probably just being anti–Semitic," suggested Cohen in the locker room.

"Nah," disagreed Fortunado. "He's being anti–Hispanic."

McCarter looked over at Pablo (without actually ever discussing it, there seemed to have been a universal decision made to keep calling him that instead of switching to the unfamiliar Moe). "What do you think, Pablo? Is Diggs madder at you for being Jewish or for being Mexican? Or for finding a way to be both?"

"I think," Pablo responded equably, "that a good curveball has no ethnicity."

Whatever public resentment might have been engendered by Pablo's admission to being a closet Goldberg pretty much disintegrated in any case when I brought him into a game in San Antonio in the seventh inning and he blew out his elbow throwing a breaking ball. It finished him for the season, and given that Pablo was keenly aware that he was nearing the end of his big-league days in any case, he decided it was the appropriate moment to call it a career. So all the scribes who had been mocking or even outright hostile about the Moe/Pablo metamorphosis suddenly ceased questioning Moe's motives and instead became elegiac about the plucky little southpaw and the unique multi-ethnic career he had somehow managed to create for himself out of an effective screwball and an even more effective imagination. Except for Diggs, of course. Duncan wrote a vicious column insisting the injury was God's punishment on the Jew for pretending to be a Mexican (he offered no opinion on whether The Lord would have wreaked the same havoc had it been the other way around). But since so many people—including many of his own readers—hated Diggs, that simply engendered a deluge of letters sympathetic to Garcia and calling Duncan more names than he himself had used in his somewhat colorful descriptions of Pablo. So even that worked to Garcia's advantage.

When he made the rounds of the locker room to say goodbye to his teammates (Tad Strain asked him how you said *adios* in Spanish), Garcia stopped by my office and happily told me that he had just accepted an unanticipated offer he had received to manage his old Nogales team in the Mexican League.

"Isn't that great, Mike? They know I'm Moe Goldberg, and they told me no one would care. I went down there for the press conference three days ago, and it was true. Everyone was so warm and friendly, they treated me like a prodigal son returned from the foreign wars. And they all asked if they could still call me Pablo. So my old name is my new nickname. I am now Pablo Goldberg."

"Pablo Goldberg?"

"*Sí.* Is not baseball a strange and wonderful country?"

Knuckleball

I HAD NEVER SEEN our General Manager look more haggard. I waited patiently as behind his desk Cole fiddled with a pen, moved some papers around, picked up a notebook, put it down, then finally looked out the window as if expecting someone to come through it. Finally he sighed and faced me. Since Cole Boone had always been someone who said whatever he had to say straight out and without fanfare, I had no idea why he was behaving so uncharacteristically. Even so, what he had to tell me left me as disoriented as he himself seemed to me.

"*What?*" It was a pretty weak response on my part, but it was all I could manage.

"Our owner—our new CEO, the junior Mr. Lumpe—insists," he continued, searching for the words to explain how it had happened. "Apparently he met Smokestack Woods when they were both in the ballpark, and I had only just gotten him to agree to hire Smokestack as one of our scouts so I'd been telling him what a great eye Woods has, which he does, so Junior said hello to him and asked Woods if he'd seen anything interesting lately, and Smokestack told him about this pitcher because he thought it was interesting."

"It *is* interesting."

"Yeah. Only Junior thought it was more than interesting. He told me it was a Eureka moment."

"He said that?"

"He did. Smokestack told me Junior even said 'Eureka!' when he told him. Said it was all Junior said, so he wasn't sure what he meant."

"And now we know."

"Yeah. And wish to hell we didn't." He gave me a look that was part pitying, part sharing the nightmare. "I don't know how you handle this, Mike, but you're the one who has to. You're the skipper. Just try to keep the ship from falling to pieces."

Cole assured me he'd take care of all the logistics, including locker room details, and would send Jay out to deal with the press as much as possible so that I wouldn't have to do it myself. In short, he promised he would oversee as much as he could. But we both knew that I would have to deal with the team, both as individuals and as a group. He told me he didn't envy me. I told him I didn't envy me either.

I told Pepper first. For the first time in my memory, he said not a word. He just shook his head, looked at the sky, then at me, shook his head again, then walked away.

Before I met with my players, I asked to meet with Woods so that I was at least armed with whatever information was available for the inevitable storm that must already be brewing. Smokestack, who had been a smart and crafty catcher in his day and knew the game the way an evangelist knew scripture, was apologetic.

"I'm really sorry, Mike. Never meant to put you on the spot like that."

"I know, Smokestack."

"I was just telling Junior 'cause it made a good story, you know? Old Ellis Carroll's kid. You remember old Ellis's knuckleball?"

"I remember no one could hit it."

"No one could catch it, either. I was one of the only backstops who could even block that thing. Added at least three years to my career, being his personal catcher. Remember when Boston traded me and then had to trade their second baseman to get me back 'cause no one else on the team could catch that knuckler Ellis threw?"

"I do, actually. My dad told me about it. He thought it was great."

"Yeah, Halfway Harry always had a sense of humor." Smokestack smiled fondly at the mention of my dad. "And a helluva screwball. Which he was himself. No offense."

"None taken. He said that too."

"He would. Anyway, I was there to see this other kid who's playing in this independent league 'cause he wants to beat the draft system and be a free agent so he can take the best offer from anyone instead of just from Baltimore which he figures will low-ball him 'cause they do that to all their draft choices and of course he's right and they will if they get the chance so Cole wanted me to see if he's worth the bonus he wants."

"Is he?"

"Not to me. He looks like Tarzan but hits like Jane. His swing is long and has a hole low and inside, he's got speed but no clue how to use it, and he's dumb as a post. I spoke with him afterwards about mental errors since he tried to steal third with two outs and his team down by three runs, and he said to me, 'How could I make a mental error? I never even been to college.'"

"So..."

"So I'm there to watch him, but this pitcher comes in for the other team, and just coming in from the bullpen causes quite a stir in the crowd, and I see the kid's name is K.C. Carroll and as I remember that's the name of old Ellis's kid. And damn if the kid doesn't strike out the next six hitters. In a row. None of them even hits a loud foul. And every last pitch is a knuckleball. Looks a lot like Ellis's. Maybe even better."

"And you told Junior."

"It was a story. You know, just to pass the time. I never thought ... well, you know."

"Yeah. I know."

When I got to the locker room, I didn't have to call a team meeting; every last member of the Buffalo Buffalo was gathered there together, and they all went dead silent upon my entrance, many of them addressing me not with words but rather with eyes pleading in silent desperation to tell them it wasn't true. Problem was that it was.

"It's true," I said as soon as I walked in. No point throwing it anywhere but over the plate.

A collective groan tested the room's acoustics.

"It can't be," moaned Blasingame.

"Don't be a fool," Garrett told him. "Man just said it was."

"Like we haven't got enough problems," Crockett contributed.

I let the others fill the air with complaints until the last one had died down and the room was again silent.

"Anyone else?" I inquired. There wasn't. They all waited for me to say something.

"This is the way it is. K.C. Carroll is one of our teammates. The transaction has been approved by the Commissioner's office. It's official. Those of you who have a problem with it, get over it. Any questions?"

"When does our new teammate arrive?" asked Cohen.

"Tomorrow. Any other questions?" There were none, at least none that anyone felt like expressing aloud just then. I nodded to them and went into my office, feeling the buzz that erupted behind me as much as hearing it.

It was several hours before game time the next day when there was a knock at the door. I called out "Come on in" and K.C. Carroll entered, closing the door. I waved towards the chair, but my visitor just stood there sizing me up while I did the same in return.

I knew from the biographical information I had that my new pitcher was twenty-two, but she looked like a teenager, not that much older than Jenna. Her reddish-brown hair was cut short around her oval face. She stood about five-six and was slender, yet nothing about her seemed frail. There was an aura of sinewy strength about K.C. Carroll, and I found myself unexpectedly relieved. We shook hands with an odd formality.

"K.C. Welcome to the Buffalo."

"Thanks, Skip." Now she sat down.

"You probably think you have some idea what you're in for, K.C., but you don't. The pressure, the attention, the microscope..."

"I've had them all before."

"Yeah, but this time, it's not likely to stop. It won't even level off, not for a good long while. It didn't for Jackie Robinson and it won't for you. You're the first woman to play in the major leagues. Everywhere you go, every town you play in, you're the circus and everyone will be watching it. To be honest, I don't know how anyone could possibly be ready for what you're going to have to go through."

"I won't say I'm ready for it," she admitted, "because I'm probably not. But I *will* say that I can handle it. My dad taught me more about big league life than just throwing the knuckleball."

I regarded her for a long moment. "You look around my daughter's age."

"I'm not."

"How do you know?"

"I googled you," she replied evenly. "Your daughters are in high school."

"It may actually be a good thing you look younger than you are," I mused. "We'll see. Anyway, if any of the guys act ... inappropriate, you just let me know and we'll make sure they don't."

"I'll let you know if there's anything I can't handle. There hasn't been so far."

"Okay."

"I want you to know I appreciate the separate room and shower you've arranged."

"You can thank Cole Boone for that."

"I already did." She hesitated. "I may not need to say this, but..." Her voice trailed off. I looked at her questioningly. She finished her thought. "I'd appreciate it if you just treated me like one of the guys."

"Well, I'm sure not going to treat you like one of the girls."

She cracked a smile, which I was glad to see.

"You'll be in the bullpen," I told her. "I won't bring you into a tight game, not at first anyway. I'll put you in as unpressured a situation as possible to begin with."

"I like pressure. If I wasn't as competitive as anyone else here, I wouldn't be here, would I?"

"Even so. Work with McCarter and Cohen as much as they're willing to let you. They haven't seen your knuckleball any more than I have, so let's find out how hard it is for them to handle. Maybe one will have an easier time than the other, I don't know. Anyhow, you've got your locker and room and uniform, anything else you need?"

"Just for the guys to judge me by what I can do out there, not what gender I was born into." She smiled, sort of. "Glad to be here, Skip. It's an honor to be a Buffalo."

Fortunately, Cole had anticipated the inevitable mob scene of reporters and arranged a press conference in the team's offices, far from our locker room where everyone dressed in peace and relative quiet, except for the attempts by some of the guys to crack jokes, most of them bad and few of them funny, about our new recruit. When the game started, all the photographers and most of the reporters were out near the bullpen, since that's where K.C. was. She answered the endless stream of flashing bulbs and all their shouted questions with an occasional smile and wave, but never a word of response. With all the microphones hanging around the relief pitchers, Jack Lee seized the opportunity and cheerfully invited everyone listening to come out to the stadium and support their local Buffalo. People tried to yell over his oration to reach K.C., but no matter what they said or did, she just smiled and waved.

Before the game, I was passed a note that came from Rafael Somosaverde, the Blue Sox manager, who wrote that he didn't think he would be comfortable coming to my office but would I meet him on the field near the batting cage and if I didn't mind, make it look like it was not an arranged meeting. I crumpled the note, told the batboy who delivered it to tell him sure, and then ambled out to the field and hung around the batting cage watching the players loosen up until Rafael came up a few feet away and leaned against the cage, carefully avoiding looking at me as we spoke.

Somosaverde had been in his day a slick infielder who was never going to hit much, so he looked for every little advantage he could find, which made him excellent manager material by the end of his career. The biggest edge he had found, though, was as unusual as it was unexpected. Rafael had originally played as Arturo Somosaverde, but when his batting average sank so low that it dipped below what Hall-of-Famer George Brett had memorably dubbed "The Mendoza Line" while watching a light-hitting infielder named Mario Mendoza struggle to stop riding the Interstate (a euphemism for batting under .200), Arturo had impulsively changed his name to Rafael. As it turned out, while Arturo couldn't hit anything at all, Rafael emerged as an effective singles hitter who could slap the ball to all fields. It didn't make any logical sense; but as Yogi Berra once famously observed, "ninety percent of this game is half-mental."

Rafael was old-school about baseball, though, and I had a pretty good notion of what he was going to say. My anticipation was reinforced by his scowl (I didn't attempt to avoid looking at him as he did me).

"This ain't right, Mike." He sounded equal measures angry and saddened.

"We're not dealing the cards, Raf. We're just playing them."

"It still ain't right."

"A lot of people agree with you."

"I know, but that's not why I'm saying it. I'm saying it because it ain't right. Women should not be playing major league baseball."

"My owner insists. And the Commissioner wants it too, I'm told."

"Your owner is a moron. And the Commissioner would bend over and beg to take it up the ass if he thought it would raise the television ratings one-tenth of one percent."

"He does think this will boost the ratings. Give them a shot in the arm."

"I'd like to give him a shot, but it wouldn't be in the arm."

"He's still the Commissioner."

"He's a whore." His eyes met mine, and they were rampant with desperate pleading. "*Dios*, Mike, can't we do something?"

"We can play the game. Or we can quit."

He was silent a moment, then said. "I'm going to protest the game."

"You'll have to lose it first, remember? You can't protest a win."

"I don't give a fuck. I'm going to protest anyway."

"Won't do any good, Raffie."

"I know," he admitted. "But I'm still going to do it. Even if that's all I can do, I'm not going to take this like a fucking whore with a trick."

He started to turn slowly away, but I stopped him with my voice. "Raffie?"

"What, Mike? You got an idea?"

"I hear she might be good."

He looked at me with deep sadness and walked away.

I hadn't planned to use Carroll in the game, but when we found ourselves trailing 12–2 in the eighth inning—I wondered whether our players were more distracted than they admitted—I figured why not get it over with right away rather than make it an issue by delaying the inevitable. If there was going to be a female cracking the barrier, and she was already on the team, might as well throw her into the history books immediately and get the initiation over with. So I walked down the dugout to Mack Lure, our bullpen coach. I had kept all Pepper's coaches and Junior had allowed me to select my own replacement as pitching coach. Mack was an old baseball buddy of mine who not only knew as much as anyone about the art of pitching but had a gift for effectively communicating with hurlers to help them understand any given situation. When he met with the pitchers before a game, he liked to wear a tee-shirt that read: "Babe Ruth is dead. Throw strikes."

"Get her up, Mack," I told him.

"You sure, Mike?"

"No. But I won't be any surer tomorrow or the day after. So she's coming in as soon as we take the field."

When I sent up Armstrong to hit for Vellis just as K.C. started to warm up in the bullpen, Steve thought the sudden roar of the crowd was for him. He even stepped out of the batter's box and tipped his cap to the crowd. Narcissism, it occurred to me, must be a great comfort sometimes, enabling you to experience waves of love that either weren't there, or were—as was the case here—intended for someone else entirely. The whole crowd seemed suddenly aware K.C. was coming into the game, as if everyone had received the intangible memo at precisely the same moment on a dedicated stadium internet that was somehow wired into every seat. When Armstrong grounded out, the roar rolled over the stadium in waves of rocking, rolling noise as the fans anticipated a historical event about to unfold right in front of them there and then. Armstrong tipped his cap again and came into the dugout beaming.

"First time I ever got cheered for grounding out. They must really like me more than I thought."

"They just love you, Steve," Blasingame assured him earnestly. "Just listen to all that cheering. They're going crazy."

"You think I should take a curtain call?"

"Absolutely," said Cohen. "You don't want to disappoint your fans."

So Steve stepped out to wave his cap at the crowd and, wouldn't you know it, since he had just made the last out, his appearance occurred right as K.C. started to come in from the bullpen. The deafening racket of the fans boomed even louder. Armstrong, not even glancing towards the outfield as he waved happily to the cheering masses, didn't notice our new hurler heading towards the mound. He came back down into the dugout with his face shining as though he had just seen the Lord.

"I had no idea they felt that way about me."

"Believe me, man, none of us did," Willoughby assured him.

"Maybe when my career is over I ought to consider running for office. Maybe even Senator. What do you fellows think?"

"Why wait?" Garrett asked. "Why not run now while your popularity is at its peak? We'll all understand if you want to leave us."

"I wouldn't quit on you guys."

"It'd be okay if you did," McCarter responded. "We'd do it for you."

Armstrong was still puzzling that one out as our team went back on the field. Tom picked up his catcher's mitt and said to me, "Well, I guess this is one way to make it into the record book," then went behind the plate. Steve finally noticed that everyone remaining in the dugout had their rapt attention on the slim figure that stood on the mound, calmly throwing warm-up pitches. We'd all seen harder tosses in a slow-pitch softball game, and heads started to turn to me with their silently screaming question.

"Just wait," I told them, hoping to hell I was right about that.

"Hey," said Armstrong, "isn't that the girl?"

"Appears to be," commented Jack Lee, who had come in from the bullpen so he could watch the proceedings from the bench. I looked at him.

"Just for the first hitter," he told me. "So that I can tell my grandkids. Then I'll go right back out there. And if they hit her like a piñata, I'll be ready to come in and mop up whenever you need me. Deal?"

I gave him a terse nod. Wyatt muttered audibly, "fuckin' disgrace."

Rademacher, who rarely spoke up, spoke up. "Maybe we oughta just give her a chance. So long as she's here."

"Fuck that." Wyatt turned to Pepper. "Pepper, you believe this?"

Pepper was bent over just staring at the dugout floor. I interrupted Wyatt. "Just let it ride, Morg, okay?" His answer was to spit the tobacco he was chewing into the spittoon we kept in the dugout just for him and Cook; on the Buffalo, they were the last of the tobacco chewers. Then the ump moved into position, but the batter didn't. I saw him talking to the ump as McCarter, girded in his catcher's gear, listened with apparent interest. Then the ump said something brief back, and the batter shook his head and reluctantly stepped in. Carroll went into her windup.

"Jesus fucking Christ," Morgan said before she even threw the pitch. Then the ball was on its way to the plate, drifting with an astonishing slowness that would have tempted any hitter to take the mightiest of swings. Ferguson, their center fielder, was one of the best hitters on the Blue Sox, and his eyes lit up like a Christmas tree when he saw the ball float towards him. As soon as he began his swing, though, the pitch darted down and then sideways and then down again as he swung and missed with such force that he corkscrewed himself into the ground and fell as if someone had pushed him. The crowd erupted with glee as the ball bounced blithely right past McCarter and rolled lazily towards the backstop.

Humiliated, Ferguson didn't swing at the next pitch, and watched it dance gently past him right down Broadway and into Tom's mitt for a called strike two. The following throw looked like the same hittable pitch until the ball seemed to have a heart attack two feet from home plate and dropped precipitously to the ground while Ferguson swung desperately and futilely over it.

Their next batter managed to make solid enough contact to send a fly ball sailing so directly at Willoughby that he didn't even have to move to catch it, but the following hitter saw five knuckleballs that seemed to have whimsical minds of their own, taking two for balls, fouling off two more and swinging helplessly at strike three.

I don't know which team was more shocked, us or them. K.C. trotted into a dugout that clearly wasn't sure how to treat her. Normally such a performance would elicit congratulatory pats and happy whoops, but most of the players sat there meditatively, not sure what to say or do. Jack Lee patted her on the back as he passed her on his way back to the bullpen, Cohen murmured an encouraging word, and Denny Savage smiled at her in approval. But the rest of the guys sat there as if under a sorcerer's spell, except for Wyatt, who treated her as though she had just blown a seven-run lead. Tom sat next to her and started to talk intently. Before they got too conversationally involved, I went over to her.

"Helluva job," I told her, loud enough for the others to hear.

"Thanks, Skip." Then she turned back to listen to Tom.

Since there was one more frame and the game was out of reach, I figured I might as well send her out again for the ninth. The abusive heckling—loud, vicious and clearly meant to be psychologically destructive—started its relentless roll from the opposing dugout to the pitcher's mound before she even reached it. We had every one of us heard plenty of razzing during a game, and many of us had given as good as we got. But this was different. For one thing, it was scatological, misogynistic and as vile as they could make it. Even Willoughby, who had heard every racist taunt that still existed, and Blasingame, who was our team's champion trash-talker and proudly claimed there was no obscenity that he hadn't heard or used, admitted later they had never experienced the like of what came out of the Blue Sox dugout. We were just lucky that Sammy Kleh was one of the umps in this game. The home-plate ump, Randell Pomerantz, was a younger man; and when he saw Kleh, his crew chief, walk from his first-base post to the Sox dugout, he just followed him and let Sammy handle it. I had been halfway to home to speak with Pomerantz when we both saw Kleh moving, so I stayed well behind the ump and we both watched and listened. Sammy stopped a couple of feet in front of their dugout.

"This is the sickest garbage I've ever heard, and I've heard a lot," he began. "The next insult I hear out of this dugout at that pitcher, one of you is getting tossed, and if I toss the wrong guy that's too damn bad. One obscenity, one less of you in this dugout. I don't care if I have to throw out every last one of you and you forfeit the game. What's going on here is despicable, and I won't have it. If that's not clear, say so right now. And anyone who does say so is out of the game."

There was silence until he got back to first, then a couple of barbs were flung at Carroll again. They were milder than their predecessors, but true to his word, Kleh tossed four players before their bench became totally silent.

K.C. kept as impassive an exterior as you would want, but she lost the strike zone and walked the leadoff man. Since the knuckler was such a challenge to catch as well as hit—McCarter, an outstanding defensive catcher, already had three balls get away from him in less than two innings and could easily have had twice that number had he been less adept with the glove—the runner stole second, and then third, with impunity. She walked the next man, too, and he immediately stole second without even a throw from our frustrated receiver, who was so busy blocking the prancing pitch with his body that he had no chance at all to throw out the runner. The only reason the man on second didn't steal third was that his teammate was already on it. She got the next batter on a weak bouncer to Crockett, who looked both runners back, but then her control fell apart and she walked the bases full. I was deciding whether to bring in Hicks or Garcia when suddenly, there was Wyatt standing right in front of me.

"Send me in."

I must have shown my surprise, because he continued impatiently, "You're gonna take her out of there anyway, right? I figure you don't want to kill all her confidence in her first game. Someone's gonna go out there to take over. So put me in."

"You're a starter, Morg. I've got a bullpen full of relievers who are there for times like this."

He shook his grizzled head impatiently. "You don't get it." Since I didn't, I waited for him to fill me in. He wasted no time doing it.

"I don't think a girl's got any business in this game, but she *is* here and we're playing the game, and right now those pansy-ass chickenshit punks are disrespecting my teammate. Put me in, Skip."

I glanced at Pepper, who was next to me. He cocked his grizzled head; an old-time mischief sauntered approvingly into his eyes. I waved my hand at Wyatt in affirmation.

"Warm up quick. I'll buy you some time out there."

"I won't need much," he told me, and I knew he wouldn't. As he and Cohen quickly hustled down to the bullpen, I walked out to the mound as slowly as possible. My pitcher was waiting for me stoically.

"Sorry, Skip. Don't know what happened, but the ball's just not doing what I want it to." She didn't display any outward emotion at all. But I felt the volcano within her fighting to erupt, and knew instinctively that she would rather drop dead on the pitcher's mound here and now than shed a single tear where anyone could see it.

"You did great." I hoped she could tell I meant it. "They couldn't hit you at all. Let's call it a day, okay? It's one you can be damn proud of."

Pomerantz came out from behind home plate and suggested that I either leave her in or take her out. I reached for the ball, and she handed it to me. The ump turned to leave.

"Hey, ump."

He turned. "Yeah?"

"She's really something, isn't she?"

K.C. controlled her surprise. Pomerantz didn't hide his. Then he recovered. "I'm an umpire. I can't respond to a question like that."

"I know you're an ump," I said. "But you were a human being once, too, weren't you?"

"Still am, on my good days. Yeah. She's really something."

As he left, I said, "There you have it," and gave her the encouraging pat on the back that managers always give pitchers when they are removing them from the game and letting them know that they've done their job well. She gave me a grateful look—the first sign of any emotion she had displayed at all—and started towards the dugout. The fans stood and cheered their voices hoarse as she walked off the field, but she never acknowledged any of it. I figured she never would in a game where she felt she hadn't done her job as well as she should.

I was glad she stayed on the bench instead of going right to the locker room. I'm a believer in that anyway; players should stay in the game and cheer their teammates on even when they themselves are no longer playing. That's part of what it means to be on a team. And if they watch the game they are no longer on the field playing, they might even God Forbid learn something, which would certainly be a bonus. But in this case I wanted her to see what I knew was about to happen.

Wyatt always strove to be intimidating when he was on the mound, but even Pepper, who had watched Morgan for his whole career, told me afterwards that he had never seen him look as fearsome as he did this day. Their hitter seemed to sense that, and stepped out three times before Wyatt threw his first pitch. When he did, it was a fastball directly into the batter's ribs. He crumpled into a heap while a run crossed the plate. Raffie had to send in a pinch-runner for the Sox while Wyatt shook his head sadly as if it had all been a terrible mistake.

Morgan hit the next guy squarely in the back. He stayed on the ground for a long moment while Pomerantz went out to the mound to warn Wyatt. I knew what they were saying with such certainty that I could have scripted the lines: the ump saying do that once more and you're gone, Wyatt saying it just slipped out of my hand, ump, why would I want to hit a guy with the bases loaded and let them score another run, and the ump regarding him suspiciously and returning back behind home plate.

With the bases still full, Wyatt stared in at the hitter; he had an open stance at the plate, so that he was almost facing Morgan. Wyatt threw two breaking balls too far outside to even tempt the batter, then came inside with a fastball that drilled him right in the chest. He fell like a shot deer. The Blue Sox dugout started to empty with angry players, but the ump had already thrown Wyatt out of the game the moment the ball hit the batter, and Morgan was already walking off the mound as I signaled for Hicks to come in.

On his way to the locker room, Wyatt passed Carroll where she sat on the bench. She quietly said, "Thanks."

He paused. "For what? All three of those runs are gonna be charged to you."

"It was worth it," she told him even more quietly. He grunted gruffly and kept on going, disappearing down the tunnel.

"Guess we showed them you can't fuck with the Buffalo," said Strain. I wasn't sure if he was kidding.

"You can *fuck* the Buffalo, though," observed Cohen. "We're down 15–2, Tad, have you noticed?"

Armstrong shifted uncomfortably on the bench. "Hey now, fellas," he remonstrated a bit too loudly. We all looked at him, then Cohen glanced at K.C. while Tad looked embarrassed. She met Dave's glance evenly.

"Fuck, guys, you don't have to watch your fucking language because of me. I'm just another member of the fucking team, say anything you fucking want to, I could fucking care less. I mean, fuck it. Besides, Dave is right, we *are* getting fucked."

Everyone laughed except Armstrong, who looked appalled. When the hilarity died down, we watched Fast Eddie, with no pressure whatsoever in this situation, unerringly locate his blazing fastballs on both the inside and outside corners.

"Damn," said Cohen admiringly to no one in particular, "why doesn't he ever do that in close games?"

"Pressure, David," replied Denny Savage. "There's just no telling how someone's going to react to pressure until you see them do it. That's why they call it 'pressure' instead of 'having fun.'"

Strikes and Babes

THERE WAS NO GAME the next day, so I had a rare chance to sleep late, which in this case was a euphemism since Donna had arranged to stay home that day as well and, with both girls at school, we actually had four solid hours to recreate everything we used to spend four hours doing with each other when we were in college, had an empty dorm room, and were able to let both our bodies and our imaginations blast away at full capacity. At least it felt like everything we used to do. If there was anything missing, I sure didn't notice it, and she assured me she didn't either. When we finally slowed down, I tried to remember, but couldn't, when I had last seen her so relaxed and at ease. I wondered whether she was thinking the same thing about me.

We were grinning at each other as sappily as teenagers at the prom when the younger of our actual teenagers came through the door. As she passed us, Laura said quickly, "Don't go all horrified parent on her, okay? It wasn't her fault." Then she bounded up the stairs and out of the line of any impending fire. Before either of us had a chance to even compose a question, Jenna walked through the door, removing the need to ask what had transpired. It was all too clear what had occurred; the question was why.

My wife was nothing if not a relentless problem-solver always calm in a crisis. She sat Jenna down and examined her right eye—she was going to have a beautiful shiner tomorrow—and made sure that none of the bruises and cuts around her face were major.

"You want to tell us what happened?" Donna inquired as she worked.

Skilled lawyer that she was, there was nothing in her voice to suggest the presence of the fervent emotions I knew were roller-derbying within her.

"I got in a fight."

"No kidding," I said. They both looked at me with different levels of danger alert, so I let Jenna continue to weave her section of the conversational tapestry.

"Before you go ballistic or anything, you should know that both guys look a lot worse than I do."

"That will cheer your father up, but it doesn't do much for me," her mother told her. "Why were you fighting?"

"These two jerks were insulting our family. To my face, and Laura's. I couldn't just let them do that in front of everyone. What would Laura think? Besides, I figured I could take them if I could taunt them into going at me one at a time, since I was a girl. And I was right. Suckers."

"In what way," Donna asked quietly, "were they insulting our family?"

Jenna's hesitation was brief as she sneaked a glance at me. "Daddy," she mumbled.

It was hard not to react, but I controlled myself with an effort. Donna gave me a glance of silent approval; let her say it, don't push. She asked our daughter with deceptive (and I knew just how deceptive) gentleness, "How do you mean, sweetheart? What were they saying?"

"All sorts of garbage."

"Such as?"

"You know, really dumb stuff."

"But you felt it required punching them."

"Actually, I gave Denny a roundhouse kick. Just flattened him. I am *so* glad you let me take karate."

"Darling, we're going to sit here all night if that's how long it takes for you to tell us what this was all about."

Jenna's reluctant sigh contained a tinge of relief at being able to share the information. Evidently she didn't really want to keep her story a secret.

"Soon as we got outside after class, Denny and Webb were calling Daddy all sorts of horrible names for letting a woman onto a baseball team. I mean, really horrible names, I didn't even know they knew them."

"Did you try to reason with Denny before you got into a fight with him?"

"Actually I did, but I would have had a better chance reasoning with his dog. I told Denny that not only was he being a male chauvinist moron, it wasn't even Dad who had put her on the team, it was Mr. Lumpe Junior, that Dad was just doing his job. But he just kept saying that Dad was ruining everything great about America and that if he cared about baseball or Amer-

ica he would ... well, I'm not going to repeat the rest of what he said. I knocked him down right about then."

Now I did dare to speak. "You know, Jenna, K.C. stood on that mound in front of thousands of people with the Blue Sox yelling stuff at her that would shrivel your friend Denny to even hear, and she never even blinked. She made the Mona Lisa look emotional."

"She sounds really cool," said Jenna. "She's my new hero. By the way, they also said really horrible things about Mom, too, mostly for being married to you."

"Is he at home now? I'll go over and knock him down again."

"Knock it off," Donna told me, but her eyes smiled slightly even as her tone of voice remained stern.

"He's not home. Far as I know, he's still in the hospital."

"Jenna!" Donna was rarely shocked, but she was now.

"It's nothing, Mom, it was only precautionary because he was such a crybaby when I knocked him down. I didn't really hurt him. He was the same jerk afterwards that he was before."

Donna launched into a monologue specifying, in some detail, why most things were not worth exploding in anger about even when you know you were right. She did it really well, but Jenna's anger at the absent Denny did not noticeably abate. Her mother kept at it while Jenna periodically defended herself, occasionally nodding in reluctant agreement. When Donna was done and Jenna seemed to have nothing more to say, our elder daughter went up to her room. Donna and I talked about it for a while, both of us realizing this was just the beginning of what promised to be a difficult passage to navigate, and trying now to anticipate at least some of what might be headed our way and how we might best handle it.

Eventually, we had reached the limit of what we could figure out ahead of time, and I went upstairs and knocked on Jenna's door. A muffled voice told me I had permission to enter. I did. Jenna was hunched over a book that I doubted she was reading, but she clearly wanted to give the impression she was terribly busy working awfully hard.

"Jenna?"

"Yeah."

"Just a quick thought."

"Okay."

"Just in case it's of any use to you."

"Okay."

"There's a western called *Conagher*." Now she glanced up from the book she wasn't really reading anyway. "Pretty good one, actually."

"And you're telling me this ... why?"

"There's a good line in it that you might want to use at school in the next day or two. Should the occasion present itself. Which I'm sure it will."

"A line?"

"Yeah. The hero rides up to a farm, and he's got a black eye. The young boy who lives there looks at this tall, quiet stranger who looks so tough but has this shiner and asks him who gave him the black eye. Conagher says to the boy, 'No one gave it to me, son. I fought for it.'"

"He says that?"

"He does."

"That's pretty good."

"I thought so."

"Thanks, dad."

I ruffled her hair and for once, she didn't seem to mind. "No," I said softly. "Thank *you*."

"Sure thing."

"But don't do it again, okay?"

"Okay." She paused. "Unless I have to."

I smiled at my Conagher of a daughter and left her in peace, knowing how unlikely I was to find much of that when I got to the ballpark.

The noise sounded like a street riot as I approached the team's section of the parking lot. When I exited the car, I was glad we were fenced off from the rest of the vast parking area, because the clashing demonstrators were screaming at each other just beyond the chain link barrier that suddenly seemed to me a lot less sturdy than it ever had been previously.

Some carried signs that said things like "Women have better curves" and "Diamonds are a girl's best friend" while those on the other side of the swaying sea of people waved slogans such as "Women shouldn't play the field" or "The only Babe in baseball should be Ruth." Ignoring all the nut-cases screaming abuse at me as I walked to the club entrance wasn't that tough, but even so I was taken aback by the depth of the vituperation being mindlessly tossed my way like so many hard, flat fastballs with no move-ment.

Charlie Luposo shook his head when I came in. "I been a clubhouse man a lot of years, Skip," he said. "I seen a lot of crazy things. I ain't never seen this."

We were playing the Stallions that night, and they must have heard about both the show Wyatt had put on and Sammy Kleh's sheriff act, because they were strikingly non-belligerent all game. A sort of tacit kinship seemed to have spread over both dugouts; the field was manned by two groups of multi-millionaire ballplayers who were flat-out being required to behave in a game that now had a woman on one of the teams, while the stands were populated by thousands of excessively choleric citizens—too many of them drunk—either promoting or opposing what apparently seemed a social earthquake. The players, having thought about the situation, were not inclined to protest enough to be fined large amounts of their money simply because one of the owners seemed to have turned unexpectedly feminist; whereas the fans were, well, fans, a volunteer army known for turning previously semi-rational humans into raving members of a screaming mob. "Fan" is, after all, the root of "fanatic."

The game was clean and quick. We were facing Sandy Hammond, who believed in throwing strikes and had enough control to throw them, and we started Big Jake, who never liked wasting time on the mound. Characteristically enough, Ellerbee had offered no opinion whatsoever about the Buffalo having become coed; if something was not relevant to his own pitches, Big Jake rarely displayed much interest in it. As for the crowd's insults, well, even before Mashinamdev had spent his week with us, Ellerbee had been indifferent to any crowd comment anyway; now that he had had an opportunity to glean from the guru suggestions regarding how to focus even more on achieving inner serenity during intense activity, Jake seemed totally oblivious to anything except his relationship to the ball he threw.

So with a close game I had no reason to bring her into anyway, two teams who didn't want to hear about it and two hurlers who weren't even listening, the crowd eventually became weary of pretending the fate of the nation was at stake and stopped yelling as though it was the seventh game of the World Series. I knew that the embers of this particular fire would in all likelihood flare up again the next time I brought Carroll into a game, and that it was bound to be a lot worse on the road than it was at our own park where the denizens of the stadium—most of them anyway—actually rooted for us to win; but we seemed to have bought ourselves a little bit of breathing room. Even if not much, and if only for the moment.

K.C. hadn't been kidding when she had told me that her dad had taught her more than how to throw a knuckleball. Despite the fact she never even warmed up in the bullpen much less played in the game, there was a throng of reporters frantically waiting for her in the large press area that Greenberg had arranged so that they could poke and prod at her without the team being exposed to it. I stood in the back of the room and watched with admiration the cool aplomb with which she handled all the hysterically shouted, and mostly silly, queries.

"K.C.! K.C! How did you feel about not getting into tonight's game?"

"Were you watching it? They couldn't touch Big Jake. Would *you* have taken him out for me or anyone else?"

"Yes!"

"Well, now we know why you're a reporter instead of a manager," she responded, and most of the room laughed.

"K.C.!" came another voice. "Are you involved sexually yet with any of the players?"

She didn't even bat an eye, and I realized she must have expected that one. Probably had heard it before elsewhere. "No," she said easily. "Are you?"

Another laugh, and then, "Since coming to the majors, what's the most challenging obstacle that you as a woman have faced so far?"

"Answering questions like that one."

"What do you think of your teammates?"

"They're great guys."

"Any of them giving you a hard time?"

"No. They're great guys."

"Any of them been really supportive?"

"Sure. They're great guys."

"Did your father give you any advice when he heard you were going to pitch in the big leagues?"

"Yes," she said, and didn't continue. The reporter finally got it and asked,

"What was his advice?"

"Throw strikes."

"Has your manager or pitching coach said anything to you that has already helped you as a pitcher?"

"Yes."

"What did they say?"

"Throw strikes."

"K.C." asked Wolf, making sure his camera was on his own face so the TV audience would be sure to see him, "Have you heard that some of the team's fans are organizing a strike of the games because of you?"

"No. I'm sorry to hear that. They'll miss some good games."

"Do you feel responsible for what they're doing?" he persisted.

"Why? I'm just trying to *throw* strikes, not cause them."

"Young lady." Duncan Diggs was flaunting his most pompous tones. "Can you tell us why you feel it's necessary for you to damage baseball with your presence?"

"Well, I don't see how I could damage it with my absence." Duncan's face flushed as his colleagues laughed. Carroll continued, "And obviously I don't agree with you that I'm damaging it."

"Then what would you say you *are* doing?" he demanded.

"Giving you something to write about?"

"K.C.," called out a young local scribe for one of the smaller papers. "Do you think there's any chance at all that some day, you might get into the Hall of Fame?"

"Sure," she said deadpan, and everyone stopped what they were doing and stared except Diggs, who appeared on the verge of apoplexy. "Actually," she continued, "I've already been there. Visited Cooperstown last winter, and they let me inside so I could see the place."

I slipped out during the ensuing mirth. She wasn't going to have much of a problem with the press, that seemed pretty clear.

Still, the atmosphere in the clubhouse had altered as if the oxygen we breathed there was laced with some invisible element that made almost everyone more self-conscious. There were a couple of exceptions: there was Big Jake's cultivated indifference, of course, and Jack Lee remained a galaxy of one. But everyone else, however subtly, seemed ready to either defend her presence or grouse about it. She became, however tacitly, an issue; and distractions are a problem for any team. I wondered what was to be done, and who would be the one to do it.

Blame It on the Stones

IN THE NEXT DAY'S GAME, Zapata hit a ground ball to the shortstop and jogged to first as he was easily thrown out to end our half of the inning. Before he crossed first base, I was already signaling Rademacher to grab his glove. When Angel returned to the dugout, I motioned him over to sit between me and Pepper.

"I'm putting Rademacher in for you. Since you're so tired."

He seemed startled. "I'm not tired. Why you think that?"

"Because you sure looked tired running to first. Or rather, *not* running to first," I amended, trying to banish the anger that made me want to scream in his face.

He seemed more peeved than abashed. "I was going to be an easy out."

"That's what he's saying," Pepper chipped in. "Why make it easy for 'em?"

"If I run hard, I am still out, not close."

"Angel," I reminded him, "you're a shortstop yourself. You think the other shortstop might bobble the ball once in a while? Or drop it? Or make a bad throw? That ever happen to shortstops?"

He just stared straight ahead, doing his best not to hear what was being said. Pepper looked frustrated. I tried another tack.

"Angel, of all the Latino ballplayers you ever watched, who was the one you admired the most?"

He replied without hesitation. "Clemente. Roberto was a king. He was before my time, but I see him on the TV many times often. He was Puerto Rican and I am Dominican, but on the field he was royalty. A man of great dignity and honor."

"And skill," added Pepper.

158

"And passion," I threw in.

"*Sí*. Skill and passion. As noble a great player as I ever see."

"As *anyone* ever sees," opined Pepper.

"So, Angel. All the times you ever see Clemente, you ever see him hit a ball *anywhere* and not run it out hard?"

As he absorbed my comment, Pepper contributed his. "Not Clemente. Roberto runs out the most routine ground ball like he has a chance for a hit. Which is one reason why he always has a chance for a hit."

Angel spoke slowly. "I do not want to look like a fool." The effort it took him to say that was apparent.

"Did Clemente look like a fool?" I asked him.

"It was a different time."

"Look, Angel," I tried to stay as patient as I knew I needed to, but it was becoming more and more of a strain. "You get paid what, five or six million a year, to play a game we all started playing for free. It's a privilege for any of us to be here. For that five-six million you get up four, maybe five times a game. When you hit the ball, what else have you got to do for the next five seconds besides run hard? If the fielder messes up, you're on base when you won't be otherwise. Even if he fields it clean, and you run as hard as you can, the fielder sees that and maybe next time he takes his eyes off the ball before it's in the glove or throws a little quicker than he meant to and draws the first baseman off first base because he knows he's dealing with a quick *hombre* who hustles. And the fans will love you if you always give it all you got. When they called Pete Rose 'Charlie Hustle' it was with respect."

"Pete runs to first base when they *walk* him," Pepper added. "Runs! And he is a Hall of Famer."

"Well...," I began.

"Okay, he's maybe not *in* the Hall of Fame, but he's still a Hall of Famer. Forget the gambling. Anyway, he doesn't rack up more hits than any-one in history by not running everything out."

"He was not Clemente," said Angel.

"Nobody is," responded Pepper.

"So what do you say?" I asked Zapata. "Shall we play it like Clemente?"

I wondered what Angel was brooding about that gave him such pause. The whole subject seemed to me such a no-brainer. Finally, staring at the ground, he muttered, "The girl don't run it out."

I felt as bewildered as Pepper looked. "Huh?" I finally said stupidly.

"She don't have to run fast. Why me but not her?"

"Carroll?" I was still trying to figure out what the hell he was thinking. "She's never been up to hit."

"She don't have to run hard."

"She would if she ever hit the ball."

"She just stand there and throw the knuckleball."

"What's that got to do with you running out ground balls?" I truly wanted to know the answer to that, but Zapata just said, "Is not fair."

I wondered fleetingly whether his reaction was related to some sort of Latino self-image, but only briefly; after all, neither Fortunado nor any other Hispanic member of the team seemed the least bit bothered by their new teammate. At least not for that reason. I decided to think about all this later since I needed to concentrate on the game we were currently playing. When I heard the voice speaking, it was only as a kind of background noise. I was perusing the middle infield, trying to determine whether there was any way our defensive alignment could more accurately anticipate where their offense would hit the ball, when I felt Pepper nudge me and then do it again. I looked around.

There was Tad Strain, down at the far end of the dugout, speaking cheerfully to whomever was on the other end of the line. On his cell phone. In the middle of the game. Everyone in the dugout noticed, but just sat there, waiting to see what I would do. I walked over to him and stood directly in front of him. He said "Wait just a sec" into the phone, then looked up.

"Tad," I asked as evenly as I could manage, "what the hell do you think you're doing?"

"Just talking to my agent, Skip." He looked sincerely confused as to why I was asking him.

"We're in the middle of a game."

"Yeah, but I'm not in it or on the field or anything. Is it a problem?"

"Yes, it's a problem." I tried to control the anger I felt rising inexorably in me. "You don't make phone calls in the middle of a game, Tad. You're supposed to be paying attention to it. You know, watching? As if you're actually involved with the team? There are no cell phones on a baseball diamond during the game. Christ, Tad, how fucking disrespectful can you get?"

He looked hurt. "It's sort of connected to the game."

"What?"

"It's my agent. I was just asking him how high he figured I'd have to raise my batting average for him to be able to get me an appearance fee for whatever charity appearance he could line up for me. So it is kind of related to the game, sort of, you see?"

Without fully realizing I was doing it until it was done, I casually snatched the cell phone out of his hand, snapped it shut, and hurled it as far as I could down the tunnel to the locker room. There was a faint crack as it landed somewhere in the unseen distance. He looked at me stupefied.

"What'd you do that for?"

"So you could go get it. And Tad, when you do reach it, don't come back. Keep going to the locker room, take a shower and go home. If you don't consider yourself a committed member of this team, I don't see why we should pretend that you are one."

"What do you mean?"

"I mean you're suspended. As of right now. Go home and discuss *that* with your agent."

He slowly rose to go as everyone on the bench studiously avoided looking in our direction. Whatever I might have expected from him in the way of a reaction, it wasn't what he actually said.

"You wouldn't do this to the girl," he said accusingly.

It took me a second before I could collect myself enough to answer.

"I wouldn't have to!" I shouted. "She would never do this!"

"You wouldn't do it to her," he repeated dully, then went down the tunnel.

I turned towards the bench. Now almost everyone was watching me. "Anyone else have something to say?" I challenged the collective of enigmatic visages. Jack Lee raised his hand as though he was in class.

"Yeah, Jack. What?"

"I just wanted to say, Skip, that you still seem to have a pretty good breaking ball. I could barely hear that sucker land when you threw it."

Slumping

THE PROBLEM WITH TAKING credit for something when you don't really deserve much is that when the good times change to bad ones, you're going to get more blame for the bad ones than you ever got credit for the good ones. So when we went on our longest winning streak of the season for no reason I could figure out, I wasn't that anxious to take bows for it. A lot of people told me not to be so modest, but I wasn't being modest. I was simply aware that no matter how high in the air you throw the ball, sooner or later it's going to come down. And I didn't want it to land on my head any harder than it had to when that time came.

So I gave plaudits to the players at every opportunity. That's a good tack to take anyway. First of all, the players are far more likely to be loyal to you if you give them the credit instead of grabbing it for yourself. And secondly, it was true in any case. Whatever we were doing that was enabling us to win more often, they were the ones doing it. As Casey Stengel once pithily observed after being congratulated on yet another World Series Championship, "I couldn't have done it without my players."

Then, sure enough, we started to lose. First a couple of series, then a couple more, then the drops of water began to turn into a stream that threatened to become a flood. It wasn't as if everyone was simultaneously awful; it's more that instead of playing just well enough to win, we found ourselves competing just badly enough to lose. If the pitching was decent that night, we didn't hit. When the lineup scored some runs, the pitching gave them back. When games were teetering in the balance, we found a way to make a damaging error, either physical or mental, that changed the result from a possible victory to a certain defeat.

We knew we weren't going to make it into the playoffs, for several reasons. (We were instructed to always refer to them as The League Championship Series, but I'd never met anyone who ever called them anything but the playoffs, except for a football coach who always referred to the entire postseason as "the tournament.") For one thing, we just weren't a good enough team to be at the top of the league; we were improving, but we were still a season or two away even if everything broke right, which it has a habit of not doing. For another, we were too many games out even if we weren't in the tailspin that seemed to have overcome us. And finally, there were three teams ahead of us. When you trail only one team, you can always hope that team completely collapses; but when there are three squads and they all play each other, you can't reasonably expect every result to favor you every time.

Yet even so, losing was becoming a habit that we had to break sooner rather than later. Losing often is infectious and can readily become a plague, and the first casualty is usually the manager, because it's far easier to replace the skipper than to fire the entire team. We all knew I had to do something—anything—to change our luck. It could be senseless, bizarre or insane, so long as it worked and somehow, mysteriously, altered the air we were breathing from an atmosphere in which we knew we would lose to one in which we were confident there was nothing to prevent us from beating the guys in the other uniforms.

Yet those of us who had long dwelled in the land of baseball lived with a deep inner awareness that the baseball gods were not noticeably fair. Mischievous, yes. Playful, surely. Random, often. Cruel, often enough. But fair? You're talking about a game in which screaming line drives can turn into double plays while bad swings sometimes produce pathetic squibs that turn into hits just because no one is in position to reach them in time. The only thing in baseball that's fair is the ball when you hit it in play. Expecting good luck would be not merely inadvisable but also unenlightened. So something in me kept glancing up at the sky to see if there was yet another ball about to fall on top of anyone's head. Especially mine.

Everyone tried—maybe too hard—to break the streak. Guys who were clean-cut grew beards, guys who already had them shaved them off. Garrett showed up completely bald. Jack Lee showed up with different color socks on each foot, though with Pluto no one could be sure that was a deliberate gesture. Our organist tried changing the music that introduced relievers into the game. Armstrong told us he prayed every day, though with him that wasn't exactly anything new; even with his added piety, however, no deities were cutting us any breaks so far as we could tell. Things got so bad that the one game in which we had a ten-run lead was rained out before the fifth inning and was thus wiped out instead of becoming an official game. Then Ellerbee pitched a one-hitter and lost when the single he allowed was followed by a stolen base, a ground out and a sacrifice fly.

The manager generally looks pretty smart when his team is winning; when they're winning a lot, he can seem like a genius. It's a lot easier to keep a clubhouse relatively calm and cheerful when things are going well; even players frustrated with their playing time, or with anything else, usually know enough to keep their mouths shut when the team is rolling. If they complain when the team wins, it generally makes them seem like the self-centered egotistical narcissists some of them can occasionally be. But when the weather gets really bad, you'd better have the raincoat and the umbrella ready, because the odds are that you're going to feel it pouring down. You earn your stripes in this game—the invisible ones scourged across your back as well as the admired ones on your baseball card—by navigating your way through rough storms and choppy seas, not by sailing effortlessly in sunshine on untroubled waters. So the more we found strange and baffling ways to consistently snatch defeat from the jaws of victory, the more I felt like Wyatt Earp patrolling the streets of Tombstone, wondering which alleys contained back-shooters wielding loaded weapons.

The sense of ambush certainly flashed quickly across my consciousness when I turned my car into our driveway and almost smashed into Laura's bike. I slammed down hard on the brakes and sat shaking for a moment as Laura came out of the house, apparently drawn by the sound.

"Why the hell are you leaving the bike in the driveway?" I yelled at her. "I could have run right into it, for Chrissake!"

She looked stricken. "I was just coming out to ... going to move it to...," she stammered.

I got out of the car. "Look, Laura, I..." but she had sprinted back into the house and was gone. When I went upstairs and knocked on her door, she didn't answer.

When I told Donna what had occurred, she looked at me far too carefully for comfort. "She needs to watch what she's doing," I said, sounding lame even to myself.

"Clearly," answered my wife.

The Ball Doesn't Care

It was unusual for Donna to wait for me in the parking lot after a game. When I noticed that she had parked her car next to mine and was leaning against hers, my first thought was that something had gone seriously wrong with her Accord SE, and my second thought was that the way things were going with the team these days, that figured. But the way she was looking at me—I'd seen that intense searchlight of a stare before, though not for quite a while, and it had always presaged hard-breaking sliders I wasn't going to be able to hit—made it immediately evident that whatever was on her mind had more to do with her husband than her Honda.

"Get in," she instructed me.

"I've got my car right here."

"I can see that. I'm taking you for a ride."

"What about my car?"

"What about it? I'll bring you back, don't worry. It won't run away. If it gets lonely, I'll buy it some flowers."

She didn't say anything on the drive to Delaware Park, so I didn't either. To my genuine surprise, she continued her silence as we walked along Hoyt Lake. I had decided to let her dictate the pace of this conference, but the park brought back too many memories of family outings, so I spoke first.

"Remember Jenna telling us about Elizabethan theatre last year when they did that all-female Shakespeare in the Park?"

She nodded. I tried again. "And Laura thinking it was so funny when we came here that the sign for the zoo was being held in that fake elephant trunk?"

"Yes," she said tersely. I decided it was a good sign that she was speaking at all, so I figured I'd push my luck. "And that amazing *Mirrored Room* at the Art Gallery, by you know, what's his-name."

"His name is Lucas Samaras. And you didn't even want to see it. I had to drag you to the Albright-Knox Gallery."

"But I went with you."

"Only when I told you I'd get a divorce if you didn't. Otherwise you would have stayed home all day watching video of Van Vellis' pitching mechanics."

She took me to the Japanese Garden, and in a few seconds, I knew why. The garden's tranquil, flowing, natural design was meant to make it a sanctuary of sorts, and I could feel some of the tension deep inside my system dissipating even as she stopped near one of the bridges and regarded me as though we were both in court and I was the one on the witness stand.

I tried without success to think of something I had screwed up, but it had been a long decade and seemed to be getting longer, and I was tired and drained and exhausted from running around in mental circles trying to figure out how to help break the team out of this debilitating slump; so I just shrugged helplessly and asked, "What's the problem?"

"Why don't *you* tell *me*?"

"What do you mean?" It was clearly the wrong question. Her words were sawtooth blades cutting crisply through pine.

"What do I mean? I mean you haven't said ten sentences to me the last three days, you walk around looking like someone shot your dog and you don't even *have* a dog, if something's bothering you that much don't you think you should maybe talk to me about it, I mean I am your wife, am I not? Remember me? The woman you married? The one who wanted to share everything with you for better or for worse? Well, that *does* include for worse, does it not?"

So I started talking. I was hesitant at first—not because I wanted to keep anything from her but because I found it difficult to articulate a welter of emotions that I hadn't yet figured out myself. Saying them aloud was confusing even to me, while trying to articulate them in a way that would make sense to another human being—even Donna, whom I trusted more than anyone else in this world—was unexpectedly daunting. As I kept talking, though, the words connected more and more easily to the feelings they were endeavoring to express, and began to roll out like ocean waves: unintimidated, unhurried and unending. I murmured about the deleterious effect of losing games on one's own psyche and how impossible it became not to question your own abilities when no matter what you tried, it didn't work. I mumbled about the corrosive effect it all had on the atmosphere in the locker room, where even guys who thought they liked you had no hesitation in doubting your choices. I reminded her of what Casey Stengel had once noted about the 25 players in his charge: that 15 of them didn't give a damn about him one way or the other. "My job," Casey had shrewdly observed, "is to keep the five who hate my guts away from the five who haven't made up their minds yet."

I pondered aloud Bob Lemon's comment that as manager, he had never taken a loss home with him, but had always left it at the nearest bar. I confessed to her that I wasn't sure how much rope I had here; I was after all unknown and new at this, and could not be too surprised if Junior decided to fire me should the trend of losing remorselessly continue.

"Has he given you any indication that he's considering firing you?"

"How could he *not* be considering it? *I'd* be considering it if I were him."

"That he's *planning* to?"

"No. He hasn't given me any sign that he's planning to."

"Then why worry?"

"Because I don't want to get fired. I love my job."

"You're the one who always told me that all managers are hired so that they can someday get fired."

"I know, but I still don't want it to happen to me. Not yet, anyway. I haven't accomplished anything yet. I want to accomplish something before they get rid of me."

I finally understood one reason she was approaching all of this so intensely, when she asked me if I realized I had been brusque with the girls lately. I started to insist somewhat indignantly that I had not been any such thing, but the glance she gave me encouraged me to reconsider what I was going to say before I actually said it. I asked her did she really think I had done that. She asked me if I thought for even an instant that she would say such a thing if I hadn't *clearly* done that. I admitted that the only rational response to that question was no.

"When? How?"

"Yesterday, when you yelled at Laura, for one."

"I almost ran into her bike."

"Did you look around when you turned into the driveway?" she asked as if I were a witness under her cross-examination. "We always look for anything that might be around—cats, dogs, lawnmowers, bikes—before we drive into the garage, do we not?"

I began to protest, but then the memory of the scene returned to me swiftly and vividly. I nodded silently.

"Then," my wife continued, "Jenna tried to talk to you about her soccer team."

"Don't tell me I yelled at her too."

"You didn't."

"Good." I sighed in relief.

"You didn't even listen to her."

"Of course I did."

"Really?" She raised an eyebrow. I remembered her doing that the very first date we'd ever been on, when I'd said something that struck her as inane and she'd made it very clear that being interested in me was not remotely synonymous with agreeing with any dumb thing I said. "Then what did she say about the other midfielder? And about the uniforms?"

"Okay," I admitted, with no answer to either question. "Point taken."

"I'm not trying to score points. I'm trying to remind you that we have two teenage daughters who are every bit as bright as we think they are, more vulnerable than either one of them would admit under torture, and who miss very little, if anything. They're people, not plants. Young and small, maybe, but human beings. If they think you're absent in their presence, they'll blame themselves. I thought you knew that."

"I did. I guess I was just too preoccupied to remember it. And," I couldn't help adding, "they're not that small."

"Not any more," she agreed. "But they're still kids. They have to be able to rely on us. Both of us. Absolutely. To be fully supportive—and responsive—at all times. Particularly hard times. Especially then."

"Do not alibi on bad hops," I muttered to myself.

"What?"

"Nothing. Maybe I should revisit this daddy thing. And this husband thing."

"You planning to re-read the instruction manual?"

"Real men don't read instruction manuals."

"They don't?"

"Nope. Thought you knew that. Only doorknobs read instruction manuals. Real men tough it out."

"Who told you that?"

"Your cousin Georgie."

"Georgie is a doorknob."

"Ah. Well, that would explain it, wouldn't it?"

She regarded me for what seemed a long moment. "Sweetheart, I don't want you to be anyone different. I would never have married you if I wanted you to be different. I just need you to be more yourself. Okay?"

"Okay."

She ran her fingers distractedly through her curly mane. "Look, I know how consuming it gets when you love what you're doing, you know that. That's why—well, one reason why—I fell in love with you, because you had the same passion I do, even it's not always for the same thing. When I'm in court representing a client whose life has been decimated by one of these inhuman corporations that really believes people don't matter but profits do, I absolutely love getting those bastards on the stand and letting everyone see what slime they really are. I grew up fantasizing about defending the innocent and getting them acquitted, but there aren't enough defendants who are innocent and I got sick and tired of defending the guilty and now that I'm working with Annie and Peter and Mark this is the most fun I've ever had. Forcing those scum to pay settlements that make them choke is so much more satisfying than just watching them go to prison. This way, my clients get rich for all they've been through and I get to watch those corporate sons of bitches suffer. I love it. But I know I get all absorbed in the court prep like you do with the team. So I understand. But we've got the girls, Mike. And we've got each other. I want it all. I don't want to lose any of it. But I only get to keep it if you help me. So will you help me? So that you don't force me to make your life miserable and hate you and resent myself when I'd much rather we were both extremely fine and extravagantly dandy? Will you do that for me?"

The last thing I had anticipated at the start of this conversation was engaging in passionate kissing with my wife in Delaware Park, so I was pretty astonished to discover ourselves doing exactly that. It seemed crazy and strange and unexpected and, well, teenage. And it felt really, really good.

Perfect Game

I WASN'T GOING TO do it, but it didn't seem as though I had much choice. A rainout had forced a double-header and I had no one left to pitch the second game.

I might have considered pulling Cook in from the bullpen as a spot starter and letting him throw as long as he could last, but Pete had suffered an unusual (to say the least) injury: he had sprained the wrist on his pitching hand in an ill-advised effort to impress his teammates by trying to rip a telephone book in half. Vellis was the only starter rested enough to pitch, but Van had come down with food poisoning the night before. "I should fucking know better than to eat fucking seafood on the fucking road," he managed, his face an unhealthy shade of mottled green. "Unless we're in Baltimore."

"We're not in Baltimore."

"I was afraid of that." Then he vomited again.

So it was an emergency start, and as we hadn't announced anyone but Van—who was so weak from all his retching that he couldn't throw a ball across his hotel room, much less home plate—and since we were on the road anyway, I figured what the hell, and told K.C. she was starting.

She tried not to seem as surprised as she obviously was, so I explained to her why I was doing it. "Just give us a couple-three solid innings. We'll just play this one by bullpen committee. Give us whatever you can for as long as you can and don't worry about a thing."

"I'll give you all I've got."

"I know you will."

The guys were also surprised, you could tell; but the novelty had worn off somewhat by then, so there was kind of a collective shrug tinted with an equally invisible, yet palpable, sense of nervousness about whether we might

170

be in for an extremely long day. Not so much because she was starting—knuckleball pitchers don't get tired, because the pitch doesn't require velocity and can be tossed all day long (there were times when a knuckleballer had effortlessly pitched both ends of a double-header)—but because when the knuckler stops knuckling, it's batting practice for the other team.

I wasn't expecting Cohen when he came into my office and told me he had been coming in early and working with K.C. in the bullpen over the past few days and found that he was able to catch her knuckleball better when he shifted his receiving stance slightly to the side so that he could pivot on either foot if the pitch broke sharply in an especially odd direction. "I may not catch it clean," he admitted, "but I can block it most all the time." Impressed as much by his initiative as by his confidence, I gave McCarter the day off and put Dave in the lineup.

We were up first and didn't give Ben Ephraim much trouble. The first three batters went down meekly: Marcus waving at what seemed to be a fastball until it broke into the dirt, Terry tapping a backdoor slider on three hops to the shortstop, and Dante admiring a third strike on the low outside corner as though it were a rediscovered Rembrandt. Garrett, who had been on deck, came back to the dugout to get his glove before he went out to third base. "Uh-oh," he said.

The Wolves had of course never seen K.C. before, and seemed unduly agitated facing her for the first time. Maybe it was a rapport with her catcher or maybe she was just more relaxed since she'd now pitched for us already—or maybe it was just the weather or the wind, in baseball you just never know for sure what makes anything happen, you just know what did happen when you look back on it later. But whatever the cause, Carroll's knucklers danced into the hitters as though they were Gene Kelly's steps while he was trying to impress Fred Astaire. The pitches that the hitters took floated teasingly in for strikes, while those they swung at seemed to gleefully avoid their bats as if the baseball had abruptly discovered an allergy to wood.

In the fifth, Garrett went the other way with an outside pitch and doubled off the wall, Crockett singled him home, Cohen hit a seeing-eye grounder through the infield that sent Jim to third, and Bo Johnson hit a fly ball deep enough to sacrifice him across the plate. In the sixth, though, Ephraim zipped through us with such ease that I found myself wondering what the chances were we would score again. I turned to Cohen, sitting next to me on the bench.

"Think she's got enough in the tank for another inning?"

"You watching the game, Skip? They can't touch her. Haven't hit a ball hard all day." We looked at each other and, I think, realized it at the same time. As if to affirm our shared thought, we both simultaneously glanced at the scoreboard. There it was, all right: the confirmation of what we simply hadn't been paying attention to because we'd been too caught up in the game inning by inning. The zero posing prettily under "R" for runs of the Wolves was matched with another zero under "H" for hits. Cohen grinned and went out to the plate to catch some more knucklers.

After that inning, everyone in the ballpark realized she was throwing a no-hitter. You could feel it across the stadium, a tacit awareness breathing silently from the stands. Six innings without giving up a hit; three more and history would be made right in front of all of us this very day. Nine more outs.

Guys started sitting far enough away from Carroll to give her plenty of room on the bench. She was as familiar as the rest of us with the old baseball superstition; talking to a pitcher in the midst of his (now her) no-no was considered bad etiquette and worse luck. No one wanted to be the one to taunt the baseball gods, especially during our current pathetic play. So not even Cohen spoke to her between innings.

Not that there was any need to in this case; since all she was throwing was the knuckleball, there was no reason to discuss how to pitch to any of the upcoming hitters.

As I watched their leadoff man come up to start the seventh, it hit me. None of them had reached base yet. This wasn't just a no-hitter going; nine more outs, and our female hurler would have a perfect game. I glanced at McCarter sitting nearby. He was watching me and somehow I knew he was entertaining the same thought I was. I said without even thinking,

"Be pretty tough to say she doesn't belong after *that*."

"Already is, Skip. Already is."

She knocked them down in the seventh as if they were bowling balls, and we did no more damage to Ephraim than they were doing to her. You could feel the tension palpably thicken in the eighth; but her knucklers blithely danced up to the plate as she faced the bottom of their lineup. They pinch-hit for both their eighth batter and their pitcher, but their first pinch-hitter barely connected on what became a weak popup that Crockett handled easily, and the second swung so mightily at a third strike that I worried he might have broken his back. The knuckler slipped playfully past him as his bat viciously attacked the unconcerned air.

We got two runners on in the top of the ninth but stranded them.

When K.C. took the mound for the bottom of the ninth, the stadium was as quiet as a Kansas cornfield at three in the morning. Their leadoff man, Randy Haynes, watched the first pitch flutter towards him and suddenly shifted into a bunting stance, tapping it towards the third-base side. But a knuckler is harder to bunt than a fastball, with its unpredictable movement and varying speed, so he pushed the bunt harder than he should have. K.C. was off the mound with a speed few of us expected, fielding it cleanly and throwing him out easily though her throw to first had only moderate velocity to it.

"Bunting for a hit to break up the no-no," Pepper muttered to me. "That's kind of a dirty trick to try."

"But fair. She must have seen that in the minors. Looks like she can field her position well enough."

"Sure. Fielding good ain't the same thing as throwing hard. Serves them right. Now we got who?"

"Wells and Pete Brown."

"Wells does not hit a loud foul off her all day so far. But Brown ... Pete is the best hitter they got. He is the last one we want to see up there."

"Hopefully, he will be."

Wells fidgeted in the batter's box for quite a while before he stepped in; then just as Carroll was going into her windup, he held up his back hand to the ump. Called time, then stepped out again. It was hardly surprising; one of a hitter's tools is to try to break a pitcher's rhythm in the hope of throwing off the hurler's timing. In this game, any microscopic edge can make a difference. Like great actors, the most thoughtful of ballplayers live for nuance.

But K.C. just grinned at him. We could see it from the dugout. Rather than making her nervous, his predictable attempt to unnerve her instead seemed to relax her. When she settled back in, she tossed him a floater that he started to swing at, checked, then feebly lunged at as it settled primly into Cohen's big glove.

"Steeerike!" yelled the ump.

Wells stepped out again, shook his head in frustration, then dug in. He let the next pitch flutter by because it was outside all the way, until suddenly it wasn't—it abruptly sneaked over the outside corner at the last moment, fooling the batter but not the ump.

"Steeeerike two!" he shouted.

The entire team was now on the top step of the dugout, except for Tad Strain (I had ended his suspension) who probably wouldn't have bothered to stand up to get a decent view of Christ at The Last Supper; but when

Garrett's gaze fired icy daggers in his direction, even Tad realized that perhaps he should not be the only member of the team seated indifferently while all his mates were crowding the top step of the dugout in palpable excitement. So he joined the mob at the dugout edge to watch the next pitch.

The two-strike pitch was like all the others that day except for one thing: its darting unpredictability stopped just before it arrived at the plate so that for one seemingly endless moment, it hung in the air, waist high and centered, like a piece of cheesecake on a tray just begging someone to consume it. Wells was so astonished by the opportunity that he swung tentatively and late. But he made contact, and the very half-heartedness of his swing worked in his favor, as so often improbably happens in this game. The ball spun in a lazy arc off the end of his bat into short right-center field. Blasingame raced desperately out from second base while Johnson (Bo today) thundered in from right; even Willoughby dashed madly over from center field even though he had no chance whatsoever of arriving there in time. The ball fell impudently just beyond Terry's reach and several feet from the charging Bo for a clean single—a dumb-luck cheapie Texas Leaguer, sure, but an indisputable hit. Bo finally grabbed it and fired to Crockett at first, but Wells was already standing on the base watching by that time.

The perfect game was gone. So was the no-hitter.

K.C. stood on the mound, glove hand dangling, pitching hand on her hip, her head down, staring at the mound.

It began slowly. At first it was barely a rustle; a sort of collective sigh that streamed through the body politic as if the universe was slowly exhaling. Then the sound started. A slow, almost distant clapping morphed into a birth of rolling thunder until the overwhelming applause rocked the stadium so mellifluously that its concrete foundations wondered what was up. Everyone, it seemed, was on their feet contributing to the oceanic ovation that washed over the diminutive hurler like giant waves in a hurricane. It lasted less than a minute, but not much less; when it finally died down, I started my trek out to the mound.

I didn't mind the chorus of boos that rained down on me. I would have been disappointed if they hadn't. I saw Crockett start to come over and waved him back to first. The other infielders saw that and stayed where they were. When I arrived at the mound, K.C. held the ball, ready to hand it to me.

"There's no one warming up." She looked surprised. "There will be as soon as I get back to the dugout," I added, "but it's still your game if you want it."

"I want it," she said simply.

"If Pete gets a hit, you're gone. But I'm going to give you a chance to finish this. You've earned it."

"I won't be able to keep Wells from stealing," she reminded both of us.

"Nobody's kept Wells from stealing since he's been born. Don't worry about it. I don't care if he steals second *and* third. He's not the tying run. Just get the batter. One way or another, Pete's the last guy you face today. I don't care about the shutout, but I do want to win the game. So just keep him in the yard, okay?"

"Okay," she answered, her eyes shining. Or maybe they were gleaming. I'd figure it out later.

"Okay." I started walking back to the dugout. By my fourth step, everyone realized I was leaving her in, and the applause then was at least as loud as the boos had been. I sat down next to Pepper.

"Ohhhh-kay," he said.

Her first pitch to Brown was outside and high, and Wells stole second. Her next pitch was inside and low, and Cohen had no chance at all to throw him out as he stole third. K.C. took a deep breath and threw a knuckleball that barely knuckled.

It was right over the plate. It did dip when it arrived there, but not impressively. Pete's quick, compact swing put his bat on the ball in a hurry. His vicious line drive rocketed towards left so quickly that few of us actually saw the ball scream straight into Garrett's glove. If he had had to move or even reach for it, it would have been by him; if it had hit him, it might have killed him. But it headed straight for his glove as if it had been predestined to end its journey there. Joe stepped on third base—the lead Wells had taken gave him no chance at all to get back in time—for the unassisted double play. Ballgame.

K.C. walked slowly off the mound as the crowd cheered wildly—it evoked an oddly disorienting sensation when the other team's fans did that for a visiting player—and I stepped out of the dugout and swayed back and forth to catch her eye. When she saw me I touched the tip of my cap. She got it, and tipped her cap to the fans who were cheering her. I didn't think the cheers could get much louder, but I believe they did. When she reached the dugout, her teammates clapped her on the back, traded fist pounds and generally surrounded her in a happy mob. Her spectacular grin gave me the impression that whatever she had been through for the past decade, this moment had made it all worth it.

Resurrection Blues

"He's back."

Jay Greenberg's voice on the phone, just speaking those two words, sounded simultaneously excited and terrified. I somehow knew instantly why he had called and to whom he was referring.

"How? When?"

"The doctor called me and said he had simply come out of his coma. It was hard to miss; Simon apparently woke up and started bellowing for someone to get in there and explain what in buffalo-hunting hell was going on. They did. He doesn't seem to remember anything except firing Pepper. Had no idea what he was doing in the hospital, and told them to get him out of there pronto or he'd fire them all. One of the nurses inadvisably told him he didn't own the hospital so he couldn't fire anyone in it. He asked if he was still in Buffalo. When they said yes, he told them he'd *buy* the damn hospital and then fire them all. They decided to let him go home."

He didn't stay home for long. When I got the message to come see him, it instructed me to do so in his office at the Dome. When I arrived he looked thinner—his face was noticeably gaunter than it had been—but otherwise he looked remarkably good for someone who had only just emerged from a coma. I greeted him warmly and he nodded. It was when I saw his eyes that I first got the feeling that something had changed, at least for the moment. It was Simon, all right, but there was a flickering, intense disorientation about him that made me wonder how recovered he really was. It seemed clear, though, that this was a question he was disinclined to ask himself. He waved me to a chair.

"I hear you've done a good job, Mike."

"Thank you, sir."

"So it's nothing personal. But I've got to replace you as manager of the team."

I was too taken aback to say anything but, "You do?"

"Afraid so. I'm the boss, you know."

"I know." I willed myself to stay calm and ignore the despair bouncing off the walls of my brain.

"And you're Junior's hire. He's a good kid. Crazy as a loon, doesn't know his ass from his elbow, understands less about baseball than my ashtray, trusts the wrong people, and talks as though he's a fortune cookie. But he's my boy, and he's a good kid. Done some good things. The Buffalo Buffalo, for instance. I would never have thought of that, but it's caught on; we're selling more merchandise than we were before, and it's gotten us some free publicity, which is my favorite kind, since we don't have to pay for it. And bringing up the girl, this K.C. Carroll. I never would have gone for that either, but she brings in more fans to see her pitch, and the commissioner tells me it helps the sport's TV revenue stream, which is after all what baseball is all about. So I give Junior credit for that. Underneath all that space-cadet new age gobbledygook, he may have the makings of a closet capitalist. The old Lumpe gene for turning a profit. It's in his DNA. Has to be, right? Since it's in mine. Anyway, he's done okay. But he's not ready to run this team yet. He's still got a lot to learn. And since I'm still around, he can learn from a master, if he doesn't take it into his airy-fairy head to fly back to India and memorize proverbs from that guru pal of his. That guru isn't getting one red cent from me to contribute to any temple-building, by the way. I called him to tell him that and the wise guy said he would pray that I recover my harmonious balance with the universe. Can you believe the nerve of that asshole? Who is he to tell me I don't have harmonious balance with the fucking universe? So I asked him that and he said he was indeed searching for his own and that my example would help him seek it. How in hell do you argue with a guy like that?"

"It can be difficult," I agreed.

"Damn right. Anyway, Mike, I have to fire you because I have to hire someone, and it can't be you, can it, since Junior already hired you. If I leave you there I'm acknowledging that Junior knows better than I do, and I can't do that. I've got to show everyone that I'm in charge. So I've got to hire my own man. Don't know who yet, but it can't be you, since you're *his* man."

"You're the one who originally hired me," I reminded him.

"Well, yes, but not to manage. I have to assert my authority, you see? Show everyone who is top dog around here. The alpha male. The one in charge. Which has got to be *me*. I hope you understand."

"Sure. I understand."

"I'm glad to hear that, Mike. I wouldn't want you to be one of these whiny victim types who think my firing you has anything to do with you. Because it doesn't. I'd have to fire you even if you were someone else. Whoever manages the Buffalo has to be someone I hire to do that. But I do appreciate all the good work you've done, Mike. I'll remember that. And I'll never forget it."

And so I got fired as unexpectedly as I had gotten hired. Pepper had been fired (again) as well—Simon was adamant about that—so it was back to MommaDaddy's where I joined Pepper in knocking back some Blues. We assured each other that the other one would get another chance somewhere in the league, but it was clear neither of us necessarily believed that. We both agreed that we would miss the game itself more than the particular members of the team—"there's too many of them anyway you're lucky you don't have to see again," Pepper reminded me—and agreed that we would both miss the atmosphere, the feel of the game itself, its emerald surfaces and geometric angles, a lot more than the traveling, the fickle skepticism of the fans, or the surroundings in general. Not to mention Simon, which neither of us did. What we also didn't mention is that without baseball games to look forward to and be involved in, both of us felt like lost souls.

Since I was still collecting my salary for *not* managing, I didn't have to go searching for new employment in any hurry; which was just as well, since I really didn't feel like dealing with the world of baseball ownership just yet. Normally, Donna would never have let me sit around feeling depressed and not doing much besides mowing the lawn and reading—but this wasn't normally, and she was remarkably patient with my meditative brooding. The girls weren't, though. They continued to watch the Buffalo games on TV, and sometimes it was hard to avoid watching some of it myself.

"Why is Mr. Sheehy sending up Mr. Strain to hit against Mr. Juantamoreno?" Laura wondered aloud. Simon had hired Jimbo Sheehy to replace me, and could have done a lot worse; Jimbo had worked his way up through the minor leagues and had done a fine job with our Triple A club. He was a fiery, demanding guy, but he knew—and respected—the game. "Mr. Juantamoreno *owns* Mr. Strain. He's only one for eleven against him." Jenna looked at her, and Laura responded defensively, "I remember from when I researched them."

"Impressive," I told her. "Now let's watch and see *why* he's only one for eleven." The first pitch was low and broke outside; Tad's bat waved at it uselessly. "There you are."

"*Where* I are?" inquired Laura.

"Tad's a first-ball fastball hitter and a dead low-ball hitter. Alberto knows that; hell, everyone knows that. So he threw him a low outside slider, which looks like a fastball until it breaks down into the dirt. Tad's swinging at a pitch out of the strike zone, and even if he hit it—which he won't—all he'll do is bounce it to the second baseman or pop it up. He's actually lucky he missed it. All a pitcher has to do is throw him pitches that look like low fastballs but aren't strikes, and Tad will get himself out *for* them."

"Why doesn't he just take the pitch?" Jenna wondered logically enough.

"Because he's a bible hitter."

"A bible hitter?"

"Thou shalt not pass."

"You mean he swings at everything he can reach," Laura clarified.

"At everything he *thinks* he can reach," her sister corrected her.

"Right. So all a pitcher needs is enough command of location to just miss the strike zone. The good ones thrive on that."

"A pitcher who hasn't control hasn't anything," Laura recited.

"Mr. McCarthy's commandments?"

"Right," she grinned at me. I couldn't help grinning back. If there was any cure for lingering depression, it was my two daughters. Still, it was too hard for me to stay there and watch the game just then, so I wandered into another room and read a story from Denis Johnson's collection *Jesus' Son*. I had read it before, but there are some things you can always re-read with pleasure—*Gatsby* and "The Dead" spring to mind, and so do *Don Quixote* and *Alice in Wonderland*—and anyway, I was in the mood for uncompromising excellence. As I was so familiar with this piece already, though, it wasn't a problem when Donna came in with the clear intent of interrupting me. Her sitting opposite me and staring until I put down the book was, it seemed to me, a pretty good indication of that purpose.

"I was wondering," she started without preamble—for a sharp lawyer, my wife wasn't much for preamble—"whether this was long enough."

"Whether *what* was long enough?"

"The wallowing in self-pity. It's somewhat justified, maybe—but justification isn't everything, you know."

"This from a lawyer."

"This from your partner in life. You've got two sensational daughters…"

"I sure do."

"…and a wife—hold the flattery on that one—not to mention an entire life to lead."

"I know. I just find it kind of dispiriting to be tossed out the window like that, for no good reason."

"You're unfortunate to have been fired like that, but you were incredibly fortunate to have been hired in the first place."

"True enough."

"And you did a good enough job to be considered for another one, if one opens up, and another team gets really desperate."

"You really know how to make a guy feel good about himself."

"Come on, sweetheart. Get over it. We all will if you will. And we won't if you don't. So either continue to stress out your children and make us all miserable and tense, or get past it and get back to enjoying the incredibly lucky life you've been given. I know it's a difficult decision, but as we used to say during plea-bargaining, the choice is yours."

I couldn't argue that. So I went to Jenna's soccer games—she had switched to midfield because, as she told me, "scoring is great but it is *so* much fun to keep someone else from doing it and getting them all frustrated and helpless"—and I watched in restrained awe at Laura's class presentation of software program applications that no one had yet developed yet but, she assured us, someone shortly would. And I spent all kinds of time becoming reacquainted with my wife in ways that made me wonder why I had ever been such an idiot as to waste time being depressed when we could be doing, well, all the things we once again found ourselves doing. I began questioning how, as I got older, I could possibly have lost track of the personal Donna-centric pleasures that had made me feel so amazing when we had first chosen to be teammates for life.

In fact, I began to enjoy myself so much I didn't even hear about K.C. until Jenna told me. She was tight-lipped with barely restrained fury and resisting tears with all of her considerable will power.

"They can't send her down to the minors. How dare they! She threw an almost no-hitter!"

"Yes, but she hasn't gotten anyone out since," I reminded her.

"She would if you were still there," Jenna almost snarled. "If she was with people who really believed in her."

"Maybe," I grudgingly acknowledged. "But it is what it is."

"If she was a guy—"

"Then they might have sent her down earlier. It may have nothing to do with gender."

"Of course it does."

"Look—she can be extremely effective when she's got her control and nobody's on base," I explained in my most reasonable tones, though I knew that was as likely to drive her crazy as it was to keep her calm. "But she walks people, and anyone she does walk can steal second and usually third because she's got no pickoff move and even if she did the knuckler makes it nearly impossible for the catcher to throw anyone out anyway and the knuckleball is her only pitch. In essence, with anyone on base she's got to strike people out to be effective, and you can't strike out everyone, not at this level. For the moment, she's a one-trick pony. It's a good trick, maybe even a great one, but it's the only one she's got."

She listened with an intensity that reminded me forcefully that she was her mother's daughter, then repeated slowly, "For the moment?"

"She should learn another pitch. It doesn't have to be a blazing fastball; a solid curve or a sinker or even a good changeup might do it. Most importantly, she needs to develop a pickoff move. But this isn't a developmental league, this is The Show. That's why the Lord invented minor leagues."

She nodded slowly. "That sounds fair enough," she admitted. "But I can't help wondering whether it really is. You told me that she was distracting too many of the guys, one way or another."

"She is. And sending her away will be a bonus in that regard. I don't deny it. But we—they—might have to do it even if she was universally welcomed by everyone."

"Couldn't she work on those things here? It's not as if the team is a playoff contender. What can we—I mean they—lose?"

"Games. Respect. A sense of purpose. And anyway that's not even the point. First of all, the team's not completely out of it yet; they haven't been mathematically eliminated from the wild card spot. And even if they had been, it's still not right. It's also not fair to her. If she's going to earn her way to a big-league roster spot, she shouldn't be trying to do it at a disadvantage. She'll have a much better shot if she develops ways to compensate for her limitations."

"I hate this," she confessed. "You know that if they send her down, everyone will take it as proof that a woman isn't good enough to play at this level. And don't say that you can't help what people think."

"I can't. But they'd be wrong. And anyway, everyone knows she's *good* enough. The almost no-hitter established that. She's just not *complete* enough. Not yet, anyhow."

"Isn't there any way at all..." She didn't finish the sentence. Or have to.

"A major league team is not affirmative action and it's not a democracy. They need players who can help them win. She might be one of them next season, or the one after that, but maybe not now. I promise you, honey, that if she works hard enough—and she will—developing more skills at Triple-A will be the best thing that ever happened to her. Let's hope so, anyway."

Jenna plopped on the couch opposite me, curled up with the adolescent muscular flexibility that we never think will be any less effortless than it is when we're teenagers, and regarded me as if I was a recent arrival from Saturn. It was a look that boded trouble, so I can't say I was too surprised when she asked me with a bit of an edge to her voice whether I would have cut *her* from the team if she'd been in K.C.'s place.

"If you only had one pitch?"

"You told me Lefty Grove only had one pitch."

"Yeah, but no one could hit it."

"No one hits her knuckleball either."

"You know what made Sandy Koufax's fastball so unhittable, Jenna? His great curve. And he could throw both for strikes. You can't get major league batters out if you don't know yourself whether your pitches are going to be in the same neighborhood as the strike zone."

"You mean like Steve Dalkowski."

"You remember him?" I asked without thinking. She gave me the dark, seething look she got when she thought she was being patronized. I quickly said, "I'm impressed, that's all."

"Why? Who could forget Steve Dalkowski?" she asked in such disbelief that for a moment there, that question made sense even to me.

"I *do* mean like Steve Dalkowski," I agreed. Dalkowski was a legend not so much among fans, most of whom had never heard of him, but among the baseball-playing fraternity. He supposedly threw as hard as anyone who ever lived—upwards of a hundred miles an hour, some said—and no one could hit the guy; but since he had no idea where his pitches were actually going, no one *had* to hit him, just wait until he had pretty much walked the ballpark. So even with his staggering natural talent, he had never made it out of the minor leagues. One scout in awe of Steve's fastball had written, "God can see it, but I don't know if even He can hit it." Another scout had registered the following observation regarding Dalkowski's extraordinary ability to make the baseball into an unguided missile: "He's a freak. I'm not even saying he's any good. I'm just saying he's a freak."

"But K.C. will be back," I assured my daughter. She searched my face to see if I was pandering to her. The look on her face made me mighty glad I wasn't.

"You think so?"

"I do. She's smart. And dedicated. She knows what she has to do, and I don't doubt she'll figure out how to do it. I've got confidence in her. Don't you?" I inquired innocently.

"I think," she replied deliberately, "that she could fly to the moon, hit fungos to Ursa Major, take off in her spaceship and catch them all before they fell. If she really wanted to."

"Then why worry? All they're asking her to do is develop another pitch."

She regarded me with the same minatory gaze she was prone to give the opposing pitcher in a softball game when Jenna was guessing what the next pitch would be. "Dad?" The sweetness of her tone would have put me on guard even without that look. "Would *you* have sent her down? If it was *your* call?"

There was no point even pretending to think it over. Never lie to your daughter, especially when she's too smart for you to get away with it. "No," I admitted. "We're having a good year as a team, but that just means we're getting better. We're not making the playoffs and she could grow with the team and learn from the pros. Plus the more the guys get used to her the better in the long run."

"So you disagree with yourself."

"Well, I'm of two minds, put it that way. On my good days, they tend to be more or less in agreement. This happens not to be one of my best days."

"Right." She headed towards the door, but my question stopped her.

"Ursa Major?"

"Oh. That. I'm just still into Bears. The Buffalo Buffalo just seems, well, kind of redundant, y'know?"

When I arrived at the airport gate, K.C. seemed surprised to see me. I had found out her flight and thought I'd wish her well on her way down and, I hoped, back up again.

"Real nice of you, Skip."

"You know what you need to do to be back, right?"

"Yup. I'll be a lot better player if I develop another pitch I can throw for strikes without their taking my head off with it, and if I don't develop a better pickoff move, well, I won't be able to keep runners from just moving right around the bases whenever they feel like it. Believe me, Skip, I know how important it is for me to play up here. But I also know how much it matters that I'm good enough to stick on merit. I need my teammates to just absolutely know that I can come into a game and help win it for them. Because if *they* know that and *I* know that, well then, anyone who makes a big deal out of the girl thing is just doing that and nothing else. Which is the way it needs to be, seems to me. Right now, if they get nervous when I come into the game, I can't much blame them. And I need to be able to blame them. You know what I mean?"

I nodded. "You know R.A. Dickey?"

"The knuckleball ace? Of course. He's one of my heroes."

"He once said about baseball, 'This game is about how to handle regret, it really is.'"

"Wow." She grinned in a way I had never seen from her; the smile transformed her face into human sunshine. "Okay, then. Be seeing you." She walked away.

Junior, who had been frustrated with his dad's decision to send her back down, told me much later (when, over a cup of green tea, I gave him Glen Hirshberg's *The Book of Bunk* as a birthday present) that when he had called Mashinamdev and invited him to agree that sending Carroll back down was a terrible idea, the guru had offered the thought that developing additional skills—"a more advanced state of consciousness in her pitching endeavors" was the phrase he apparently employed—could only add to K.C.'s general state of enlightenment. I couldn't help thinking that a couple of months ago none of us would ever have expected anyone in baseball owner-ship to consult an Indian guru in order to validate a baseball decision, but—as Mashinamdev himself had once observed to me—you don't really know what you know until you know it. If then.

Poor Mrs. Poffenberger

I DIDN'T EVEN KNOW I had been brooding until Jenna sat down on the floor right in front of me in a lotus position and asked me why I was still being so mopey. That's one of the genuine advantages having teenage daughters; when you're pouting like a teenager, they let you know it without artifice or ceremony. I told her I wasn't aware that I was. She gave me a look I had never seen on her before—though I had seen it more than once on her mother, many years ago, when Donna and I started dating—as though she was searching for an answer to an unasked question, an answer that was mysteriously hidden but must be there somewhere if the searcher could only find the right spot to seek. I watched her start to say something, hesitate, think better of it, change her mind, start again, hesitate again. Then I saw the determined flash in her eyes that announced before she spoke that she had decided to just go for it, whatever "it" was. She spoke carefully, as if saying something in a language she had never spoken before.

"Smead Jolley," she pronounced.

I wondered if I looked as startled as I felt.

"Huh?"

She repeated the name.

"What about him?"

"Nothing about him, dad. It's just that he's an old-time ballplayer."

"I know."

"With kind of a weird name."

"Well, yes."

"So ... well ... Laura and I were talking about your kind of seeming sorta down, kind of, lately, and I don't remember how exactly it came up in conversation, but ... well, we just thought since you and Pepper always

185

used to cheer yourselves up by saying all those crazy names out loud, maybe that would help. Though I don't know why it would. But I—that is, we—figured it couldn't really hurt, could it? It's sort of dumb, I know that, but if it cheered you up, it'd be worth it, you know? I mean, who cares how dumb it is if it makes you feel better, right? And we didn't know what else would make you feel better, so ... well..." She ran out of verbal fuel and parked her sentence by the conversational curb.

I wanted enormously to hug her; I don't know why I found myself unable to do it. Instead, I just lowered my chin to my chest and closed my eyes. When I opened them again, Jenna hadn't moved, but her expression had altered. She regarded me with a gentleness that almost broke my heart.

"Let yourself feel better, Dad. Would you? Please?"

"I'd like to," I admitted. "I just feel so ... well..."

"Lousy?"

"Pretty much, yeah," I confessed.

"We all want you to. And Mom *needs* you to, even though she probably wouldn't admit that under torture. Even Flash is acting all edgy with you feeling like this."

"Flash is a cat."

"Well, duh, I sort of know that, Dad. Cats can be edgy. They pick up people's moods better than people do sometimes. By the way, whatever made Mom name her Flash? She's probably the slowest cat I've ever seen."

"I don't know," I replied more morosely than I meant to.

She acted as though my tone was normal, cocked her head and asked cheerfully, "Do you think it was Mom's advanced sense of irony? Or do you think she was working so hard on that trial that she went all oblivious again?"

"Luscious Easter," I said after a moment. She broke into the widest smile I'd seen in some time, from anybody, rose quickly to her feet and gave me an impulsive hug. "Thanks, Dad," she whispered, and left the room. I wasn't sure whether her departure was due to a concern that she might get emotional or a fear that I might.

I was thinking about that when Laura came in and sat herself on the couch, facing me gravely.

"So did Jenna try names on you?"

"Yes."

"Which ones?"

"Smead Jolley."

She shook her head in amusement. "That was the only one she could consistently remember. Jenna's got amazing concentration when she's playing basketball, but give her a book or put her in front of a computer and she suddenly starts acting like a teenager."

"She *is* a teenager."

"Yeah, that's just what I mean. All that maturity stuff goes sailing right out the proverbial window. I still can't figure out why Mr. Jolley was so easy for her and the others she just blanks on when we quiz each other."

"You quiz each other?"

"Well, sure. How else could we be sure we remember the names correctly? Anyhow, that's one thing I can do better than her. I'm really good at remembering stuff that doesn't matter."

"So you have others for me?"

"Sure. Slim Sallee."

"Ossee Schcreckengost," I responded.

"He sounds like a character in some Dickens book."

"Maybe he was."

"Don't be silly, Dad. Luscious Easter."

"That's the one I gave back to Jenna."

"Oh. Okay. Shovel Hodge, then."

"Cletus Elwood Poffenberger," I offered.

"Really? What was poor Mrs. Poffenberger thinking, do you think?"

"That's a very good question."

"Yeah, I'm working on asking better questions. It's actually more interesting sometimes than trying to find answers, you know?"

"I agree with you."

"So does that cheer you up?"

"You and Jenna? Oh, yes. You surely do."

"So do you feel less mopey now?"

"A lot less, yes. Thank you."

She nodded firmly in approval. "Good. Mom said she didn't know if our trading names with you would be any help at all, but she also said you can't hit the ball if you don't swing the bat. Which Mr. McCarthy said also."

"They're both right."

"That's what we figured. So I'm really glad if it helped and you're not lying about it just to make us feel better, because you need to feel better more than we do. We're fine. We're both fine. Jenna gets mad at these two boys in her class sometimes because one doesn't pay enough attention to her and the other one pays too much, but they're just stupid boys and she knows that and basically she's as fine as I am."

"I'm glad to hear that," I assured her. She got up to leave the room but stopped in the doorway.

"Speaking of poor Mrs. Poffenberger. Can I ask you something?"

"Anything, honey."

"How could any mother name a boy Hazen Shirley Cuyler? Unless she hated the kid or was a sadist or something."

"I guess that's why they called him Kiki."

"I guess so. But maybe if you hit .321 over eighteen years, you get to be called whatever you want to be called, huh?"

"I guess so," I agreed.

She smiled at me. "Feel better, dad, okay? We all really, really want you to." Then she was gone.

Never Was a Cowboy

DURING THE NEXT COUPLE of weeks, I found that my instinctive desire to watch the games was consistently counterbalanced by my depression in watching other people make mistakes I knew that I wouldn't have (I would have made entirely different mistakes). But I was adapting, albeit slowly; Donna and the girls made me feel like an idiot for doing anything other than enjoying their company much more than I had previously been able to. If it had continued like that for a while longer—say, a decade or two—I might have recovered completely from the consuming addiction to baseball that seemed so impossible to shake. But I was making progress, seemed to me. Then Jimbo Sheehy decided to have one more drink during dinner at the upscale restaurant he was enjoying with his female companion.

As it turned out, his attractive companion turned out not to be his wife. Which wouldn't have mattered that much except that they had a disagreement that quickly escalated into an abrasive—and loud—argument. That it wasn't his third, or even his fourth drink, probably didn't help much. Before the wait-staff could calm him down, Jimbo stood up and belted the young woman so hard that she was flung into the next table, demolishing some fairly decent china and what had apparently been a pleasant evening for the unsuspecting elderly couple seated there (the septuagenarian lady was cut by a shard of flying glass and was taken to the hospital). Since there were lots of witnesses to not only the blow but also to the torrential obscenity with which Sheehy accompanied it, it made the news promptly and prominently. Faced with the multiple ways in which the incident tarnished the team's image—it turned out that, in addition to the other issues involved, the girl was barely legal—Simon fired his new manager even more rapidly than he had hired him.

What stunned me was not Sheehy's dismissal—it would have been more shocking had Simon done otherwise—but the hard-to-comprehend reality that the next day, I found myself once again, and most unexpectedly, facing Simon in his office. I stared at him to make sure I had just heard what I thought I had heard, though I knew well enough that I had; it was too strange to be anything but true.

"Junior never should have suggested I fire you in the first place," he said. For a fleeting moment I considered pointing out that it had been *his* idea to fire me, not Junior's; but clearly introducing actual truths into this conversation could be detrimental to my already tenuous career, so I took Shakespeare's advice (often a good idea in any case) and decided to let discretion be the better part of valor.

"On the other hand," Simon continued blithely, "Junior also suggested that I re-hire you. Got to give the young man some credit for having a good idea, even when it's *my* good idea he's having.

"Anyway, Mike, we've been doing worse without you than we were doing *with* you, which proves I was right to hire you in the first place. Plus we're not playing with that old school spirit, and I know you know about that old school spirit. It'll be good to have that back again. And most of the players hated Sheehy, which I wouldn't have minded if he had won more; and they seem to like you, which frankly I wouldn't care about except that like I say, you were losing less than he was. Plus after he slugged that girl—what was he thinking, anyway, slugging a girl, that's totally unacceptable and morally reprehensible, especially in public where anybody can see you and even take pictures that end up all over the internet—anyway, after he slugged the girl and that poor old lady had to go to the hospital for stitches, well, his tenure here just wasn't viable any more, he had to go. After all, I fired Pepper, and he at least hit a grown man who was a lot bigger—and younger—than he was, which took some guts even if it was a stupid thing to do. So you can have your job back managing the team if you want it, Mike, that's what I'm saying. Just for the rest of the season, mind you, then we'll re-evaluate, but we would do that anyway, so what difference does that make, really? So how's about it, Princeton? You want to shepherd the Buffalo again?"

"Sure. Yes. You bet." I hoped I didn't sound as frantically eager as I felt.

"I'm glad to hear it, Mike. Enthusiasm is good. Not that I've got anything against pale-faced stammerers who aren't sure what they really want and are afraid to grab it by the horns and sail it safely to shore—I'm not prejudiced—but I just have no use for people like that. Like that piece of Danish fruitcake in Shakespeare's play. If he had simply stopped dithering around and just killed the S.O.B. instead of agonizing over every little thing, a lot of corpses at the end would have still been alive leading useful, productive lives as nobles or noblettes or whatever they did for a living. A lesson to us all, I guess. Don't just dick around when you've got a decision to make. Like Yogi says, When you come to a fork in the road, take it."

"I'll take it."

"Good for you, Mike. That's why you're the man to be chief of the Buffalo. You're decisive. Decisive is good. Better than indecisive, anyway. And of course, you're smart, too. Intelligent and all that crap. And you know, the more I know about this game—I know a lot, obviously, but I figure even I can keep learning more—anyway, the more I know the more I think you're right that there are times baseball can seem pretty complex. It really can take some smarts sometimes, I can see that now. In fact, baseball is a lot like chess, only without the dice."

So I once again became the manager of the Buffalo Buffalo. The players seemed mostly pleased at my return. Some of them, as Simon said, had simply hated Sheehy. Others were relieved to see a devil they knew rather than a devil they didn't. Still others probably didn't care at all but didn't despise me enough to send out any negative karma. And it was always possible that a couple of them were actually glad I was back. Bo Johnson, for one. "You treat us like men," he told me appreciatively. "You let us wear earrings." Anyway, it sure felt good to be back in the saddle again. Though, as I observed to Jack Lee when he welcomed me back, I had been unceremoniously tossed from this particular saddle before.

"Never was a horse that couldn't be rode," Jack reminded me, evoking his youthful rodeo days in Wyoming. "Never was a cowboy couldn't be throwed. The important thing is to get back on that saddle and ride like hell till you get where you're going."

Love of the Game

WE HAD WON the game that night—I was 2–0 in career managerial debuts—and it was one of those games in which everything had gone so right you found yourself wondering how anything went as wrong as often as it actually did. When you're hitting the ball safely, catching it cleanly, throwing accurately, pitching successfully, running the bases intelligently—when you're playing the game the way it was meant to be played—there is nothing more beautiful than the game of baseball. I would of course never say that to my wife, but it didn't really matter, because Donna already knew that I felt that way.

A lot of baseball aficionados since the last years of the nineteenth century had previously observed what the social satirist George Carlin made us laugh about in one of his most inspired comedy routines (though there was little routine about Carlin's routines), but Carlin had really nailed it: the vocabulary of baseball is a wonderful window into the soul of the game. In football, you *ram* the ball across the *goal line*, *kick* a field goal, drag defenders on your back as you score a touchdown. In hockey, you *shoot* the puck, unleash a *slap shot*, start a *power play*, *body-check* your opponent. In basketball, you *dunk* on an opponent, *block* shots, and, of course, *shoot* and *foul* (as is the case with hockey as well). Baseball is the only one of these sports where you score not by delivering the ball forcefully into a goal, but rather by sending the ball far enough away to enable you and your teammates to *reach home safely*. You reach first *base*; hit a *home* run; are *safe at home*. Skillful pitchers don't deliver devastating physical blows to the opposition; they paint the corners.

When you knock out an opponent in football or hockey, they carry him off on a stretcher; when you knock out a pitcher in baseball, he is simply replaced by another one who may theoretically repair the damage done.

Football is full of blitzes and sacks and being thrown for a loss; basketball has its flagrant fouls and its hard picks; hockey players who don't drive their opponents headfirst into the sideboards are regarded with disdain (and with offensive vocabulary) by their fellow warriors on the ice. Only baseball reveres the "sacrifice" bunt or fly ball in which you give yourself up so that your teammate can advance in his path around the bases. Only baseball encourages a hitter to selflessly move the runner along on his homeward journey by slapping the ball to the right side of the infield, thus enabling the runner already on his way to reach third base. Football linemen are called "guards" and "tackles"; late-inning pitchers provide "relief."

"The game is all counterpoint," observed Bartlett Giamatti, the once-commissioner/scholar/philosopher of baseball (it tells you all you need to know about the soullessness of modern owners that they fired the late great Bart's heir and successor, the erudite and thoughtful Fay Vincent—who committed the ultimate blasphemy, to them, by musing aloud that the national pastime was a sacred trust that "sometimes requires putting self-interest second"—and replaced him with a used-car salesman who made their profits somewhat higher by selling out the fans in preference to TV revenue, starting postseason games so late at night for TV purposes that entire future generations of potential fans were deprived of memories to cherish and, therefore, of the essential reason to remain fans). The blessed Bart went on, "*Home* is an English word virtually impossible to translate into other tongues. No translation catches the associations, the mixture of memory and longing, the sense of security and autonomy and sensibility, the aroma of inclusiveness, of freedom from wariness, that cling to the word *home* and are absent from *house* or even *my house*. *Home* is a concept, not a place; it is a state of mind where self-definition starts...."

Basketball scores run into the hundreds; combined football points often total fully half that amount. In contrast, scores in hockey and baseball tend to be low, so a single score can matter enormously. But a hockey goal, with its quick, violent origins, often needs to be re-run in slow motion for a viewer to even be able to see what actually happened; while in baseball, you can most of the time see the potential run taking shape while the exquisite, immutable geometric patterns on the field take inexorable form in front of you. When a runner rounds third and heads for home plate (now there's an image that provides comfort and familiarity) even as the outfielder gathers up the ball and hurls it homeward, the almost unbearable anticipation of what will happen when the runner and the sphere arrive almost simultaneously keeps our mesmerized attention glued to the unfolding events at hand. In the other games, the score itself is what matters most. In baseball, what grips the mind and sears the soul is the *process* by which the score does or doesn't happen. Will the ball arrive in time? Will the tag on the runner stealing second be made within the split-second required, or will the pitcher's motion be a shade too slow, the catcher's release ever-so-slightly delayed, the runner's slide into the base somehow imperfect? Will the majestically sailing fly ball that the batter has just struck with such impressive force sail over the leaping outfielder's desperately extended glove into the welcoming bleacher seats, or will the defender manage to snatch unexpected victory from the jaws of impending and apparent defeat? When the hitter bounces a ground ball up the middle, will the lunging shortstop's dive somehow arrest the ball's progress, or will the infielder's reach exceed his grasp by an agonizingly slight margin?

Aristotle wrote that the highest happiness was to be found in contemplation. There's no evidence that Aristotle ever stood on a mound and pondered whether he should throw a fastball or breaking pitch to the batter facing him; but there's also no question that of all the games that serve America as a form of modern religion, baseball is far and away the most reflective by nature. Indeed, the leisurely pace of the game is consciously defiant of the racing up and down the arena that so strongly characterizes football, basketball, hockey and their similarly rushed sports brethren. Charles Schulz, beloved creator of the *Peanuts* comic strip, was such a hockey devotee that he built himself his own rink to skate around on. But when he chose a game for his comic-strip kids to play, he selected baseball, because its particular pastoral essence lends itself uniquely to philosophical musings in the middle of a game. Lucy often comes in from the outfield to share her reflections with Charlie Brown, who is perennially pitching haplessly on the mound; in one comic strip, the kids gather on the mound to have a theological discussion in mid-game. There is even an entire book, *Who's on First, Charlie Brown?* devoted to Schulz's baseball comic strips. The introduction is by Hall of Famer Cal Ripken, Jr., who observes that humor is a necessity in baseball "because the game can be so humbling."

They say baseball is a game of inches, and it is (so are the others). But it is also a game of images, of gorgeous geometry, of infinite and timeless self-reference. Above all, it is a game of exquisite anticipation. In spring training, every team dreams of reaching the World Series. Between pitches, every participant in the game (at least, those who are using their brains for actually thinking) is meditating on the various, and seemingly infinite, possibilities that will accompany the next pitch. If he hits it to me, reflects the third baseman to himself, do I go to second and try for a double play, or throw to first for the sure out? How fast is the runner, relative to how hard the ball may or may not come at me? Can we afford to give up another run or not? Can I trust our new second baseman to make the double-play pivot on time? What kind of pitch is our pitcher throwing, to what part of the strike zone, and how might that determine whether the batter pulls the ball, and with how much authority? And does our pitcher still have his velocity, or control? Those are just some of the questions that might flick across the fielder's mind in the brief, vital moments before the catcher calls the pitch, the pitcher nods assent, the hitter digs in, and the ball is tossed his way.

In football, teams value overweight behemoths who may not be able to move much but who can knock other men down. In basketball, a forward who is only (!) six foot nine or a guard who is a mere six-two can be considered "undersized." In hockey, teams put enormous value on a token thug or two whose penalty minutes greatly exceed his number of goals and whose value to his squad is expressed in the approving description of him as an "agitator," though if you're not his teammate he is widely referred to as a "goon." But in baseball, you can be of enormous value to your team whether you're small but fleet of foot and a superior defender, or if you're slow as a tax return but can hit for average or power; whether you're a crafty hurler with little velocity but excellent control, or a pitcher with a lot to learn still, but who nonetheless possesses a blazing fastball or a knee-buckling curve. In what other sport could a one-armed hitter be an MVP, as was Pete Gray for Memphis of the Southern Association in 1944, when he hit .333 (which I was never able to do with two arms) with 5 homers and 68 stolen bases, achievements that earned him a Major League stint with the St. Louis Browns? Or a one-armed pitcher who threw a no-hitter, as did Jim Abbott? What other sport could offer similar opportunities to Chicago Cub hurler Mordecai "Three Fingers" Brown, so nicknamed because his throwing hand had only three fingers, which forced him to throw the ball with an unexpected movement that helped him rack up six consecutive twenty-win seasons?

An apparent physical handicap does not necessarily preclude a successful career in baseball, as these men demonstrated. The other side of that same coin is that the optimization of one's skills is necessary to play effectively, which is not always the case in all other sports. A football lineman might actually be even more efficient with a broken arm because he would be able to use his cast as he might a club; no baseball player with a similar injury could play well, because he could neither grip a bat nor throw a ball. An NHL hockey player who was once reeling after root-canal surgery was nonetheless sent out on the ice by his coach, who explained succinctly, "He doesn't skate with his teeth." Though truth be told, if he was playing hockey at that level he like as not didn't have many of his own teeth remaining anyhow. But then, the NHL has a division, as well as a major award, named after a coach who once informed his team that "If you can't beat 'em in an alley, you won't beat 'em on the ice." Could such a comment (minus the ice, of course) be imaginable coming from a football coach? You bet. But from a baseball manager? Perish the thought. And if (heaven forbid) it ever did, it would invite contempt rather than reverence from his players.

It is true that soccer, like baseball, makes every score of utmost importance, which is perhaps one reason for soccer's enormous popularity internationally; but how can you compare baseball, a game in which any nuance of every ability you possess could and should be utilized, to a contest in which competitors are not allowed to use their hands?

All these sports have followers who devote themselves to their teams with passions so similar to zealous faiths than they are demonstrable evidence these sports are themselves modern religions. But football and hockey worship violence; and NBA basketball, at least as it is played today, celebrates showmanship over teamwork. Baseball has a dedicated following which understands well that failure is the norm and to be expected; that you need the entire team in order to win; and that it's a long season. Equally true is that the faithful of baseball know—or soon learn—that fate is unfair, that the baseball gods are whimsical, that victory is in the beauty of the game rather than merely in the final score, that history is enduring and important, and that no matter what happens, you should regard each game, as Ripken suggests, with amusement and joy.

The poet—and devout baseball *aficionado*—Donald Hall once wrote: "In the country of baseball days are always the same." That is as profoundly misleading as it is true. While every game is similar to all those tucked securely away in the vaults of our collective (and individual) memories, any notable play evokes the remarkable unforgotten feats that serve as both comparison and precedent. To put it another way, every game is reminiscent of those that have preceded it, yet in any game you are likely to witness something you have never seen before, at least not quite in that way or in that context. When Yogi Berra describes that phenomenon as "*Déjà vu* all over again," we all know what he means.

In *Bull Durham*—far and away the greatest baseball movie ever made, possibly because writer/director Ron Shelton is the only filmmaker to have spent years in a (Baltimore Orioles) minor-league system (*Sports Illustrated* lists it as the greatest *sports* film ever made, period)—Annie Savoy gets it right when she says in the film's opening voiceover: "I've tried them all, I really have—and the only church that truly feeds the soul, day in and day out, is the church of baseball." Of course, any religion becomes instantly more appealing when Susan Sarandon is its representative acolyte; but even so, her character is right about the religion of baseball feeding the soul daily, whether it's the nourishment provided by the summer season, or the fall classic, or the Hot Stove League when fans everywhere consider their team's hopes and prospects and mentally arrange helpful if unlikely trades. It's no coincidence that the opening shots of *Bull Durham* show fabulous still photographs of striking and memorable images from baseball's storied past while the soundtrack plays gospel music. Baseball is indeed a religion, we are being told; but it's a constantly self-renewing one steeped in memories, honoring its traditions, and constantly blessing its congregation with a joyful sound.

Unlike Annie Savoy, I hadn't tried them all, but I'd tried plenty. I'd congregated with parishioners from my native Catholic to Baha'i; double-majored in History and Classical Literature at college; been a political junkie in Presidential election years; watched movies with a devotion akin to religion; read the poetry of Millay and Cummings with a passion I had previously reserved for Shakespeare himself; and been in love with the state of being in love before I had met Donna and she had personified it all for me. And there were our daughters, who were the prayers in my atheist's universe. But like Annie Savoy, I had found that one truth remained constant to me: that the only church that truly feeds the soul, day in and day out, is the church of baseball.

Yo La Tengo

I WAS FEELING GOOD when I arrived in my office. I had just met with Cole Boone, and the GM had acceded to my request to include K.C. in our September call-ups from the minors. I had then called Carroll on the phone and told her how much I was looking forward to seeing her throw that knuckleball again, and again, and again. She was ecstatic to hear the news, assured me that she had been working diligently on both a forkball and a pickoff move, and promised she would show me that in baseball at least, one could indeed teach a young dog new tricks.

It was a beautiful day for a game, which made it kind of a pity that we played in a dome instead of outdoors the way the gods of baseball and of nature intended it. I should have known that this was going to be one of those games you don't forget when Vellis, our starting pitcher, had a 2–1 count on their leadoff man. Van threw a pitch that Richert fouled off for strike two and as soon as the ball left his hand, Vellis clutched his left elbow and grimaced. The thing was, Van was right-handed. Nothing had hit him or happened to him, and this was his non-pitching arm. But when I went out there and he tried to throw a warm-up pitch, it was obvious that something had inexplicably attacked his left elbow.

"Got no idea what the hell this is, Skip. I don't even throw with it. But it hurts." So I sent him to the showers and brought in Bobby Lee Milner, whom we had just brought up from AAA. Bobby Lee was from Crumpler, North Carolina, which, he had told us, basically consisted of a combination general store/gas station attached by its side to a Post Office. That *was*, he assured us, the town. When he had arrived in Buffalo, he had promptly lost money to a cabbie when Bobby Lee bet the guy that Buffalo was the biggest city in the world. He was a tall, lanky kid who seemed gawky until he wound up and tossed a baseball, which he did with an explosive grace that was as unexpected as it was effective. None of us had the slightest idea how he'd do in a big-league game, though. This seemed as good a time as any to find out.

"You know what you need to do, right, Bobby Lee?" I asked him when he arrived from the bullpen and stood on the mound, looking around at all the people in the stands.

"Sure, Skip. Get 'em out."

"Just give us some innings, Bobby Lee."

"You bet."

"Go as long as you can."

"You bet."

"Don't worry about throwing it past everyone. You've got eight players backing you up if they hit it."

"You bet."

McCarter chimed in with some excellent advice. "Since I know the hitters, kid, and you don't, just throw what I call for. Fair enough?"

"You're the boss."

"Actually, I'm the catcher."

"You bet."

Tom and I exchanged a glance, then he put his catcher's mask back on and returned behind home plate while I went back to the dugout.

"You think he knows what he's doing?" Cohen asked me on the bench.

"Pitching is pitching everywhere," I reminded him. "You throw the ball and try to miss wood."

"It's aluminum in college," he replied, just as Milner threw a fastball that arrived so quickly Richert barely had time to swing and miss. "But then again," David continued without missing a beat, "We're not in college any more."

He struck out the next batter, which brought Killer Miller up to the plate. Killer liked to say he got his nickname from the ferocity with which he attacked the baseball, which was fair enough; but his explanation might have been more persuasive absent his acquittal, on grounds of self-defense, in a manslaughter trial prompted by an incident when two exceedingly ill-advised thieves tried to mug him outside a nightclub and, with his bare hands, Miller had managed to kill one of them and hospitalize the other. Drunk or sober, Miller was very, very strong. He stood in the batter's box menacingly, waiting for the pitch. Bobby Lee blinked and threw it.

Sometimes a batter hits the ball so high it seems to take forever to descend, even though when it does so it hasn't traveled all that far and often ends up in an infielder's glove. We call that a "major league popup." This wasn't quite that. Miller struck the ball a mighty blow that might have sent it far into the upper deck had he hit anything resembling a line drive, but he didn't. This ball rose high and far, but more straight up than far away. It sailed so high into the outfield that Willoughby, in center, waited for it patiently, then suddenly began shifting his position nervously, and we knew that he must have lost sight of it. Then something happened—or rather, didn't happen—that no one in the ballpark expected (least of all Marcus out there with his glove extended hopefully). The ball, which had soared to such heights, didn't come down.

Every member of the team believed in the laws of physics, even those players who couldn't spell it—but this was one baseball that went up without coming down. Impossible? Sure. But that's baseball.

It took a while before anyone—including the umpires—could figure it out, but eventually someone on a TV camera crew got word to the teams that the fly ball had risen so high in the air that it had actually reached the dome roof and become stuck between a couple of steel support rods. While the umpires huddled to figure out what to do about it, Miller circled the bases uncertainly—when Miller reached third, Garrett playfully faked tagging him out, and Miller actually slid into the base before sheepishly rising to his feet and continuing homeward—and then waited for the umpires' verdict along with the rest of us.

I turned to Glen Collins, my bench coach, whom I had hired when Simon had refused my pleas to let me bring Pepper back. Pepper had actually recommended Glen, a personable, sharp-eyed baseball lifer who missed nothing that occurred on the field and whom all of us who respected the game not only admired but liked as well. There was a perennially mischievous air to Glen; you always got the impression that if he wasn't up to something, he was actively considering it.

"You ever seen anything like that before?" I asked him.

"Lots of times," he answered. "But never like that."

Not knowing what else to do, the umps finally decided to call it a ground-rule double. Before I could decide whether to rush out and argue that it might have been caught, Tommy Hyde, the Warriors manager, raced out first to insist that it might have been a home run. None of us really had any idea what would have happened, since it hadn't, so I figured I'd let him lose the argument instead of me. Ultimately, Miller was sent back to second. Three pitches later, McCarter called time with a 1–2 count on the hitter and came over to the dugout pretending he had some problem with his catcher's equipment. I went over to stand next to him while he faked fixing the non-existent difficulty.

"Miller's stealing our signs, Skip," he said. "He's watching me from second, and somehow he seems to know what I'm calling for, and he's signaling the batter whether it's a fastball or a breaking pitch."

"Really."

"Yup."

"Okay," I told him. "Go have a word with the kid and tell him you're going to call for a pitchout but he should throw it right down the middle."

"Got it," he said, and went back to do it. Sure enough, the batter relaxed with the windup and gazed in astonishment as strike three sailed right past him. Killer shot me a dirty look from second base which made my day, until I remembered how he had achieved his nickname.

After that things proceeded peacefully enough until the fifth—though in the fourth, Crockett never swung at a single pitch as their All-Star ace, Rhonnie Silvertree, threw three fastballs right by him, all straight down Main Street on the proverbial platter. After simply watching all three whiz past him without the bat ever leaving his shoulder, Jim returned to the bench and complained, "Man, they just don't make these ash bats like they used to. Maybe I ought to switch to maple."

But in the fifth, Diskant, their right fielder, led off for them and worked the count full. At 3–2, Bobby Lee—pitching as though the plate was high and outside—hurled a fastball on which Diskant checked his swing. Pomerantz, the umpire behind the plate, called it ball four, and Diskant trotted to first with his base on balls. The pitch, meanwhile, bounded off either Tom's glove or Diskant's bat and careened foul down the first-base side. McCarter turned and heatedly argued with the ump that the bat had actually tipped the ball, so it should be a foul instead of ball four. Milner, who clearly agreed with him, ran in from the mound to join the verbal fray. The Warrior first-base coach, seeing that Tom hadn't chased after the bounding ball, frantically yelled at Diskant to run to second, which he promptly started to do. Seeing this, Blasingame chased the errant sphere and fired it to Zapata, who was standing in his customary shortstop position, which of course gave him no play on Diskant as the latter approached second base. Then the fun really started.

Caught up in his argument with Tom, Pomerantz had reflexively handed our catcher a new ball. Hearing the shouts from our dugout, McCarter looked up and saw Diskant arriving unimpeded at second. Since there was no play to be made at that point, he didn't even attempt a throw; but our startled rookie pitcher grabbed the ball out of Tom's mitt and hurled it frantically towards second base, which remained unpatrolled by any member of our infield. The ball sailed into center field and Diskant, seeing a baseball zoom past him into the outfield, headed for third. He hadn't taken three steps before Zapata, who hadn't moved, casually reached out and tagged him with the ball in his glove as the runner went by.

Well, the conundrum of the ball stuck in the rafters was simplicity itself next to *this* play. After all the umpires had huddled together long enough to rewrite the Book of Prophets, they signaled that Diskant was out. Tommy Hyde came tearing out of the dugout again, enraged. The umps had finally come to the conclusion that since Diskant had been tagged with the original ball, which was still in play, he was out. Hyde yelled, screamed and turned purple arguing that his baserunner couldn't possibly be expected to know that the baseball thrown past him was not the one in play at the time. He was of course right about that, but that didn't affect the call at all, and Tommy simply became increasingly apoplectic until Winston finally thumbed him out. Glen and I watched and speculated on how many names, and which ones, Hyde was calling the ump, and of course casually betting on which particular insult would result in his finally being tossed out of the game.

"And before you ask," Collins quickly said to me, "The answer is no, I've never seen that happen. In rookie ball once we had a runner on third and the other team's catcher deliberately threw a peeled potato past our third baseman and then when our runner came home, he tagged him with the ball, but not only did the ump call our guy safe, he tossed the catcher out of the game for purposeful and unsportsmanlike deception. The league actually suspended the catcher indefinitely because the potato was peeled and they concluded that was proof he had brought it to the park planning to deceive a runner. Guess if he'd thrown an unpeeled potato he could have just argued that he'd found it in the dugout or something. Then again, if it hadn't been peeled it wouldn't have been white enough to be mistaken for a baseball, would it? But no, I've never seen anything like what just happened right here in front of us in a major league ballgame, no-sir-ee Bob, Mike."

We got to the ninth a run ahead, but Hicks, who had relieved our set-up man who had relieved our long man who had relieved Milner, walked the first batter and hit the next one, so I took a trip out to the mound to try to calm him down. Unfortunately, Crockett was already there, standing on the first-base side of the mound while McCarter planted himself firmly on the other side. By the time I arrived, our first baseman was characteristically in full panic mode.

"Don't lose this next guy," Crockett was pleading with Fast Eddie.

"Chill," Tom told Crockett.

"If you choke," Jim continued heedlessly, "everyone will boo us and the papers will rip us apart tomorrow and our won-lost record will—"

"Jim," interrupted McCarter, "shut the fuck up."

"Guys," I told them, "go back to your respective positions, will you?" As they did, I looked at Hicks, who seemed nervous. "Eddie," I told him, "relax."

"Okay," he replied, seeming to become even more anxious.

"Look, Eddie, just challenge him with fastballs. Throw it right down the middle if you want, just make him hit it, okay? If we lose, we lose, but let's make them earn it, what do you say?"

"Sure, Skip."

"Just put it anywhere in the strike zone, Eddie. That's all I ask."

"Okay."

I returned to the dugout and watched him throw a pitch way outside. Ball one. The next one bounced in the dirt; Tom was lucky to block it and keep the runners from advancing. Ball two. The third pitch almost hit the batter. 3–0.

"Be great if he swung at the next one, wouldn't it?" Glen asked me rhetorically. "Fat chance. Think Fast Eddie could find the strike zone if we maybe drew him a map?" Sure enough, the next pitch was high and outside—but to our mutual disbelief, for reasons I couldn't begin to fathom, the batter swung at it anyway. "Jesus Hallelujah Christ," said Glen softly.

The hitter lofted a pop fly into short left field. Zapata ran out for it while Tambellini charged in and the runners quite properly moved a little less than half-way between bases, not sure whether or not it would be caught. Even from the dugout, we could all hear Angel scream at the top of his voice, over and over, "*Yo la tengo! Yo la tengo! Yo la tengo!*" He stopped, planted his feet and reached up to snare the ball just as Tambellini ran full speed into him, knocking him rudely to the ground and jarring the ball out of his glove. The baseball rolled uselessly across the turf as both Dante and Angel lay dazed on the outfield turf, Angel lying woozy and Dante sitting staring stupidly at the ball moving away. Both runners chugged around the bases and scored before Willoughby arrived from center and threw the ball, far too late, to home plate.

Hicks struck out the next three hitters, seemingly liberated by no longer having a lead to protect. When everyone arrived in the dugout, I took Dante aside.

"Couldn't you hear Zapata calling for the ball?" I asked him. "Hell, we heard it loud and clear from here, and you two were right near each other and getting closer with every step. How could you possibly not have heard him?"

"I heard him all right, Skip. But I didn't know he was calling for it."

"Why did you think he kept yelling 'I got it!' if he wasn't calling for it?"

"I thought maybe he was calling for *me* to take it."

"You didn't hear him screaming *yo la tengo?*" I asked in disbelief.

"Hell, Skip, I don't speak no Spanish, I didn't know *what* he was screaming. Actually, it sounded to me like he was yelling, 'Yo! Latin go!' so I figured maybe he was telling me he was going to get out of the way and *I* should catch it."

There was not much I could say to that, so I didn't say it. We mounted a rally in the bottom of the ninth but didn't score, so we lost the game. Which was more frustrating than usual, because this was a game I had really wanted to win, since it had turned into a game that was clearly going to be recalled and discussed in times to come.

Which is to say that it was a baseball game just like any other baseball game, only different. Just like all the others.

The Last Out

MY DAD HAD ONCE taken me to a game in which the home team had been down by four runs heading into the bottom of the ninth. When the first two batters meekly bounced out, I reached for my jacket.

"Where are *you* going?" my dad asked me.

"Well, the game's about to end," I pointed out.

"The game's not over," he told me, "until the last man makes the last out." That was the best advice I ever got; and as if to demonstrate the veracity of his theory, the next three hitters loaded the bases with a bloop single, a walk and an infield hit; their number eight hitter hit his first triple in three years, clearing the bases; then a pinch-hitter notorious for his inability to hit the ocean if he was standing on the seashore slammed a two-run homer off a star reliever for the unlikeliest of victories.

Roger Angell, the matchless baseball scribe who has with reason been called the poet-laureate of baseball—though he himself wrote that "I decline the honors. It seems to me that what I have been putting down for a quarter century now is autobiography: the story of myself as a fan"—once observed that "Baseball is not life itself, though the resemblance keeps coming up."

I was thinking about that one evening at dinner. Donna had chosen the Stowaway Room at the Anchor Bar because she liked the nautical theme ("I feel at sea so much of the time anyway," is how she put it). We were alone for the evening: Laura was accompanying her sister on Jenna's mission to determine which of the hundred plus Greek restaurants in Buffalo, every one of which claimed to be "home of the original souvlaki," actually had the best souvlaki. Jenna had decided to try them all. "I'm just doing what you always say, Mom," Jenna had told Donna. "Obtain all the available evidence so that you have a valid basis for your verdict."

The season was drawing to an end. We were going to end up a surprisingly respectable third place in our division, and Simon was pleased enough to have decided to keep me on for next season, or as much of it as I was going to survive before the team inevitably fell into a losing streak and he would in all likelihood fire me yet again. But that was all yet to come. Right then I felt great because I loved what I was doing every day of my life; I was doing it well enough for the team to be playing the game hard and with passion (all you can ever ask of any player is the best of which he or she is capable, after all); and because looking across the table at the astonishing woman who had for whatever reasons decided to marry me made me keenly aware how amazingly lucky I really was. That she was smarter than me only made me feel even luckier. I wasn't always sure what she saw in me, but I was always eternally grateful that she seemed to see it.

She saw me looking at her and, as was her habit, smiled to let me know she knew what I was feeling without my having to say it. I reached out for her hand, and she took mine in hers.

"There's something I've been meaning to ask you for quite a while," I confessed.

She squeezed my hand with her own, and her smile somehow added another dimension without losing the one that was already there.

"What would that be?" she inquired lovingly. She looked into my eyes as I gazed romantically into hers.

"What do you suppose," I murmured dreamily, "that Bill Lattimore could possibly have done with the 1908 Cleveland Indians—in only four games, mind you—that earned him the nickname 'Slothful Bill'?"